When the giant ape pushed Jane roughly aside to meet Tarzan's charge, and
she saw their relative sizes, her heart
quailed. How could a man defeat such a
mighty enemy?

Like two charging bulls they came
together, and like two wolves they
sought each other's throats. The long
teeth of the ape battled the thin blade of
the man's knife.

Jane watched. Her lithe young form
was flattened against the trunk of a great
tree, hands pressed tight against her rising and falling chest, eyes wide with
mingled horror, fascination, fear, and
admiration. She watched the primeval
battle of ape and man for possession of a
woman: for her.

TARZAN

ʼʼ OF THE APES ʼʼ

EDGAR RICE BURROUGHS

Edited, with an Afterword,
by Jonathan Kelley

 THE TOWNSEND LIBRARY

TARZAN OF THE APES

TP THE TOWNSEND LIBRARY

ISBN-13: 978-1-59194-010-4
ISBN-10: 1-59194-010-9

Library of Congress Control Number:
2003100038

TABLE OF CONTENTS

CHAPTER 1

OUT TO SEA

The man who told me this story really should not have done so. We were enjoying a fine wine in his home, and he began to relate an incredible tale. I expressed some doubt early on, after which his pride required him to furnish proof. He produced musty manuscripts and official records of the British Colonial Office to support much of his narrative.

The written records tell us that a certain young English nobleman, John Clayton (titled Lord Greystoke), was instructed to investigate the conditions in a British colony on the west coast of Africa. Another European power was said to be recruiting the local Africans into an armed force, and using them to extort rubber and ivory from the tribes further inland. The remaining natives of the British colony complained that many of their young men were enticed away with promises of reward, but that few ever returned. The local Englishmen supported the natives' complaint, saying that the recruits were held in virtual slavery. Since they could not read the European language in which their enlistment was written, their officers dishonestly continued to tell them they had several more years to serve.

Clayton typified the best sort of Englishman. He was mentally, morally and physically strong. He was of above average height, with gray eyes and strong, healthy features. He carried himself with dignity. He had begun his career in the army, and had sought a transfer to the Colonial Office out of political ambition. He was elated by this delicate and important work in the Queen's service, and felt that it would further his career.

On the other hand, he had been married to Lady Alice Rutherford for barely three months, and the idea of taking this fair young girl into the dangers of tropical Africa appalled him. For the new Lady Greystoke's sake, he would have refused the appointment, but she would not have it. She insisted that he accept and that she go with him. The opinions of other family members are not recorded.

On a bright May morning in 1888, Lord Greystoke and Lady Alice sailed from Dover for West Africa. A month later they arrived at Freetown and chartered a small sailing vessel named the *Fuwalda* to take them to their final destination.

And here John Clayton, Lord Greystoke, and Lady Alice, his wife, vanished from the eyes and from the knowledge of men.

Two months after they hoisted anchor to leave Freetown, half a dozen British warships began scouring the south Atlantic for traces of them. Very early in the search, on the shores of the island of St. Helena, the Navy found a wrecked vessel. This suggested that the *Fuwalda* had gone down with all hands, and the search ended before it really got started. All the same, hope lingered in the lost couple's loved ones for many years.

The *Fuwalda* was a typical south Atlantic coastal vessel. Most of the crews of such ships were composed of lowly characters, including murderers and cutthroats of every nationality and race. The *Fuwalda* was no exception; her officers were bullies, hating and hated by the crew. The captain was a capable seaman, but brutal to the men. The only arguments he used in dealing with them were the revolver and the belaying pin—a shipboard tool often used as a club—and it is unlikely that the type of men in his crew would have understood any other form of persuasion.

From the second day after leaving Freetown, John Clayton and his young wife witnessed scenes on the deck of the *Fuwalda* that they had believed only happened in fictional sea stories. On that morning, a chain of events began that would lead to the life of a man whose story is like no other— a man who would become known as Tarzan of the Apes.

Two sailors were washing down the decks of

the *Fuwalda*, the first mate was on duty, and the captain had stopped to speak with John Clayton and Lady Alice. The sailors were working backwards toward the little party, who were facing away from them. Closer and closer they came, until one of them was directly behind the captain. In another moment he would have passed by, and this strange narrative would never have been recorded.

But just that instant the captain turned to leave Lord and Lady Greystoke, tripped over the sailor, and went sprawling headlong onto the deck. This overturned the water-pail, and drenched him with its dirty contents. For an instant the scene was humorous, but not for long. The officer swore a volley of awful oaths, and got to his feet in a red-faced, humiliated rage. With a terrific blow, he knocked the sailor to the deck. The poor sailor happened to be small and rather old, but his fellow deckhand was neither. He was a huge, dark-haired bear of a man with a great bull neck, massive shoulders, and a large moustache. He pounced on the captain and crushed him to his knees with one mighty blow.

The officer's face went from scarlet to white, for this was the crime of mutiny, and he knew how to deal with mutineers. Without rising, he whipped a revolver from his pocket and fired point-blank at the great mountain of muscle towering before him. As quick as he was, though, John Clayton was almost as quick, and the young lord struck down the captain's arm. The bullet intended for the sailor's heart lodged in the massive leg instead.

Clayton and the captain had words, the lord making clear his disgust with the brutality shown to the crew, and saying that he would tolerate nothing further of the kind while he and Lady Greystoke remained passengers. The captain was about to make an angry reply, but thought better of it and stalked away with a scowl. He did not care to annoy an English official, for the Queen's arm wielded an instrument of punishment feared on every sea: the Royal Navy.

The two sailors arose, the older man assisting his wounded comrade to his feet. The big fellow, known among his mates as Black Michael, tried his leg gingerly. It held him, and he turned to Clayton with a word of gruff thanks, then limped away without further discussion.

They did not see Black Michael again for several days, nor did the captain offer them more than a surly grunt. As was the custom with noble passengers, they continued to have their meals in the captain's cabin, but the captain made sure that his duties kept him from joining them for dinner.

The other officers were coarse, illiterate fellows, little better than the villainous crew they bullied. They were glad to avoid social contact with the polished English noble and his lady, so the Claytons were left very much to themselves. They were glad for peace, but it also kept them unaware of the daily happenings on board, which were leading the craft toward bloody tragedy.

On the second day after the wounding of Black Michael, Clayton came on deck just in time to see the limp body of one of the crew being carried below by four others while the first mate, a heavy belaying pin in his hand, stood glowering at the little group of sullen sailors.

Viewing this scene, Clayton did not need to ask any questions. The following day, as the great lines of a British battleship appeared on the horizon, he pondered demanding that he and Lady Alice be transferred to safety. He increasingly feared that only harm could result from their remaining on the sullen *Fuwalda*.

Toward noon they came within speaking distance of the Navy vessel, but when Clayton had nearly decided to ask the captain to take them aboard, he suddenly realized how ridiculous such a request would seem. What sane reason could he give the captain of Her Majesty's ship for desiring to go back in the direction he had just come? If he complained that two rebellious seamen had been treated roughly by their officers, they would laugh to themselves and think him a coward.

John Clayton did not ask to be transferred to the British man-of-war. Late in the afternoon he saw the last of her shape fade below the far horizon, but not before he learned something that confirmed his greatest fears and made him curse his pride. As he and his wife watched the warship disappear, the little old sailor worked his way near them while polishing brass. He said to Clayton in an undertone:

"Hell's to pay, sir, on this here craft, an' mark my word for it, sir."

"What do you mean, my good fellow?" asked Clayton.

"Why, hasn't ye seen wat's goin' on? Hasn't ye heard that devil's spawn of a captin an' his mates knockin' the bloomin' lights outen half the crew? Two busted heads yeste'day, an' three today. Black Michael's as good as new agin an' he's not the bully to stand fer it, not he, an' mark my word for it, sir."

"You mean, my man, that the crew contemplates mutiny?" asked Clayton.

"Mutiny!" exclaimed the old fellow. "Mutiny? They means murder, sir, an' mark my word for it, sir."

"When?"

"I'm not a-sayin' when, an' I've said too damned much already, but ye was good t'me t'other day an' I thought it no more'n right to warn ye. But keep a still tongue in yer head, an' when ye hear shootin', git below an' stay there. That's all, only keep a still tongue in yer head, or they'll put lead between yer ribs, an' mark my word for it, sir," and the old fellow went on with his polishing, which carried him away from where the Claytons were standing.

"Cheerful outlook, Alice," said Clayton.

"You should warn the captain at once, John. The trouble may yet be avoided," she said.

"I suppose I should, but from purely selfish motives I am tempted to 'keep a still tongue in my head.' Whatever they do now, they will spare us because I saved this fellow Black Michael, but if they find that I betrayed them, they would show us no mercy."

"You have but one duty, John, and that is to support lawful authority. If you do not warn the captain, you are as much a party to these events as though you had helped to plot and carry them out."

"You do not understand, dear," replied Clayton. "My first duty is to think of you. The captain has brought this condition upon himself. Why should I risk subjecting my wife to unthinkable horrors in a probably futile attempt to save him from his own brutal folly? You have no idea, dear, of what would occur were this pack of cutthroats to gain control of the *Fuwalda*."

"Duty is duty, John, and no excuses may change it. I would be a poor wife for an English lord were I to cause him to shirk his clear duty. I realize the danger which must follow, but I can face it with you."

"Have it as you will then, Alice," he answered, smiling. "Maybe we are borrowing trouble. While

I do not like the looks of things on board this ship, they may not be so bad after all, for it is possible that our friend the 'Ancient Mariner' was thinking wishfully. Mutiny on the high sea was common a hundred years ago, but in this good year 1888 it is the least likely possibility."

He stopped for a moment and looked. "But there goes the captain to his cabin now. If I am going to warn him, I might as well get the beastly job over, for it sickens me to talk with the brute at all."

So saying, he strolled carelessly after the captain, and a moment later was knocking at his door.

"Come in," growled the deep voice of that surly officer.

And when Clayton had entered, and closed the door behind him, "Well?"

"I have come to report a conversation I heard today. While it is possible that nothing may come of it, you should be warned that the men contemplate mutiny and murder."

"It's a lie!" roared the captain. "And if you have been interfering again with the discipline of this ship, or anything else that is none of your affair, you'll take the consequences and be damned, English lord or not! I'm captain of this here ship, and from now on you keep your meddling nose out of my business!"

The captain had worked himself up to a purple-faced frenzy of rage, and he shrieked the last words at the top of his voice, thumping the table loudly with one huge fist, shaking the other in Clayton's face. Greystoke did not flinch, but stood eying the excited man with a level gaze.

"Captain Billings," he drawled finally, "if you will pardon my candor, I might remark that you are something of a fool." The nobleman then turned and left with calm confidence, which was even more infuriating to a man like Billings than any hostile outburst. Had Clayton attempted to placate him, the captain might easily have come to regret his tirade, but he was now too angry for that, and their last chance for cooperation was gone.

"Well, Alice," said Clayton, as he rejoined his wife, "I might have saved my breath. The fellow proved most ungrateful and acted like a mad dog. He and his blasted old ship may hang, for all I care, and until we are safely off, I shall look only after our own welfare. And I rather fancy that I should first go to our cabin and look over my revolvers. I am sorry now that we packed the larger guns and the ammunition with the stuff below."

They found their quarters in disorder. Clothing from their open boxes and bags were strewn around the little apartment, and even their beds had been torn to pieces.

"Evidently someone was more anxious about our belongings than we were," said Clayton. "Let's have a look around, Alice, and see what's missing." A thorough search revealed that nothing had been taken but Clayton's two revolvers and their small supply of ammunition.

"Those are the very things I most wish they had left us," said Clayton, "and the fact that they only took the weapons is most sinister."

"What are we to do, John?" asked his wife. "Perhaps you were right in that our best chance lies in remaining neutral. If the officers are able to prevent a mutiny, we have nothing to fear, while if the mutineers are victorious, our one slim hope lies in not having attempted to hinder them."

"Right you are, Alice. We'll keep in the middle of the road."

As they started to straighten up their cabin, Clayton and his wife both noticed the corner of a piece of paper protruding beneath the door of their quarters. As Clayton stooped to reach for it, he realized that it was being pushed inward by someone from outside. Quickly and silently he stepped toward the door, but as he prepared to throw it open, his wife grasped his wrist. "No, John," she whispered. "They do not wish to be seen, so we cannot afford to see them. Remember that we are keeping to the middle of the road."

Clayton smiled and dropped his hand to his side. They stood watching the little bit of paper until it finally remained motionless on the floor just inside the door. Then Clayton bent and picked it up. It was a bit of grimy, white paper roughly folded into a ragged square. Opening it, they found a crude, barely legible message warning them not to report the loss of the revolvers, nor to repeat what the old sailor had told them—on pain of death.

"I rather imagine we'll do as they say," said Clayton with a rueful smile. "About all we can do is to sit tight and wait for whatever may come."

CHAPTER 2

THE SAVAGE HOME

They did not have long to wait, for the next morning, as Clayton was emerging on deck for his walk before breakfast, a shot rang out, and then another and another. What he saw confirmed his worst fears. Facing the little knot of officers was the entire motley crew of the *Fuwalda*, led by Black Michael.

At the first volley of pistol shots from the officers, the men ran for shelter. From behind masts, wheelhouse, and cabin they returned the fire of the five men whose authority they so hated. The captain's revolver had shot two of the men, who lay between the combatants. But then the first mate fell forward onto his face, wounded or dead, and at a shouted order from Black Michael, the mutineers charged. The mutineers had been able to find only six firearms, so most were armed with boat hooks, axes, and crowbars.

The captain had emptied his revolver and was reloading as the charge came. The second mate's gun had jammed, so there were only two weapons to oppose the charge of the mutineers. The officers began to retreat before the infuriated rush of their former crew. The combination of the curses and oaths of both sides, the sounds of gunfire and the screams and groans of the wounded turned the deck of the *Fuwalda* into a madhouse.

Before the officers had taken a dozen steps backward, the men were all over them. An ax in the hands of a burly African split the captain's head, and an instant later, the others were dead or wounded from dozens of blows and bullet wounds. It had been short and grisly work.

Through it all John Clayton had leaning carelessly against the door that led below decks, puffing calmly on his pipe as though he had been watching a dull cricket match. As the last officer went down, he thought it would be best if he returned to his wife before the crew found her. Though outwardly calm and indifferent, Clayton was quite worried that his wife's safety rested in the hands of these ignorant brutes.

As he turned to descend, he was surprised to see her standing on the steps almost at his side.

"How long have you been here, Alice?"

"Since the beginning," she replied. "Oh, how awful, John! What can we hope for at their hands?"

"Breakfast, I hope," he answered, smiling bravely in an attempt to allay her fears. "At least I'm going to ask them. Come with me, Alice. We must act as though we expect courteous treatment."

The men had surrounded the dead and wounded officers, and heartlessly proceeded to throw both living and dead overboard, including their own dead and dying. Presently one of the crew spied the approaching Claytons, and with a cry of: "Here's two more for the fishes," rushed toward them with an ax.

Black Michael was quicker. He fired once, and the fellow went down with a bullet in his back before he had even gotten close. With a loud roar, Black Michael gained the mutineers' attention, pointing to Lord and Lady Greystoke, and cried: "These here are my friends, and they are to be left alone. D'ye understand? I'm captain of this ship now, an' what I says goes," he added, turning to Clayton. "Just keep to yourselves, and nobody'll harm ye," he said, looking threateningly at his fellow seamen.

After that, the Claytons obeyed Black Michael's instructions so well that they saw little of the crew and learned nothing of their plans. Occasionally they heard faint echoes of brawls and quarreling, and on two occasions the vicious bark of firearms shattered the still air. Mostly, though, Black Michael kept the band of cutthroats under control.

On the fifth day following the murder of the ship's officers, the lookout sighted land. Black Michael did not know whether it was an island or mainland, but he announced to Clayton that if it seemed to be habitable. He and Lady Greystoke would be put ashore with their belongings.

"You'll be all right there for a few months," he explained, "and by that time we'll have been able to scatter a bit. Then I'll see that yer gover'ment's notified where you be an' they'll soon send a man o' war to fetch ye off. If we landed you in civilization, a lot o' questions would be asked that none o' us here wants to try an' answer."

"But, my good man," objected Clayton, "this is an unknown shore. It is inhuman to leave us in such a place, fair game for the mercies of savage beasts and hostile tribesmen."

Black Michael's voice grew angry. "Ye'd best be grateful for the chance. Many's the man here wouldn't give it ye." Clayton argued no further, but resolved to make the best of a bad situation.

About three o'clock in the afternoon, they sighted a beautiful wooded shore opposite the mouth of what appeared to be a land-locked harbor. Black Michael sent a small boatload of men to check the depth of the entrance and determine if the *Fuwalda* could pass through safely. In about an hour they returned and reported deep water all the way into the little basin.

Before dark the small ship lay peacefully at anchor on the still, mirror-like surface of the harbor. The surrounding shores were beautiful with semi-tropical greenery, and hills and plateaus rose in the distance. Nearly all was cloaked in thick jungle. There were no signs of habitation, but the presence of abundant bird and animal life and the shimmer of a little river suggested that the land might easily support human life.

As darkness settled, Clayton and Lady Alice still stood by the ship's rail in silent contemplation of their future home. From the dark shadows of the mighty forest came the wild calls of savage beasts—the deep roar of the lion, and, occasionally, the shrill scream of a panther. Alice shrank closer to her husband in terrified anticipation of the horrors awaiting them in the dark, lonely nights to come.

Later in the evening Black Michael instructed them to prepare to land in the morning. They tried again to persuade him to take them to some more hospitable coast with better hope of being found by civilization, but no pleas, threats, or promises of reward could move him.

"I'm the only man aboard who would not rather see ye both safely dead, and yet Black Michael's not the man to forget a favor. Ye saved my life once, and in return I'm goin' to spare yours, but that's all I can do. The men won't stand for any more, and if we don't get ye landed pretty quick, they may even change their minds about that. I'll put all yer stuff ashore with ye, yer guns included, as well as cookin' utensils an' some old sails for tents, an' enough grub to last ye until ye can find fruit and game. Ye ought to be able to live here easy enough until help comes. When I get safely away, I'll see that the British gover'ment learns about where ye be. I don't know exactly where this be, but they'll find ye all right."

After he left, they went silently below, each wrapped in gloomy worries. Clayton did not trust a word Black Michael had said. He feared that there would be some treachery once they were ashore with the sailors. Once out of their new leader's sight, any of the men might strike them down.

And even should they escape that fate, there were more and greater dangers. Alone, Clayton might hope to survive for years; he was a strong, athletic man. But what of Alice? What of the unborn life within her, launched into a primitive and dangerous world? Clayton shuddered as he considered their awful situation.

It was a mercy that he did not foresee the hideous reality awaiting them in the grim depths of that gloomy wood.

Early next morning their numerous chests and boxes were hoisted into small boats for transportation to shore. Because the Claytons had expected a possible five to eight years' residence in their new home, there was a great variety of stuff, including many luxuries as well as basic necessities.

Whether out of compassion for them, or for selfish reasons, Black Michael decreed that nothing belonging to the Claytons should be left on board. The property of a missing British official would have been a difficult thing to explain. He even insisted that the sailors return Clayton's revolvers.

The small boats were also loaded with salt meats and biscuit, a small supply of potatoes and beans, matches, cooking vessels, a chest of tools, and the old sails they had been promised. Perhaps also fearing the conduct of his men ashore, Black Michael went ashore with them. After the ship's fresh water barrels were replenished, the huge mutineer was in the last boat to return to the waiting *Fuwalda*. As the boats moved slowly away, Clayton and his wife stood silently watching, feeling utterly hopeless.

And behind them, over the edge of a low ridge, other eyes watched—close-set, wicked eyes, gleaming beneath shaggy brows.

As the *Fuwalda* passed out of sight, Lady Alice threw her arms about Clayton's neck and burst into uncontrolled sobs. She had faced the dangers of the mutiny, and the terrible future ahead, with courage. Now that the horror of absolute solitude was upon them, her nerves gave way. She was very young, barely an adult. He let her release the emotions she had long and bravely held back.

"Oh, John," she cried at last, "the horror of it. What are we to do?"

"There is but one thing to do, Alice," he said calmly, "and that is work. Work must be our salvation. We must not give ourselves time to think, or we may go mad. We must work and wait. Even if Black Michael does not keep his promise, I'm sure that relief will come quickly when it is apparent the *Fuwalda* has been lost."

"But John, if it were only you and I," she sobbed, "we could endure it, I know, but—"

"Yes, dear," he answered, gently, patting her belly. "I have been thinking of that, too, but we must face it as we do everything, bravely and with confidence in our ability to cope with any circumstance. Many centuries ago our ancestors of the distant past faced the same problems we now face. They solved them. People much like ourselves thrive on this very continent. Can we not do as well as they and our forebears have done? And are we not armed with every advantage in terms of supplies and knowledge of science? What others accomplish with instruments of stone and bone, we can do more easily with our modern tools."

"Ah, John," replied Alice, "that is a man's philosophy, but I see with my heart rather than my head, and all that I can see is too unthinkable to put into words. I only hope you are right, my husband. I will do my best to be a brave mate for you."

Clayton's first thought was to arrange a sleeping shelter for the night, to protect them from prowling beasts of prey. He first opened the box containing his rifles and ammunition. When they were both armed against possible attack, they sought a location for their first night's sleep.

A hundred yards from the beach, there was a little level spot with few trees. Here they decided to someday build a permanent house, but for now they decided to construct a little platform in the trees, above the reach of the large savage beasts whose realm this was. Clayton selected four trees which formed a rectangle about eight feet square, then cut long branches from other trees. With these he built a framework about ten feet above the ground, securing the branches to the trees with rope. Then he laid smaller branches across them as a floor, paved the platform with great leaves of a fern called elephant's ear, and laid a great folded sail from the *Fuwalda* across it all.

Seven feet higher he constructed a lighter platform to serve as the roof, and from the sides of this he hung the rest of his sailcloth as walls. When his work was completed, he had a rather snug little nest, to which he carried their blankets and some of the lighter luggage. It was now late in the afternoon, and he spent the rest of the day building a ladder so that Lady Alice could climb to her new home.

All day the forest about them had been filled with excited birds of brilliant plumage, and dancing, chattering monkeys, who watched these new arrivals and their activities with keen fascination. Despite a sharp lookout, Clayton and his wife saw nothing of larger animals. Twice, however, they had seen small monkeys come screaming and chattering from the nearby ridge, glancing fearfully back over their little shoulders as if fleeing some concealed terror.

Just before dusk Clayton finished his ladder, and, filling a great basin with water from the nearby stream, the two castaways ascended to the comparative safety of their elevated chamber. It was warm, so Clayton pushed the side curtains back over the roof. As they rested on their blankets, Lady Alice, straining her eyes into the darkening shadows of the wood, suddenly reached out and grasped Clayton's arms.

"John," she whispered, "look! What is it, a man?"

Clayton looked, and saw the silhouette of a great figure standing upright on the ridge. For a moment it stood, as though listening, then turned slowly and melted into the shadows of the jungle.

"What is it, John?"

"I do not know, Alice," he answered gravely. "It is too dark to see so far, and it may have been only a shadow cast by the rising moon."

"No, John; if it was not a man, it was some huge and grotesque mockery of man. Oh, I am afraid."

He gathered her in his arms, whispering words of courage and love into her ear. Soon after, he lowered and tied the curtain walls into place so that, except for a little opening toward the beach,

they were entirely enclosed. It was now pitch dark within their tiny nest, so they lay down to try to forget their situation for a while in sleep. Clayton lay facing the opening, a rifle and pair of revolvers close at hand.

Scarcely had they closed their eyes than the terrifying cry of a panther rang out from the jungle behind them. It continued, coming closer, until they could hear the great beast directly beneath them. For an hour or more they heard it sniffing and clawing at the trees which supported their platform, but at last it roamed away across the beach, where Clayton could see it clearly in the brilliant moonlight—a great, handsome beast, the largest he had ever seen.

During the long hours of darkness they caught only scattered moments of sleep, for the night noises of a great jungle teeming with animal life kept their nerves on edge. They were startled awake a hundred times by piercing screams, or by the stealthy moving of great bodies beneath them.

CHAPTER 3

LIFE AND DEATH

It was with intense relief but little rest that they watched the next sunrise. After their slim breakfast of salt pork, coffee, and biscuits, Clayton began work building their house. They could have neither safety nor peace of mind at night until four strong walls shielded them from the jungle life.

Over the course of the next month, he cut and assembled small logs about six inches thick, transforming the elevated platform into a one-room cabin. He plugged the gaps with clay, leaving one window and a doorway. At one end he built a fireplace of small stones set into clay, and applied more clay until he had coated the entire exterior. He put heavy wooden bars onto the window, so that it would stop even a powerful animal.

The roof was made of jungle grass laid over a framework of small branches and covered with clay. There was a moment of humor when Clayton constructed a thick door from pieces of the packing boxes, then realized he had no means to hang it. Soon, though, he managed to fashion hardwood hinges. He then went on to the easier work of building a bed, chairs, table, and shelves. By the end of the second month, they were well settled, comfortable, and as happy as one could expect, except for the constant dread of attack by wild animals and the ever-growing loneliness.

At night, great beasts snarled and roared around their tiny cabin. Soon they became numbed to these, and slept soundly the whole night through. Three times they caught fleeting glimpses of great man-like figures like that of the first night, but never near enough to tell whether the half-seen forms were those of man or animal. The brilliant birds and little monkeys grew accustomed to the Claytons, and soon were accepting little morsels of food from their friendly hands.

One afternoon, while Clayton was working on an addition to their cabin, a number of their little monkey friends came shrieking and scolding fearfully through the trees from the direction of the ridge. Finally they stopped near Clayton, jabbering excitedly to him as though to warn him of approaching danger.

At last he saw it, the thing the little monkeys so feared—the manlike brute they had occasionally glimpsed. It was approaching through the jungle in a semi-upright position, now and then placing the backs of its closed fists on the ground—a great ape, making deep throaty growls and an occasional low barking sound.

Clayton was some distance from the cabin, preparing to cut down another tree for his building operations. Grown careless from months of continued safety, during which time he had seen no dangerous animals during daylight, he had left all his rifles and revolvers inside the little cabin. Now that he saw the great ape crashing through the underbrush directly toward him, practically cutting him off from escape, he felt a vague little shiver up and down his spine. Armed only with an ax, he knew his chances were small—and Alice! Oh God, he thought, what will become of Alice?

There was yet a slight chance of reaching the cabin. He turned and ran toward it, shouting an alarm to his wife to run in and close the great door in case the ape cut off his retreat.

Lady Greystoke had been sitting a little way from the cabin, and when she heard his cry, she looked up to see the ape springing with incredible swiftness in an effort to head off Clayton. With a low cry she sprang toward the cabin, and, as she entered, gave a backward glance which filled her soul with terror. The brute had intercepted her husband, who now stood at bay, ready to meet the infuriated animal's charge with his ax.

"Close and bolt the door, Alice," cried Clayton. "I can finish this fellow with my ax."

But he knew he was facing a horrible death, and so did she. The ape was a great bull, weighing probably three hundred pounds. His nasty, close-set eyes gleamed hatred from beneath his shaggy brows, while his great canine fangs were bared in a horrid snarl as he paused in front of his prey.

Over the brute's shoulder Clayton could see the doorway of his cabin, not twenty paces distant, and a great wave of horror and fear swept over him as he saw his young wife emerge, armed with a rifle. She had always been afraid of firearms, but now she rushed toward the ape with the fearlessness of a lioness protecting its young, heedless of her great pregnancy.

"Back, Alice," shouted Clayton, "for God's sake, go back." But she would not comply, and just then the ape charged, so Clayton could say no more.

The man swung his ax with all his mighty strength, but the powerful brute seized it in those terrible hands, tore it from Clayton's grasp and hurled it far to one side. With an ugly snarl he closed in on his defenseless victim, but before his fangs reached the throat they thirsted for, there was a sharp crack, and a bullet struck the ape's back between his shoulders.

Throwing Clayton to the ground, the beast turned on his new enemy. There before him stood the terrified girl vainly trying to fire another bullet into the animal, but she was unfamiliar with the firearm, and the hammer fell futilely on the empty chamber. The charge of the great ape bowled her over.

At this moment Clayton regained his feet, and without thought of the utter hopelessness of it, he rushed forward to drag the ape from his wife's prostrate form. To his surprise, the great bulk rolled lifelessly upon the turf before him—the ape was dead. The bullet had done its work.

A hasty examination of his wife revealed no marks or injury, and Clayton decided that the huge brute had died the instant he had sprung toward Alice. Gently, he lifted his wife's unconscious form and carried her to the little cabin, but it was fully two hours before she awoke.

Her first words filled Clayton with worry. For some time after regaining her senses, Alice gazed wonderingly about the interior of the little cabin, and then, with a satisfied sigh, said:

"Oh, John, it is so good to be really home! I have had an awful dream, dear. I thought we were no longer in London, but in some horrible place where great beasts attacked us."

"There, there, Alice," he said, stroking her forehead, "try to sleep again, and do not worry about bad dreams."

That night, a little son was born in the tiny cabin beside the primeval forest, while a leopard screamed before the door, and the deep notes of a lion's roar sounded from beyond the ridge.

Lady Greystoke never recovered from the shock of the great ape's attack, and, though she lived for a year after her baby was born, she never again left the cabin, nor did she ever fully realize that she was not in England. Sometimes she would question Clayton as to the strange nighttime noises, the absence of servants and friends, and the strangeness of the furnishings within her room. He made no effort to deceive her, but neither did he attempt to make her fully aware of the true situation. She was happy with her little son, her husband's loving attention, and her delusions. Clayton knew well that, had she not partly lost her sanity, she would have been worried and apprehensive. So while he suffered terribly to see her this way, he was almost glad at times that she could not understand.

He had long since given up hope of any but an accidental rescue, so with unceasing energy, he had worked to beautify the interior of the cabin. Skins of lion and panther covered the floor. Cupboards and bookcases lined the walls. Clay vases held beautiful tropical flowers. Curtains of grass and bamboo covered the windows, and he had fashioned lumber to neatly seal the walls and ceiling and lay a smooth floor within the cabin. He loved the work, because it was for his wife and the tiny life she nurtured.

During the year that followed, Clayton was attacked several times by other great apes, but because he never again ventured outside without both rifle and revolvers, he had little to fear from the huge beasts. He had strengthened the window bars and added a locking bar to the cabin door, so that no animal could break into the little home. At first he shot much of the game from the cabin windows, but toward the end, the animals learned to fear the strange lair from which came the terrifying thunder of his rifle, and he had to venture forth to find meat.

In his leisure Clayton read, often aloud to his

wife, from the store of books he had brought for their new home. Among these were many picture books and schoolbooks for little children—for they knew that their little child would be old enough for such before they might hope to return to England. At other times he wrote in his diary, which he always kept in French, and which he kept locked in a little metal box.

A year from the day her little son was born, Lady Alice passed quietly away in the night, so peacefully that it was hours before Clayton realized it. The horror of the situation came to him very slowly, and it is doubtful that he ever fully realized the enormity of his sorrow and the fearful responsibility that was now solely his.

The last entry in his diary was made the morning following her death, and there he recited the sad details in a matter-of-fact way that tears at the heart:

"My little son is crying for nourishment—Oh Alice, Alice, what shall I do?"

And as John Clayton wrote what would be his last words, he dropped his head wearily upon his outstretched arms, resting on the table he had built for his cherished wife, who lay still and cold on the bed beside him.

For a long time no sound broke the deathlike stillness of the jungle day except the wailing of the tiny man-child.

CHAPTER 4

THE APES

In the jungle, a mile inland from the cabin, old Kerchak the Ape was on a rampage of rage among his people. The younger and lighter members of his tribe scampered to the higher, flimsier branches of the great trees to escape his wrath, risking deadly falls rather than face old Kerchak in his fit of uncontrolled anger. The other males scattered in all directions, but not before the infuriated brute had cracked a neck between his great, foaming jaws.

A unlucky young female slipped from a high branch and came crashing to the ground almost at Kerchak's feet. With a wild scream he was upon her, tearing a great piece from her side with his mighty teeth, and then crushing her skull to jelly with a broken tree limb.

Then he spied Kala, returning from a search for food with her young babe. She was ignorant of the rampage until suddenly the shrill warnings of her fellows caused her to scamper madly for safety. But Kerchak was so close behind her that she took a risk that great apes take only when in mortal danger: she made a long, desperate leap from one tree to another, causing Kerchak to narrowly miss grasping her ankle.

She made the leap successfully, but the sudden halt loosened the hold of the tiny baby ape where it clung frantically to her neck. She saw the little thing plummet, twisting, to the ground thirty feet below.

With a low cry of dismay, Kala rushed headlong to its side, now thoughtless of the danger from Kerchak; but when she gathered the small, mangled form to her chest, it was lifeless. She sat cuddling the body to her, moaning, but Kerchak did not assault her. The death of the babe had satisfied his fit of demonic rage.

Kerchak was a huge king ape, weighing perhaps three hundred and fifty pounds. His build was compact and his appearance was cruel. His awful temper and his mighty strength made him supreme among the apes. He was in his prime, and no animal—ape or otherwise—dared attack him. Alone of all the wild life, only the old elephant, Tantor, did not fear him; and Kerchak feared only Tantor. When Tantor trumpeted, Kerchak sought refuge in the trees with the other great apes.

With an iron hand and bared fangs, Kerchak ruled a tribe of some six or eight ape families, each consisting of an adult male with his females and their young, numbering sixty or seventy in all. Kala was the youngest mate of a male called Tublat, and the fallen child had been her firstborn. Despite her youth, she was large and powerful, and more intelligent than most of her kind—and with a great capacity for maternal love and sorrow. But she was still a great ape, one of a species closely allied to the gorilla, yet more intelligent. Her kind were the most fearsome of all apes.

When the tribe saw that Kerchak's rage had ceased, they came slowly down from their retreats and went back to their normal activities. The young played and frolicked. Some of the adults lazed on the soft decaying vegetation of the ground, while others foraged on the ground for tasty small bugs and reptiles. Still others searched the nearby trees for fruit, nuts, small birds, and eggs.

An hour later Kerchak called them together and commanded them to follow him toward the sea. They traveled mainly upon the ground, slowly, following the broken path of the great elephants whose comings and goings provide the only roads through the jungle. When they took to the lower trees, they moved with the swifter agility of their smaller monkey cousins. And all the way, Kala carried her little dead baby hugged closely to her chest.

Shortly after noon they reached a ridge overlooking the beach with the tiny cottage. Kerchak had seen many of his kind die before the loud noise made by the little black stick in the hands of the strange white ape. He had decided to own the deadly device, and to explore the white ape's mysterious lair. He wanted very much to sink his teeth into the neck of the strange animal he hated and feared, so he often brought his tribe to observe, hoping to catch the white ape off his guard. They no longer revealed themselves, for each time they had done so, a terrible roar of death had claimed another member of the tribe.

Today there was no sign of the man, and they saw that the cabin door was open. Slowly and silently they crept through the jungle toward the little cabin—so as not to awaken the death-dealing little black stick. Finally, Kerchak himself slunk stealthily to the very door and peered inside. Behind him were two males, and then Kala, still clutching the little dead form.

Inside the den they saw the strange white ape lying half across a table, his head buried in his arms. On the bed lay a figure covered by cloth, while the helpless wailing of a baby came from a tiny cradle close by.

Noiselessly, Kerchak entered, crouching for the charge, and then John Clayton rose with a sudden start and faced them. The sight that met his eyes must have frozen him with horror, for there within the door stood three great bull apes, while behind them crowded many more. He never knew how many, for his revolvers were hanging on the far wall beside his rifle, and Kerchak was charging.

When the king ape released the limp form which had once been Lord Greystoke, he turned his attention toward the little cradle. But Kala was there before him and snatched up the child before Kerchak could reach him. Before he could intercept her, she had bolted through the door and taken refuge in a high tree.

As she took up Alice Clayton's living baby, she dropped the dead body of her own baby into the empty cradle. The wail of the living had answered the call of universal motherhood within her wild heart. High up among the branches of a mighty tree, she hugged the shrieking infant, and soon the tiny man-child felt the familiar comfort of motherly love, quieting him.

In the meantime the other beasts were warily investigating the cabin. Once satisfied that Clayton was dead, Kerchak turned his attention to the thing which lay covered on the bed. When he saw the body of the woman beneath, he tore the cloth roughly from her and seized the still white throat in his huge hands. Realizing that she too was dead, he left both bodies alone and returned to his exploration of the cabin.

The rifle hanging on the wall caught his first attention. He had long desired this strange, death-dealing thunder-stick, but now he scarcely had the courage to seize it. Cautiously he approached the thing, ready to flee immediately should it thunder

as it had before. Its voice had been the last sound many of his kind had heard. Somehow he knew that the thunder-stick was dangerous only when in the hands of one who could manipulate it, yet it was several minutes before he dared touch it. He paced back and forth, his eyes never leaving it, occasionally uttering the ear-piercing scream of his kind—the most terrifying noise in all the jungle.

Presently he halted before the rifle. He nearly

touched the shining barrel, only to withdraw it once more and continue his hurried pacing and roaring, working up his nerve. Again he stopped, and this time he touched the cold steel, snatching his hand back immediately. After a few tentative touches, he finally tore the rifle from its hook. Finding that it did him no harm, Kerchak began to examine it closely. He felt it from end to end, peered down the black depths of the muzzle, fingered the sights, the breech, the stock, and finally the trigger.

All this time, the apes inside the cabin sat huddled near the door watching their chief, while those outside strained to see. Suddenly Kerchak's finger pulled the trigger. There was a deafening roar in the little room, and the crowded apes fell over one another in their wild haste to escape. Kerchak was equally frightened, so much so that he quite forgot to throw aside the thunder-stick, and bolted for the door with it tightly clutched in one hand. As he passed through the opening, the front sight of the rifle caught upon the edge of the door with sufficient force to close it tightly behind him.

When Kerchak halted a short distance from the cabin and discovered that he still held the rifle, he dropped it like a red-hot iron. The noise of the thunder-stick was too much for his brute nerves, but he now believed that the terrible thing was quite harmless by itself.

It was an hour before the apes could again bring themselves to continue investigating the cabin. They then found to their annoyance that the door was so tightly closed that they could not force it. Clayton's cleverly constructed latch had fallen into place. Nor could the apes find entry through the heavily barred windows. After roaming about the area for a short time, they started back the way they had come.

Kala had remained aloft with her little adopted babe, but now Kerchak called to her to descend with the rest. As there was no note of anger in his voice, she dropped lightly from branch to branch and joined the others on their homeward march.

Those apes who attempted to examine the strange baby were repulsed by Kala's bared fangs and low menacing growls. When they assured her that they meant the child no harm she permitted them to come close, but not to touch. She seemed to know that her baby was frail and delicate, and feared that their rough hands might injure the little thing.

She did one other unusual thing. Remembering the death of her own little one, she clung desperately to the new babe with one hand, whenever they were on the march. The other young rode upon their mothers' backs, their little arms tightly clasping the hairy necks before them, while their legs were locked beneath their mothers' armpits. Not Kala—she held the small form of the little

Lord Greystoke tightly to her chest, where the tiny hands clutched her long black fur. One child had fallen from her back to a terrible death, and she would take no further chances with this one.

CHAPTER 5

THE WHITE APE

Tenderly Kala nursed her little babe, wondering silently why it did not gain strength and agility like the others. She cared for him nearly a year before he would walk alone, and as for climbing—my, but how backward he was! Kala sometimes talked with the older females about her young hopeful, but none of them could understand how a child could be so slow in learning to care for itself. Why, it could not even find food alone.

Had they known that the child was thirteen moons of age when Kala had found it, they would have considered it absolutely hopeless, for their own little apes were as far advanced in two or three moons as was this little stranger after twenty-five.

Tublat, Kala's husband, was sorely frustrated. Only her careful watching kept him from disposing of the defective child. "He will never be a great ape," he argued. "Always you will have to carry him and protect him. He will only be a burden to the tribe. Let us leave him quietly sleeping among the tall grasses, that you may bear stronger apes to guard us in our old age."

"Never, Broken Nose," replied Kala. "If I must carry him forever, so be it."

So Tublat went to Kerchak to urge him to force her to give up little Tarzan, for so they had named him, meaning "White-Skin." But when Kerchak spoke to her about it, Kala threatened to run away if they did not leave her and her child in peace. The right of the jungle people to leave the tribe is sacred, so they stopped bothering her. Kala was a fine clean-limbed young female, and they did not wish to lose her.

As Tarzan grew he made more rapid strides, so that by the time he was ten years old he was an excellent climber, and on the ground could do many wonderful things which were beyond the powers of his little brothers and sisters. They often marveled at his superior cunning, but in strength and size he was lesser. At ten, the great apes were fully grown, some of them towering over six feet, while little Tarzan was still but a half-grown boy.

Yet such a boy!

From early childhood he had swung from branch to branch like his giant mother, and as he grew older, he spent hours daily doing so with his brothers and sisters. He could spring twenty feet across space at the dizzy heights of the forest top, then smoothly and precisely grasp a wildly waving limb. He could drop twenty feet at a stretch from limb to limb in rapid descent to the ground, or he could climb to the top of the loftiest tropical tree with the ease and swiftness of a squirrel. At ten, he was fully as strong as the average man of thirty, and far more agile than the most practiced athlete ever becomes. And day by day his strength was increasing.

His life among these fierce apes had been happy, for it was the only one he had known. He was nearly ten before he realized how different he was from his fellows. His tanned little body suddenly caused him intense shame, for he realized that it was entirely hairless, like a reptile's. He sought to correct this by plastering himself from head to foot with mud, but this dried and fell off, and felt so uncomfortable that he decided he preferred the shame.

One sultry day in the dry season, he and one of his cousins had gone down to the lake to drink. As they leaned over, both little faces were mirrored on the placid pool—the fierce and terrible features of the ape beside those of the young nobleman.

Tarzan was shocked. It had been bad enough to be hairless, but to be so ugly! He wondered that the other apes could look at him at all. That tiny slit of a mouth and those puny white teeth! How weak beside the mighty lips and powerful fangs of his more fortunate brothers! His nose looked thin and pinched compared to the wide, flat, handsome nostrils of his companion. It certainly must be fine to be so handsome, thought poor little Tarzan.

But when he saw his own eyes—ah, that was the final blow—a brown spot, a gray circle and then blank whiteness! Frightful! Not even the snakes had such hideous eyes.

He was so intent on this shocking vision that he did not hear the great body moving stealthily through the jungle. His companion was drinking too noisily to hear the sinister threat either. Not thirty paces behind them crouched Sabor, the lioness. This particular Sabor was huge and very hungry. Cautiously she moved a great padded paw forward, noiselessly placing it before she lifted the next, and in this way she made her low advance—a great cat preparing to spring upon its prey.

Now she was within ten feet of the two unsuspecting little playfellows. Carefully she drew her hind feet well up beneath her body, the great muscles rolling under the beautiful skin. She was crouching down, nearly flattened to the earth. The tail lay quiet and straight. A wise hunter, she knew that her leap would make noise anyway, and that her fierce cry tended to freeze her poor victims just long enough for her mighty claws to sink into their soft flesh and prevent escape. She paused for an instant; then, with an awful scream, she sprang!

So far as the ape was concerned, Sabor reasoned correctly. The little fellow crouched trembling just an instant, but that instant was quite long enough to prove his ruin.

Not so, however, with Tarzan, the man-child. The dangers of the jungle had taught him self-confidence, and his mind was sharper and quicker than those of the apes. So Sabor's scream sent little Tarzan into instant action.

In front of him lay the deep waters of the lake, behind him certain death. Tarzan had always hated water, except as something to drink, because he connected it with the chill and discomfort of heavy rains, as well as the frightening thunder and lightning. His wild mother had taught him to avoid deep waters. He himself had recently seen an ape-child, little Neeta, sink beneath its quiet surface and never come up.

His quick mind chose the lesser of these two fates before Sabor's scream and leap even finished. He felt the chill waters close over his head even before the great beast landed. He could not swim, and the water was very deep, but he rapidly moved his hands and feet in an attempt to scramble upward. Within a few seconds he was dog-paddling, and his nose was above the water's surface. Breathing easily and making forward progress, he found that he liked swimming in water.

But he had no time to think much about his new ability. He was now swimming parallel to the bank, and there he saw the cruel beast crouching on top of the still form of his little playmate. Sabor was intently watching Tarzan, expecting him to return to shore, but the boy had no such intention.

Instead he raised his voice in the tribal distress call, adding the warning which indicated the danger of Sabor to would-be rescuers.

Almost immediately there came an answer from the distance, and presently forty or fifty great apes swung rapidly and majestically through the trees toward the scene of tragedy. In the lead was Kala, for she had recognized the tones of her most beloved, and with her was the mother of the little ape who lay dead beneath cruel Sabor.

Though more dangerous than any one ape, Sabor had no desire to meet so many enraged adults, and with a snarl of hatred she disappeared quickly into the brush.

Tarzan now swam onto dry land. He felt happy and refreshed. Thereafter, he lost no opportunity to take a daily plunge into a lake or a stream. Kala had difficulty getting used to the odd sight. Her people could swim when necessary, but did not voluntarily enter water.

Tarzan long remembered the lioness adventure with fondness, for his daily life was mostly dull: search for food, eat, sleep. His tribe roamed an area extending roughly twenty-five miles along the seacoast and some fifty miles inland. They moved continually about this area, occasionally remaining in one portion of it for months, but able to cover the entire territory by speedy movement through the trees. Their movements were dictated by food supply, climate, dangerous animals, and Kerchak's tendency to get bored with one place. At night they slept, sometimes covered with the great leaves of the elephant's ear. In the cold, they cuddled together for warmth, and in this way Tarzan had slept in Kala's arms nightly for all these years.

The huge, fierce brute loved this child of another race, and he in turn gave to the great, hairy beast all the affection that would otherwise have belonged to his fair young mother. When he was disobedient, Kala cuffed him, but never cruelly, and was more often caressing him than chastising him.

Tublat, her mate of the crooked nose, always hated Tarzan, and on several occasions had nearly ended his youthful career. For his part, Tarzan never lost an opportunity to show that the feeling was mutual. Whenever he could safely annoy Tublat, make faces at him, or hurl insults at him from a safe position, he did so.

His superior intelligence and cunning permitted him to invent a thousand diabolical tricks to play on his foster father. Early in his boyhood, he had learned to form ropes by twisting and tying long grasses together, and with these he was forever tripping Tublat or attempting to hang him as he passed under a branch. In time he learned to tie crude knots, and make sliding nooses, and with these he and the younger apes amused themselves. They tried to imitate him, but he alone was good with ropes and knots.

One day while playing, Tarzan had thrown his rope at one of his fleeing companions, tightly grasping the other end. By accident the noose fell squarely about the running ape's neck, bringing him to a sudden and surprising halt. Ah, here was a fine new game, thought Tarzan, and immediately he attempted to repeat the trick. And thus, with much practice, he learned the art of roping.

Now the life of Tublat became a living nightmare. In sleep, while on the hunting march, night or day, he never knew when that quiet noose would slip about his neck and nearly choke the life out of him. Kala punished him, Tublat swore dire vengeance, and old Kerchak warned and threatened, but all to no avail.

Tarzan defied them all, and continued to try to hang Tublat at every opportunity. The other apes were very amused, for old Broken Nose was widely disliked anyway.

In Tarzan's clever little mind many thoughts revolved. If he could catch his fellow apes with his long arm of many grasses, why not Sabor, the lioness?

It was the germ of a thought, one destined to mull around in the back of his mind until it resulted in magnificent achievement.

But that came in later years.

CHAPTER 6

JUNGLE BATTLES

The tribe was often near the closed and silent cabin. Tarzan's inability to gain entrance magnified his desire to see what lay inside. It was a place of mystery and pleasure, one he imagined full of wonderful creatures. He would peek into the curtained windows, or climb up onto the roof to peer down the chimney, all in a vain effort to puzzle out its contents.

It had not yet occurred to him to try the door, because it seemed as solid as the walls. But on his next visit after the adventure with old Sabor, he noticed that the door seemed different than the rest of the wall. For the first time it occurred to him that it might offer a way in.

As was usual when he visited the cabin, he was alone, for the tale of the thunder-stick had lived on and grown among the apes over the years. The white man's deserted abode was weird and terrifying, best avoided.

He had never been told the story of his own connection with the cabin. The language of the apes was inadequate to describe the cabin's interior, especially the strange people and their belongings. The tribe had long forgotten the details. Only Kala had vaguely explained to him that his father had been a strange white ape, but he did not know that Kala was not his real mother.

On this day, determined, he spent hours examining the door and fussing with its mechanics. Finally he stumbled on the right combination, and the door creaked open before his astonished eyes. For some minutes he hesitated, but eventually his eyes became used to the dim interior. He slowly and cautiously entered.

In the middle of the floor lay a skeleton, still covered with the moldy remnants of what had once been clothing. A similar but smaller set of bones lay on the bed, while in a little cradle nearby was a third, tiny skeleton. Tarzan was unmoved; dead or dying animals were common sights in his wild jungle world. Even if he had known that he was looking at the remains of his own father and mother, it would not have bothered him. The furnishings and other contents of the cabin, however, were fascinating. He closely examined the strange tools and weapons, books, paper, clothing—what little had withstood the ten years in the humid atmosphere of the jungle coast.

He figured out how to open some of the chests and cupboards, and the contents of these were much better preserved. Among other things, he found a sharp hunting knife, and immediately cut his finger on the keen blade. He experimented with it, learning to hack splinters of wood from the table and chairs. A new toy! After some time he got tired of this and continued to explore. In a cupboard filled with books he came across one with brightly colored pictures, a child's illustrated alphabet book:

A is for Archer
Who shoots with a bow.
B is for Boy,
His first name is Joe.

The pictures interested him greatly.

There were many apes with faces similar to his own, and further over in the book he found, under "M," some little monkeys like those that flitted through the trees of his jungle. But none of his own people were pictured—that is, none that resembled Kerchak, or Tublat, or Kala. At first he tried to pick the little figures from the pages, but he soon saw that they were not real, though he did not know what they might be, nor how to describe them.

The boats and trains and cows and horses meant nothing to him, but these were not quite so baffling as the odd little symbols which appeared beneath and between the colored pictures. Perhaps they were some strange kind of bug, for many of them had legs—though none had eyes and a mouth. It was his first introduction to the notion of written language.

Near the middle of the book he found his old enemy, Sabor, the lioness, and further on, Histah, the snake, coiled to strike. How wonderful it was! Never before had he enjoyed anything so much.

So absorbed was he that he did not notice the approaching dusk until it blurred the figures.

He put the book back in the cupboard and closed the door, for he did not wish anyone else to find and destroy his treasure. As he left, he closed the great door behind him, taking the hunting knife with him to show to his tribe.

He had taken a few steps toward the jungle when a great form rose up before him from the shadows of a low bush. At first he thought it was one of his own people. In another instant he realized that it was Bolgani, the huge gorilla, and too close for him to escape.

Little Tarzan knew that he must stand and fight for his life. The great gorillas and his tribe were deadly enemies, and no mercy was ever asked or given. Had Tarzan been a full-grown bull ape of his tribe, he would have been more than a match for the gorilla, but even a very muscular little English boy stood no chance alone.

His true ancestors, though, had been mighty fighters, and the training of his lifetime in the brutal jungle had awakened this heritage. He felt no fear, as we think of it, but his little heart beat faster from the excitement of adventure. With escape

impossible, he met the gorilla squarely and without a sign of panic.

Tarzan met the brute in mid-charge, striking its huge body with his closed fists like a fly attacking an elephant. But in one hand he still clutched the knife he had found in the cabin. As the striking and biting brute closed upon him, the boy accidentally turned the point of the weapon toward the hairy chest. The knife sank deep into its body, and the gorilla shrieked in pain and rage.

In that brief second, the boy had learned a use for the sharp and shining toy. As the tearing, striking beast dragged him down, he plunged the blade repeatedly into its chest.

The gorilla struck terrific blows with its open hand, and tore the flesh at the boy's throat and chest with its mighty tusks. For a moment they rolled on the ground in the fierce frenzy of combat. Tarzan's torn and bleeding arm kept striking home with the long sharp blade, but more and more weakly each time. Then the little figure stiffened, and the young Lord Greystoke was unconscious on the decaying vegetation which carpeted his jungle home.

A mile back in the forest, the tribe had heard the fierce challenge of the gorilla. As was his custom when any danger threatened, Kerchak assembled his people. This was partly for mutual protection, since there might be more than one gorilla, but also to account for all members of the tribe.

Tarzan was soon noted missing, and Tublat was strongly opposed to sending assistance. Kerchak himself had no liking for the strange little waif, so he listened to Tublat. With a final shrug of his shoulders, he turned back to the pile of leaves where he had been sleeping.

Not Kala. She had already noted Tarzan's absence, and was already flying full speed through the branches, toward the point from which the cries of the gorilla were coming.

Now it was dark, the moonlight only penetrating the thick jungle in spots. Like some huge phantom, Kala swung noiselessly from tree to tree, making rapid progress toward the scene. She knew that tragedy was occurring nearby. The cries of the gorilla proclaimed that it was in mortal combat with some other inhabitant of the fierce wood. Suddenly these cries ceased, and the silence of death reigned throughout the jungle.

Kala could not understand, for the last cry of Bolgani had been one of agony and death, but she could not tell with whom the gorilla was fighting. She knew it was improbable that her little Tarzan could destroy a great bull gorilla, so as she neared the apparent site of the struggle, she moved more warily. Her final approach was extremely cautious, peering eagerly into the moon-splashed blackness for a sign of the combatants.

Presently she found them, lying in a little open space under the brilliant light of the moon. Next to little Tarzan's torn and bloody form lay a great bull gorilla, stone dead.

With a low cry Kala rushed to Tarzan's side, gathered the poor, blood-covered body to her chest, and listened for a sign of life. Faintly, she heard the weak beating of the little heart.

She gently bore him back through the inky jungle to the tribe, and for many days and nights she tended and guarded him, bringing him food and water, and brushing the flies and other insects from his cruel wounds. The only medicine she knew was to lick the wounds to keep them clean, enabling nature's healing to work more quickly.

At first Tarzan would not eat, but rolled and tossed in a delirious fever. All he craved was water, and this she brought him in the only way she could, bearing it in her own mouth. No human mother could have cared more unselfishly for a baby than did Kala for the little orphan whom fate had brought her.

Finally the fever abated, and the boy began to mend. He was in terrible pain, but no word of complaint escaped his tight lips. A portion of his chest was laid bare to the ribs, three of which Bolgani had broken. One arm was badly mauled by the giant fangs, and a great piece had been torn from his neck. The cruel jaws had missed his jugular vein only by some miracle.

As was the custom of the great apes, he endured his suffering quietly, preferring to crawl away from the others and lie huddled in the tall grass rather than to show his misery before their eyes.

The only company he was glad for was Kala, but now that he was better, she was gone for longer times in search of food. The devoted animal had scarcely eaten enough to support her own life while Tarzan had been so ill, and was reduced to a poor thin shadow of her former self.

Little Tarzan, on the mend but having no other means to occupy himself, spent the time deep in thought.

CHAPTER 7

THE LIGHT OF KNOWLEDGE

After what seemed like forever, little Tarzan was finally able to walk again. From then on, he recovered swiftly, and in another month he was as strong and active as ever.

During his recovery he had thought much about the battle with the gorilla, and his uppermost wish was to recover the wonderful weapon he had used to defeat mighty Bolgani. Also, he was anxious to return to the cabin and learn more of its wondrous contents.

Early one morning, he set forth alone. After a brief search he located the clean-picked bones of his enemy, and near them the knife, now rusty from blood and the damp ground. To his dismay, its surface was no longer bright and gleaming, but it was still a powerful weapon. He meant to use it whenever the opportunity arose; in particular, he no longer felt inclined to run from the attacks of old Tublat.

In another moment he had thrown the latch and entered the cabin. His first concern was to understand the lock, and he studied it until he learned to lock it from inside the cabin. Now he would not be disturbed. He began a thorough search of the cabin, but the books so riveted his attention that he soon forgot about everything else. There were some children's readers, numerous picture books, and a great dictionary. He examined all of these, but the pictures interested him most, as did the little buglike shapes found on pages without pictures. It was all a great wonder.

His little face was tense in study, for he had the beginnings of a solution to the puzzling problem of the strange little bugs.

In his hands was a child's textbook opened to a picture of a little ape similar to himself, but covered, except for hands and face, with strange, colored fur, for such he thought the jacket and trousers to be. Beneath the picture were three little bugs—

B O Y

Then he discovered, in the text, that these three bugs were repeated many times in this exact sequence.

Another fact he learned was that there were comparatively few individual bugs, but these were repeated many times, occasionally alone, but more often in company with others.

Slowly he scanned the pictures and the text for a repetition of the combination B-O-Y. Presently he found it beneath a picture of another little ape and a strange animal which resembled the jackal.

Beneath this picture the bugs appeared as:

A BOY AND A DOG

There they were, the three little bugs which always accompanied the little ape.

He progressed very, very slowly, for the task was more difficult than he knew, and might seem impossible to you or me—learning to read without having the slightest idea that such things as letters and writing existed. He did not achieve this in a day, or even a year, but he did learn. By the time he was fifteen, he knew what many of the combinations of letters stood for. As to grammar, of course, he had only the faintest notion.

One day when he was about twelve, he discovered a drawer holding some lead pencils. Scratching the table top with one, he was delighted to discover that it left behind a black line. He worked so hard with this new toy that the tabletop was soon a mass of scrawled loops and irregular lines, and his pencil-point was worn down to the wood. He then picked up another pencil, but this time he had an objective: he would attempt to reproduce some of the little bugs.

It was difficult, more so because he held the pencil as one would grasp the hilt of a dagger. But he kept at it for months, until through trial and error he learned a better way to hold the pencil. Now he could draw any and all of the bugs.

Thus he made a beginning of writing. He studied diligently, and by the time he was seventeen, he could read the simple child's reading book. He knew the true purpose of the bugs.

He no longer felt shame for his hairless body or his human features, for now he understood that he was of a different race from his wild and hairy companions. He was a M-A-N, they were A-P-E-S, and the little apes which scurried through the forest top were M-O-N-K-E-Y-S. He knew, too, that old Sabor was a L-I-O-N-E-S-S, and Histah a S-N-A-K-E, and Tantor an E-L-E-P-H-A-N-T.

And so he learned to read.

From then on his progress was rapid. The great dictionary and his high intelligence enabled him to make educated guesses about things he did not understand. The tribe's migratory habits often interrupted his education, but his mind kept busy even without books. Pieces of bark, flat leaves and even bare earth were his notebooks, lessons scratched out with the knife-point.

Nor did he neglect the sterner duties of life. He practiced with his rope and played with his knife, which he had learned to sharpen on flat stones. From a picture in one of the books, he had devised a crude sheath to contain it. The tribe had grown larger in his time, for under the leadership of Kerchak, they had frightened the other tribes out of their territory. This gave them plenty to eat and minimized losses due to raids by their neighbors.

For this reason, younger males growing to adulthood preferred to find mates from their own tribe. If they captured a mate from another tribe, they tended to bring her back to Kerchak's band under his rule. It was safer than setting up a new tribe, or fighting Kerchak for leadership at home. Occasionally a very ferocious ape would challenge Kerchak, but none could defeat the fierce ape-king.

Tarzan held a unique position in the tribe. They seemed to consider him one of them, and yet in some way different. The older males ignored him entirely, or else hated him so greatly that only his wondrous agility and speed and the fierce protection of Kala kept him from an early death.

Tublat was his most consistent enemy. But it was through Tublat that, when he was about thirteen, his enemies stopped persecuting him. From that day he was left respectfully alone, except for times when one of the males would go into a fit of mad rage. At those times, no one was safe.

On the day that Tarzan gained respect, the tribe was gathered at a small natural clearing, almost circular, in a hollow among some low hills. The arena was surrounded by the mighty trees of the untouched forest, and girdled with such dense undergrowth that the only way in was through the upper branches of the trees.

Here, safe from interruption, the tribe often gathered. In the center of the clearing was one of those strange earthen drums which the apes build for their odd rites. European and African men have often heard these sounds in the jungle, and even seen the drums, but none have ever reported witnessing the ritual. Tarzan, Lord Greystoke, is surely the only human who ever actually joined in the wild, ancient ceremony of the Dum-Dum.

On this day, the tribe—now a full hundred strong—trooped silently through the lower terrace of the jungle trees and dropped noiselessly to the floor of the theater. The rites of the Dum-Dum marked important events in the life of the tribe— a victory, the capture of a prisoner, the killing of some great enemy, the death or crowning of a king—and were conducted with great ritual.

Today it was the killing of a giant ape from another tribe. As the people of Kerchak entered the arena, two mighty bull apes carried in the enemy's dead body. They laid their burden before the earthen drum and then squatted there beside it as guards, while the other members of the community curled up in grassy nooks to sleep until the rising moon signaled the beginning of the savage festival.

For hours the little clearing was absolutely quiet, except for the sounds of the many brilliant parrots and other jungle birds flitting among the vivid flowers and mossy branches. Then darkness settled, and the apes assembled in a great circle around the earthen drum. The females and young squatted in the outer ring, with the adult males in a smaller ring in front of them.

Before the drum sat three old females, each armed with a knotted branch between one and two feet in length. A small pile of similar branches lay nearby. Slowly and softly they began tapping on the resounding surface of the drum as the first faint rays of moonlight silvered the encircling tree tops.

As the moonlight brightened, the females beat the drum faster and with greater force, until the wild rhythm resounded for miles. Great predators stopped in their hunting and lifted their ears and heads to listen to the dull booming of the Dum-Dum of the apes. Occasionally one would scream or roar out an answering challenge, but none dared approach to investigate or attack.

When the sound of the drum was almost deafening, Kerchak sprang into the open space between the squatting males and the drummers. Standing erect, he threw his head far back and looked full into the eye of the rising moon. He beat upon his chest with his great hairy paws and thundered his fearful roaring shriek.

Once, twice, three times, that terrifying cry rang out through the night.

Then Kerchak slunk silently around the open circle, veering far away from the dead body lying before the altar-drum, but keeping his wicked little red eyes fixed upon the corpse. Another male then sprang into the arena, and, repeating the horrid cries of his king, followed stealthily in his wake. More males followed, their bloodthirsty screams driving out all other jungle sounds.

It was the challenge and the hunt.

When all the adult males had joined in the thin line of circling dancers, the attack began.

Kerchak seized a huge club from the pile and rushed furiously to the dead ape. Snarling as if in combat, he dealt the corpse a terrific blow. The older females beat the drum louder and faster. Each of the warriors approached the victim of the hunt and delivered his blow, joining in the mad whirl of the Death Dance.

Tarzan was one of the wild, leaping horde. His

brown, sweat-streaked, muscular body, glistening in the moonlight, shone in bright contrast to the hairy brutes about him. There was none more stealthy in this mimic hunt, none more ferocious than he in the wild ferocity of the attack, none who leaped so high into the air in the Dance of Death.

As the noise and tempo of the drumbeats increased, the dancers seemed to go mad with the wild rhythm and the savage yells. Their leaps and bounds increased, and they foamed at the mouth.

The strange dance went on for half an hour. Then, at a sign from Kerchak, the noise of the drums ceased and the female drummers scampered hurriedly through the line of dancers toward the outer rim of squatting spectators. Then, as one, the males rushed headlong upon the thing which their terrific blows had beaten to a hairy pulp.

They rarely got their fill of meat, so the taste of a fresh kill was a fitting conclusion to their wild celebration, and they turned their attention to devouring their late enemy. Great fangs tore away huge hunks, with the mightiest obtaining the best pieces. The weaker circled the outer edge of the snarling pack, awaiting a chance to dodge in and grab a dropped tidbit or bone while they lasted.

Tarzan, more than the apes, craved and needed meat. His kind were meat eaters, and never once in his life had he eaten all the meat he wanted. Now his agile little body wormed its way far into the mass of struggling, tearing apes to obtain the share that his strength alone would not have gained him. When he finally reached the fast-disappearing feast, he whipped out his sharp knife and slashed off an entire hairy forearm, more than his share, just beneath the feet of the mighty Kerchak. The king was so busy gorging that he failed to note this act of outright disrespect to his royalty. Little Tarzan wriggled out from inside the struggling mass, closely clutching his grisly prize.

Among those circling the outskirts of the banqueters was old Tublat. He had been among the first at the feast, had already eaten a huge helping, and was now forcing his way back for more. As he did, he spied Tarzan emerging from the clawing, pushing throng with that hairy forearm hugged firmly to his body. Tublat's little, close-set, blood-shot eyes shot wicked gleams of hate and greed as they fell upon the despised boy.

But Tarzan saw his arch-enemy as quickly and knew what to expect. He leaped nimbly away toward the females and the young, hoping to hide himself among them. Tublat, however, was too close on his heels for him to escape. So he sped toward the surrounding trees, bounding with great agility onto a lower limb. Transferring his burden to his teeth, he climbed rapidly with Tublat in close pursuit. Up, up he went, high into a lofty tree, onto branches that would not hold his heavier pursuer. There he perched, hurling taunts and insults at the raging, foaming beast fifty feet below him.

And then Tublat went mad.

With horrifying screams and roars, he rushed to the ground, among the females and young, sinking his great fangs into a dozen tiny necks and tearing great pieces from the bodies of the females who fell into his clutches.

In the brilliant moonlight Tarzan witnessed the whole mad carnival of rage. He saw the females and the young scamper to the safety of the trees. Then the great apes in the center of the arena felt the mighty fangs of their maddened fellow, and as one they melted into the black shadows of the overhanging forest.

One female remained in the arena beside Tublat, running swiftly toward the tree where Tarzan perched. Close behind her came the awful Tublat.

It was Kala. As soon as Tarzan saw that Tublat was gaining on her, he dropped rapidly from branch to branch toward his foster mother. Soon she was beneath the limbs where Tarzan crouched in wait. She leaped to grasp a low-hanging branch, just over Tublat's head. She should have been safe now, but with a tearing sound, the branch broke. Kala landed directly on the head of Tublat, knocking him to the ground.

Both were up in an instant, but Tarzan had been even quicker. He stood between Kala and the infuriated ape. Nothing could have made the fierce beast happier, and with a roar of triumph he leaped upon the little Lord Greystoke—but his fangs never bit into that tanned flesh.

One muscular hand shot out and grasped the hairy throat, and another plunged a keen hunting knife a dozen times into the broad chest. The lightning-like blows ceased only when Tarzan felt the limp form crumple beneath him.

As the body rolled to the ground, Tarzan placed his foot on the neck of his lifelong enemy. He raised his eyes to the full moon, threw back his fierce young head and voiced the wild and terrible cry of his people.

One by one the tribe swung down from the heights and formed a circle about Tarzan and his vanquished foe. When they had all come Tarzan turned toward them.

"I am Tarzan," he cried. "I am a great killer. Let all respect Tarzan and Kala, his mother. None among you are as mighty as Tarzan. Let his enemies beware."

Looking full into the wicked, red eyes of Kerchak, the young Lord Greystoke beat upon his mighty chest and screamed out his shrill cry of defiance once more.

CHAPTER 8

THE TREE-TOP HUNTER

The morning after the Dum-Dum, the tribe started slowly back toward the coast. The body of Tublat lay where it had fallen, for the tribe of Kerchak does not eat its own dead. Instead, they searched for food on the way back, and found fruits, nuts, birds, eggs, and small animals.

Once old Sabor crossed their path and sent them scurrying to the safety of the higher branches. She respected their number and their sharp fangs; likewise, they respected her strength and ferocity. Tarzan sat not far above the majestic, supple lioness as she moved silently through the thick jungle. He hurled a pineapple at cruel Sabor. She stopped, turned, and eyed the taunting figure above her.

With an angry lash of her tail, she bared her yellow fangs, curling her great lips in a hideous snarl that wrinkled her bristling snout and narrowed her wicked eyes to slits of hatred. Ears laid back, she looked straight into his eyes and sounded her fierce, shrill challenge. And from the safety of his overhanging limb, the ape-child sent back the fearsome answer of the ape-kind.

For a moment the two eyed each other in silence, and then the great cat turned into the jungle, which swallowed her as the ocean engulfs a stone.

But a great plan came into Tarzan's mind. He had killed the fierce Tublat, so was he not therefore a mighty fighter? He would track down the crafty Sabor and slay her also. He would then also be a mighty hunter and would gain one more thing. Reading the books had made him desire to cover his body with CLOTHES, for the books indicated that all MEN did so, while MONKEYS and APES and every other living thing went naked—and he was a MAN. CLOTHES, he reasoned, must truly symbolize the superiority of MAN over all other animals. Surely there could be no other reason for wearing the hideous-looking things.

Many moons ago, when he had been much smaller, he had desired the skin of Sabor, the lioness, or Numa, the lion, or Sheeta, the leopard to cover his hairless body, which reminded him of Histah, the snake. Now he was proud of his smooth skin, for it proved his descent from a mighty race. Sometimes he wanted to obey the books, and wear clothes. Other times he desired to wear nothing, so that all might see proof of his superior ancestry.

As the tribe continued their slow way through the forest after Sabor stalked through, Tarzan's head was filled with his great scheme for slaying his enemy. For many days thereafter he thought of little else. Today, though, he had more immediate demands on his attention.

Suddenly it became as dark as midnight, the noises of the jungle ceased, and the trees stood motionless as though paralyzed. All nature waited—but not for long.

Faintly, from a distance, came a low, sad moaning. It grew steadily nearer and louder.

The great trees bent in unison as though pressed earthward by a mighty hand. Farther and farther toward the ground they bent, with no sound except the deep and awesome moaning of the wind.

Then, suddenly, the jungle giants whipped back, lashing their mighty tops in deafening protest. A vivid and blinding light flashed from the whirling, inky clouds above. The roar of thunder belched forth its fearsome challenge. The mighty rain gushed down as the storm exploded upon the jungle.

The tribe huddled below the great trees, shivering from the cold rain. The lightning flashed, showing the torment of the trees by the wind. Now and again some ancient patriarch of the woods would be hit by lightning. It would crash in a thousand pieces among the surrounding trees, adding to the tangled confusion of the tropical jungle. Branches great and small broke off, hurtling downward to bring death and destruction to many unhappy dwellers of the world below.

For hours, the fury of the storm continued at full force. In constant danger from falling debris, paralyzed by the vivid flashing of lightning and the bellowing of thunder, the tribe crouched in pitiful misery until the storm passed.

The end was as sudden as the beginning. The wind ceased, the sun shone forth—nature smiled once more.

The leaves, branches, and the gorgeous flowers glistened in the splendor of the returning day. And as Nature forgot, her children forgot also. Busy life went on as before. But to Tarzan, the mystery of CLOTHES was now explained. How snug he would have been beneath the heavy coat of Sabor! His planned adventure now had further incentive.

For several months the tribe hovered near the cabin, and Tarzan's studies took up most of his time. When journeying through the forest, though, he kept his rope ready. Many smaller animals fell into its snare.

Once it fell about the short neck of Horta, the boar. His mad lunge for freedom toppled Tarzan from the overhanging limb where he had lain in wait. The mighty tusker turned at the sound of his fall, and saw easy prey: a young ape. Horta lowered his head and charged madly at the surprised youth.

Luckily, Tarzan was unhurt by the fall. He landed on all fours like a cat, and was on his feet in an instant. With apelike agility, he leaped to the safety of a low limb as Horta rushed futilely beneath.

In this way Tarzan learned the limitations as well as the possibilities of his strange weapon. He lost a long rope on this occasion, but had it been Sabor rather than Horta, he might have lost his life as well.

It took him many days to braid a new rope, but when it was finally ready, he went hunting again. He lay in ambush in the dense foliage of a great branch right above the trail that led to water.

Several small animals passed unharmed beneath him. He did not want such minor game. It would take a strong animal to test his new scheme.

At last came Tarzan's quarry, with sleek muscles rolling beneath shimmering hide: none other than Sabor, the lioness. Her great padded feet were noiseless on the narrow trail. Her head was high in alertness; her tail moved gracefully. Nearer and nearer she came to where Tarzan crouched motionless on his limb, the long rope at the ready.

Sabor passed beneath. She took one stride beyond the waiting hunter—and then a second, and a third, and then the silent coil shot out above her.

For an instant the spreading noose hung above her head like a great snake, and then, as she looked upward to locate the swishing sound, the rope settled around her neck. With a quick jerk Tarzan snapped the noose tight about the glossy throat, and then he dropped the rope and clung to the tree with both hands.

Sabor was trapped.

With a bound, the startled beast turned into the jungle, but Tarzan had made plans not to lose another rope. The lioness was halfway into her second bound when she felt the rope tighten around her neck. Her body turned completely over in mid-air, and she fell with a heavy crash upon her back. Tarzan had fastened the end of the rope securely to the trunk of the great tree.

So far, the plan had worked perfectly, but when he braced himself and grasped the rope, he found that Sabor was not coming easily. It was one thing to lasso a struggling, biting, clawing, screaming mass of fury, but quite another to drag and hang her from a tree. Old Sabor was immensely heavy. If she did not wish to move, it would take Tantor the elephant himself to budge her.

The lioness now saw the one who had insulted her dignity. She screamed with rage and leaped toward Tarzan, clinging to his branch. But when her huge body arrived, Tarzan was gone. He had jumped to a smaller branch twenty feet above his raging captive. For a moment Sabor hung half across the branch, while Tarzan mocked her and threw branches at her unprotected face.

Presently the beast dropped to the earth again, putting slack onto the rope. Tarzan came quickly to seize it, but Sabor now found that only a slender cord held her. Her huge jaws severed it before Tarzan could tighten the strangling noose a second time.

He was greatly disappointed. His well-laid plan having failed, he sat in safety and screamed mockery at Sabor. She paced back and forth beneath the tree for hours. Four times she crouched and sprang at the dancing figure above her, but she might as well have tried to capture the wind.

At last Tarzan tired of the sport. With a parting roar of challenge, he threw a ripe fruit that spread soft and sticky over the snarling face of his enemy. Then he swung rapidly through the trees, a hundred feet above the ground, and in a short time was back among his tribe.

Here he told the entire tale of his adventure. His swelling chest and boastful swagger quite impressed even his bitterest enemies. Kala fairly danced for joy and pride.

CHAPTER 9

MAN AND MAN

Tarzan's wild jungle life remained much the same for several years. He grew stronger and wiser, and from his books he learned more and more of the strange worlds beyond his jungle.

His life was never dull. There was always Pisah, the fish, to be caught in the many streams and the little lakes. Sabor, with her ferocious cousins, kept him alert any time he was on the ground. Sabor and her kin hunted him, but their cruel, sharp claws never quite reached his smooth hide. Sabor the lioness was quick, and quick were Numa and Sheeta, her cousins, but Tarzan was like lightning.

It is not known how, but he made friends with Tantor, the elephant. But it is known that on many moonlit nights Tarzan and Tantor walked together, and when possible, Tarzan rode high, perched on Tantor's mighty back.

He spent many days in the cabin, where the bones of his parents and the skeleton of Kala's baby lay untouched. At eighteen, he could easily understand nearly all of the varied volumes on the shelves. He could also write well, at least with printed letters. Thus at eighteen we find him, an English lord's offspring, who could write but not speak his native language.

He had never seen another human being, for his tribe's territory contained no great river to attract the tribespeople of the interior. It was enclosed on three sides by high hills, and on the fourth by the ocean. It was a thick jungle, alive with lions and leopards and poisonous snakes. There were much safer, easier places for man to live.

But as Tarzan sat one day investigating the mysteries of a new book, the ancient security of his jungle was broken forever.

From far to the east, in single file over the brow of a low hill, came a great number of humans.

In the front were fifty African warriors armed with sharp, slender wooden spears, long bows, and poisoned arrows. On their backs were oval shields, in their noses huge rings. Their curly hair was decorated with tufts of bright feathers, and their foreheads and chests bore intricate tattoos. Their teeth were filed to sharp points. They looked warlike, ready for action. Following them were several hundred women and children, the former bearing great burdens of cooking pots, household utensils and ivory on their heads. A hundred more warriors formed a rearguard, for they expected pursuit.

European troops had often harassed these

tribespeople, demanding that they collect more rubber and ivory. One day their frustration had boiled over, and they had killed a European officer and his small force of African troops. Eventually a stronger body of European-led African troops came for revenge and attacked the village at night, killing many. The sad remnant of a once-powerful tribe retreated into the gloomy jungle toward freedom.

After four days of travel, they came upon a less-overgrown area near a small river. Here they began to build a new village, and in a month their knowledge and industry produced impressive results. A great area had been cleared; huts and high, protective fences built; plantains, yams and maize planted. They lived as before. Here there were no whites, no black soldiers enforcing their rule, and no demands to gather rubber or ivory.

Several moons passed by before the tribespeople ventured far into the surrounding jungle. Several had already fallen prey to old Sabor, and because the jungle was full of her kind and their leopard cousins, the warriors remained close to the safety of their village.

But one day, Kulonga, a son of the old king, Mbonga, wandered far into the dense mazes to the west. Warily he stepped, his slender lance ever ready, his long oval shield firmly grasped in his left hand close to his sleek ebony body. His bow was slung at his back, and on his shield was a quiver of slim, straight arrows smeared with the sticky, black substance that made their tiniest puncture deadly.

Night found Kulonga far from the safety of his father's village, but still headed westward. Climbing into the fork of a great tree, he built a platform and curled himself up for sleep.

Three miles to the west slept the tribe of Kerchak.

Early the next morning the apes were awake, moving through the jungle in search of food. As usual, Tarzan searched in the direction of the cabin, so that by the time he arrived at the beach, his stomach was full. The apes scattered in small groups in all directions, always staying within range of the alarm.

Kala had moved slowly along an elephant track toward the east. She was bent over, seeking tasty bugs and mushrooms, when a faint strange noise brought her to startled attention. She looked up the trail.

Coming toward her was a strange, fearful creature.

It was Kulonga.

Kala did not wait to see more, but turned rapidly back along the trail in an effort to avoid the stranger. Close after her came Kulonga, intent upon a good feast this day, with his spear poised to throw.

For a moment she was out of his sight, but the trail straightened after a time, and he caught another brief glimpse of her. His spear hand went far back, the muscles rolled like lightning beneath his skin, and the spear sped toward Kala.

Unfortunately for Kulonga, it was a poor throw. The spear only grazed her side.

The she-ape sounded an alarm of rage and pain, and turned upon her tormentor. In an instant the trees were crashing beneath the weight of her tribemates, swinging rapidly toward the scene of trouble.

As she charged, Kulonga unslung his bow and fitted an arrow with astonishing quickness. Drawing the shaft far back, he drove the poisoned missile straight into the heart of the great ape. With a horrid scream, Kala plunged forward on her face before the stunned members of her tribe.

Roaring and shrieking, the apes dashed toward Kulonga, but the warrior was fleeing down the trail like a frightened antelope. He knew of the ferocity of the wild, hairy apes, and that he must get far away. Racing through the trees, they followed him for a long distance, but one by one they gave up the chase and returned to the scene of the tragedy.

Tarzan was the only man any of them had ever seen before, and so they wondered. What strange sort of creature had invaded their jungle?

On the far beach by the little cabin Tarzan heard the faint echoes of the conflict, and knew that something was seriously wrong. He too hastened in the direction of the sound.

When he arrived, he found the entire tribe

gathered jabbering about the dead body of his slain mother.

Tarzan's grief and anger were limitless. He roared out his furious challenge time and again. He beat upon his great chest with his clenched fists, and then he fell upon the body of Kala and sobbed his heart out in anguish. Losing the only creature in all his world who had ever shown him love and affection was the greatest tragedy he had ever known. He had lavished upon her the love and respect that would otherwise have been reserved for the fair and lovely Lady Alice, had she lived.

After the first outburst of grief, Tarzan controlled himself. He questioned the members of the tribe who had witnessed the killing. They told him of a strange, hairless black creature, similar to himself but with feathers growing from its head, who launched death from a slender branch, and then ran into the jungle as swiftly as Bara, the deer.

Tarzan leapt immediately into the branches of the trees and sped rapidly through the forest. He knew that the elephant trail wound and twisted, so he cut straight through the jungle to intercept the killer. At his side was the hunting knife of his unknown father, and across his shoulders the coils of his own long rope. In an hour he descended to the trail and examined the soil closely. In the soft mud on the bank of a tiny stream, he found footprints like his, but much larger. His heart beat fast.

Could it be that he was trailing a MAN—one of his own race?

There were two sets of prints pointing in opposite directions, indicating that his quarry had passed this point coming and going. As he examined the newer footprints, he saw evidence that the trail was very fresh. His prey must have just passed by. Tarzan swung himself to the trees once more and sped along, swift and silent, high above the trail.

He had covered barely a mile when at a distance he spotted the African warrior, standing in a little open space. In his hand was his slender bow, loaded with one of his death-dealing arrows. Opposite him stood Horta, the boar, with lowered head and foam-flecked tusks, ready to charge. Kulonga, son of Mbonga, was too focused on the nearby danger to notice Tarzan above him.

Tarzan looked with wonder at the strange creature beneath him—shaped like him, but so different in face and color. His books had portrayed this type of MAN as a NEGRO, but compared to the reality, the print and pictures had been dull and lifeless. This sleek ebony MAN pulsed with life. As the man stood there with his drawn bow, Tarzan recognized him from his picture book—

A stands for ARCHER

How wonderful! Tarzan almost gave his presence away, so excited was he at his discovery.

But things were happening below him. The

powerful arm had drawn the missile far back. Horta, the boar, was charging, and the African released the little poisoned arrow. Tarzan saw it fly with the quickness of thought, sinking into the bristling neck of the boar.

Kulonga immediately raised a second arrow to his bow, but Horta was upon him so quickly that he had no time to shoot. With a bound, the warrior leaped entirely over the rushing beast, then turned with great agility and planted a second arrow in Horta's back. He then sprang into a near-by tree.

Horta wheeled to charge once more. He took a dozen steps, then staggered and fell on his side. For a moment his muscles twitched; then he lay still.

Kulonga came down from his tree. With a knife that hung at his side, he cut several large pieces of meat, and in the center of the trail he built a fire, cooking and eating his fill. The rest he left where it had fallen.

Tarzan watched with interest. The desire to kill burned fiercely in his heart, but his desire to learn was even greater. His quarry had shown tremendous skill and deadliness. He would follow this odd creature for a while, and find his lair. He could then kill him at his leisure, when the bow and deadly arrows were laid aside.

When Kulonga had finished his meal and disappeared beyond a turn of the path, Tarzan dropped quietly to the ground. With his knife he severed many strips of meat from Horta's carcass, but he did not cook them.

He had seen fire before only when Ara, the lightning, had destroyed some great tree. Tarzan was very surprised that any creature of the jungle could produce the red-and-yellow fangs which turned wood into fine dust. Even more surprising, though, was the way the MAN had ruined his delicious lunch by plunging it into the ruinous heat. Maybe Ara was a friend with whom the Archer was sharing his food.

Be that as it may, Tarzan would not ruin good meat in any such manner. He gobbled down a great quantity of the raw pork, burying the rest beside the trail where he could find it when he returned later.

And then Lord Greystoke wiped his greasy fingers on his naked thighs and took up the trail of Kulonga, the son of King Mbonga. At this exact moment in far-off London, another Lord Greystoke, the younger brother of the real Lord Greystoke's father, sent back his chops to the club's chef because they were undercooked. When he had finished dining, he dipped his fingertips into a silver bowl of scented water and dried them with a piece of fine white linen.

All day Tarzan followed Kulonga, hovering above him in the trees like an evil spirit. Twice more he saw him hurl his arrows of swift death—

once at Dango, the hyena, and again at Manu, the monkey. In each case, the animal died almost instantly, for Kulonga's poison was as fresh and deadly as his aim was skilled.

As he followed, Tarzan thought much about this wondrous method of slaying. He knew that the small wound made by the arrow could not, by itself, so quickly kill the wild creatures of the jungle. After all, they often received much greater wounds in battle with their neighbors—yet they usually recovered. No, there was something mysterious about these tiny slivers of wood. He must investigate.

That night Kulonga slept in the fork of a mighty tree. Far above him crouched Tarzan.

When Kulonga awoke, he found that his bow and arrows had disappeared. The African was furious, but even more frightened. He searched the ground and the tree, but there was no sign of either bow or arrows, nor of the thief in the night.

Kulonga was panic-stricken. He had been unable to recover his spear, and now that his bow and arrows were gone, he was defenseless except for a single knife. His only hope lay in reaching the village as quickly as his legs would carry him. He knew he was near home, so he set forth at a rapid trot.

From a great mass of thick vegetation a few yards away, Tarzan emerged to swing quietly in his wake.

Kulonga's bow and arrows were securely tied high in a giant tree that Tarzan had marked with his knife in a special way, just as he marked all his trails and hiding places.

As Kulonga continued his journey, Tarzan closed in on him until he traveled almost over the tribesman's head. His rope was coiled at the ready, but he was anxious to discover the black archer's destination, so he delayed the kill. Presently he was rewarded, for they suddenly came in view of a great clearing. The forest ended abruptly, and two hundred yards of planted fields lay ahead. Beyond these lay many strange lairs. He must act quickly, or his prey would be gone.

Experience had taught him never to hesitate in an emergency. As Kulonga emerged from the shadow of the jungle, a slender coil of rope fell toward him from a mighty tree at the edge of the fields. Before the he had taken half a dozen steps into the clearing, a quick noose tightened about his neck.

Tarzan pulled back his prey so quickly that Kulonga's cry of alarm was choked off. He drew the struggling warrior up hand over hand until he had him hanging by his neck in mid-air. Tarzan then climbed to a larger branch, drawing the still-thrashing victim well up into the cover of the tree.

Here he fastened the rope securely to a stout branch, and descended. Without ceremony, he plunged his hunting knife into Kulonga's heart. Kala was avenged.

Tarzan examined the African warrior's body closely, for he had never seen any other human being. The warrior's knife with its sheath and belt caught his eye, and he took them. A copper anklet also interested him, and he transferred this to his own leg.

He admired the tattooing on the forehead and chest, and marveled at the sharply filed teeth. He examined and then put on the feathered head-dress. Then he prepared to get down to business, for Tarzan was hungry, and here was meat of the kill, which jungle ethics permitted him to eat.

Then he stopped to think. Tublat and he had hated one another. Tarzan had killed Tublat in a fair fight, and yet had never even thought of eating Tublat's flesh. He knew that the apes did not eat the flesh of their own kind.

But how was Kulonga any different from Horta, the boar, or Bara, the deer, or any of the countless creatures of the jungle who preyed upon one another for food? Something was different.

Suddenly he remembered. Had not his books taught him that he was a MAN? And was not the Archer also a man?

Surely he was. And with a qualm of nausea, Tarzan knew that he could not eat the flesh of the man he had killed.

Quickly he lowered Kulonga's body to the ground, removed the noose, and took to the trees again.

CHAPTER 10

THE FEAR PHANTOM

From a lofty perch, Tarzan looked across the fields to the village of thatched huts.

He saw a place where the forest touched the village, and made his way there in a fever of curiosity. These were more of his own kind! He sought to learn more of their ways, and of the strange lairs in which they lived.

They were enemies, of course. All creatures outside his own tribe were enemies except for Tantor, the elephant. Tarzan's jungle upbringing did not include sentimental notions of the brotherhood of man. The fact that they were shaped like him meant nothing to him. It was not malice or hatred—to kill was simply the law of his wild world, the greatest of his primitive pleasures. He accepted the right of others to this pleasure also, even if it was he that they hunted.

Though he killed mostly for food, Tarzan would also sometimes do a thing that no animal but man does—kill for pleasure. Yet even when he killed for revenge, or in self-defense, he did so unemotionally.

Killing was all business—the business of the jungle.

So now, as he cautiously approached the village of Mbonga, he was quite prepared either to kill or be killed should he be discovered. He proceeded with stealth, for he had learned great respect for the little splinters of wood which dealt such swift death.

At length he came to a great tree, heavy with thick foliage and giant creeper vines. In this concealed position he crouched, wondering about every feature of this new, strange place below him.

There were naked children running and playing in the village street. There were women grinding dried plantain in stone mortars, while others were making cakes from the powdered flour. In the fields other women were hoeing, weeding, or gathering. All wore strange girdles of dried grass around their hips. Many wore brass and copper anklets, armlets and bracelets, necklaces and nose rings. All the people were the same color as Kulonga.

Tarzan looked at these strange creatures with growing wonder. He saw several men dozing in the shade, while at the extreme edge of the clearing, he occasionally saw armed warriors on guard against any surprise attack. He noticed that only the women worked. No man tended the fields, or seemed to perform any of the other basic labor of the village.

His eyes finally rested upon a woman directly beneath him. She was boiling a thick, reddish-black substance in a cauldron. Next to her lay a quantity of wooden arrows. She was dipping their points into the boiling substance, then laying them on a narrow rack.

Tarzan was fascinated. Here was The Archer's secret. He noted the extreme care the woman took to avoid touching the mixture. Once when a particle spattered on to one of her fingers, she hurried to wash it off with leaves and water. Tarzan knew nothing of poison, but clearly it was this deadly substance that killed, and not the little arrow.

How he would like to have more of those deadly little slivers. If the woman would only leave her work for an instant, he could drop down, gather up a handful, and be back in the tree again before she drew three breaths.

As he was trying to think of a way to distract her, he heard a wild cry from across the clearing. He looked and saw a warrior standing beneath the very tree in which he had killed the murderer of Kala an hour before. The fellow was shouting and waving his spear above his head. Now and then he would point to the ground before him.

The village was in an instant uproar. Armed men rushed from huts and raced madly across the clearing toward the excited sentry. After them trooped the old men, then the women and children. In a moment, the village was deserted.

Tarzan knew that they had found his victim. Of more immediate interest was the fact that no one was around to prevent his taking a supply of the arrows. Quickly and noiselessly he dropped to the ground beside the cauldron of poison.

For a moment he stood motionless, his quick, bright eyes scanning the interior of the wall. No one was in sight.

His eyes rested upon the open doorway of a nearby hut. Tarzan thought he would take a look inside, so he cautiously approached the low thatched building. For a moment he stood outside, listening intently. There was no sound, and he glided into its semi-dark interior.

Weapons hung on the walls—long spears, strangely shaped knives, a couple of narrow shields. In the center of the room was a cooking pot, and at the far end hung a hammock of dry grasses covered by woven mats. Several human skulls lay scattered around on the floor.

Tarzan felt, lifted, and then smelled each item with his sensitive and highly trained nostrils. The spears were very interesting. He decided he would own one of these long, pointed sticks someday when he would not be loaded down with arrows.

As he took each article from the wall, he placed it in a pile in the center of the room. On top of the pile he overturned the cooking pot, and on top of this he laid one of the grinning skulls. To this he fastened the headdress of the dead.

Then he stood back, surveyed his work, and grinned. Tarzan enjoyed a joke.

But now he heard the sounds of many voices, long mournful howls, and mighty wailing. He was startled. Had he remained too long? Quickly he reached the doorway and peered down the village street toward the gate.

The natives were not yet in sight, though he could plainly hear them approaching across the fields. They must be very near.

Like a flash, he sprang across the opening to the pile of arrows. Gathering up all he could carry under one arm, he kicked over the boiling cauldron and disappeared into the foliage above just as the first of the returning natives entered the gate. Then he turned to watch what came next, ready to flee at the first sign of danger.

The tribespeople filed up the street, four of them bearing the dead body of Kulonga. Behind them trailed the women, making strange cries of grief. They came to the doorway of Kulonga's hut, which happened to be the very one Tarzan had investigated.

Soon those who had entered came rushing out in wild, jabbering confusion. The others quickly gathered about with excited pointing and chattering. Then several of the warriors approached and peered within.

Finally an old fellow entered the hut. He had many metal ornaments on his arms and legs, and a necklace of dried human hands rested upon his chest.

It was Mbonga, the king, father of Kulonga.

For a few moments, all was silent. Then Mbonga emerged, a look of mingled wrath and superstitious fear on his face. He spoke a few words to the assembled warriors, and in an instant the men were searching every hut and corner of the village.

Soon the overturned cauldron and missing poisoned arrows were discovered. The searchers found nothing else, and returned to report to Mbonga. The tribespeople huddled around their king in awe and fright.

Mbonga could not explain the strange events. The finding of the still warm body of Kulonga, knifed and stripped within an easy shout of the village, was mysterious enough. The amazing discoveries within the village, even in dead Kulonga's own hut, filled their hearts with dread. There being no natural explanation, the tribespeople began to suspect the supernatural. They stood in little groups, talking in low tones, casting terrified glances behind them.

Tarzan watched them for a while from his lofty perch. He had little experience with fear and none at all with superstition, and thus had no idea why they were acting this way. The sun was high in the heavens. Tarzan had not yet had breakfast, and the flavorful remains of Horta the boar lay many miles away. He turned his back on the village of Mbonga, and melted away into the leafy vastness of the forest.

CHAPTER 11

"KING OF THE APES"

$\mathbf{T}$arzan dropped from the branches into the midst of the tribe of Kerchak, arms full. With swelling chest, he boasted of his glorious adventure and showed off the spoils of conquest. Kerchak grunted and turned away in jealousy. He sought any excuse to vent his hatred on Tarzan.

The next day, Tarzan was practicing with his bow and arrows at the first gleam of dawn. Over the next month, he mastered the art—though at a cost of almost all his arrows.

The tribe continued to find good hunting near the beach, and so Tarzan alternated between archery practice and reading his father's books. During this period the young English lord found a small metal box hidden in one of the cupboards. The key was in the lock, and soon he had it open.

In it he found a faded photograph of a smooth-faced young man, a few letters, a small book, and a golden locket studded with diamonds on a small gold chain.

Tarzan examined these all intently.

He liked the photograph most of all, for the eyes were smiling and the face was open and frank. It was his father. He liked the locket, too, and he placed it around his neck in the way he had seen Africans wearing jewelry. The brilliant stones gleamed strangely against his smooth, brown hide. He could not read the handwriting of the letters, so he put them away and returned to the book.

This was almost entirely filled with fine handwriting, but while the little bugs were all familiar to him, they were combined strangely. He had long ago learned how to use the dictionary, but it was useless here. For the moment he put the book back in its box, but he was determined one day to find the solution.

Little did he know that this book held the answer to the riddle of his strange life. It was the diary of John Clayton, Lord Greystoke. It was kept in French, as he had always done. The strong, smiling face of his father remained in Tarzan's heart, but the problem of the book would have to wait. He was out of arrows and needed to journey to the village to obtain more.

He set out early the next morning, traveling rapidly, and arrived at the clearing before midday. Again he took up his position in the great tree. As before, he saw the women in the fields and the village street, and the cauldron of bubbling poison directly beneath him.

For hours he waited for an opportunity to

drop down unseen and steal the arrows, but nothing occurred to distract the villagers. The day wore on, and still Tarzan crouched above the unsuspecting woman at the cauldron. Eventually the light of day gave way to a moonless night, and only a few fires remained lit. Tarzan then dropped to the soft earth at the end of the village street. He quickly gathered up the arrows, and this time he got all of them, for he had brought a number of long fibers to bind them into a bundle.

Later, when the villagers discovered that once more their arrows had been stolen, they discussed the matter. They concluded that they had offended some great god by placing their village in this part of the jungle without showing proper respect. From then on, every day an offering of food was placed next to the great tree that grew above the poison-cauldron. The villagers hoped that it would placate the mighty god.

Tarzan could not know it, but he had laid the foundation for much future misery for himself and his tribe.

That night, he slept in the forest not far from the village, and early the next morning set out slowly homeward, hunting as he traveled. He found only a few berries and an occasional grub worm, and he was quite hungry. He was rooting under a log when he looked up and saw Sabor, the lioness, in the center of the trail not twenty paces away.

The great yellow eyes were fixed upon him with an ominous gleam, and the red tongue licked the longing lips as Sabor advanced in a low crouch.

Tarzan did not attempt to escape. He had been waiting for this opportunity, now that he was armed with something more than a knife and a rope of grass.

Quickly he unslung his bow and fitted a tar-tipped arrow, and as Sabor sprang, the tiny missile met her in mid-air. Tarzan had learned well from watching Kulonga's skillful technique. He sprang to one side, and as the great cat struck the ground beyond him, another death-tipped arrow sunk deep into Sabor's rear.

With a mighty roar, the beast turned and charged once more, only to be met with a third arrow right in the eye, but this time she was too close to the ape-man for him to sidestep the onrushing body. He drew the gleaming knife.

Tarzan went down beneath the great body of his enemy, striking deep with the blade. For a moment they lay there, and then Tarzan realized that the still body lying on top of him was beyond power to injure anyone ever again.

With difficulty, he wriggled from beneath the great weight, and as he stood erect and gazed down upon his trophy, a mighty wave of triumph swept over him. He puffed out his chest, placed a foot upon the body of his powerful enemy, and throwing back his fine young head, roared out the awful challenge of the victorious bull ape.

The forest echoed. Birds fell still, and the larger animals and beasts of prey slunk stealthily away, for few wanted trouble with the great apes.

Meanwhile, in London, another Lord Greystoke was speaking to HIS kind in the House of Lords—but none trembled at the sound of his soft voice.

Sabor did not taste very good, but hunger made up for her toughness and rank flavor. Before long, stomach full, the ape-man was ready to sleep again. First, however, he must remove the hide, for this was the main reason he had desired to destroy Sabor.

Deftly he removed the great pelt, for he had practiced often on smaller animals. When the task was finished, he carried the hide to the fork of a high tree, and there he curled up and fell into exhausted sleep.

Tarzan did not awaken until about noon of the following day. He headed immediately for the carcass of Sabor, but was angered to find the bones picked clean by other hungry jungle-dwellers. He set forth, and after half an hour he spotted a young deer. Before the little creature knew of its danger, a tiny arrow was buried in its neck.

The poison worked so quickly that the deer fell dead after taking only a dozen leaps into the jungle. Again Tarzan feasted well, but this time he hastened on home to the tribe. When he found them, he proudly exhibited the skin of Sabor, the lioness.

"Look!" he cried, "Apes of Kerchak! See what Tarzan, the mighty killer, has done. Who else among you has ever killed one of Numa's people? Tarzan is mightiest among you, for Tarzan is no ape. Tarzan is—" But here he stopped, for the ape-language had no word for man, and Tarzan could only write the word in English—he could not pronounce it.

The tribe had gathered to hear him, and to look at the proof of his wondrous ability. Only Kerchak hung back, nursing his hatred and rage.

Suddenly something snapped in the wicked little brain of the ape-king. With a frightful roar, the great beast sprang into the crowd. Biting and striking in fury, he killed and wounded a dozen before the rest could escape to the upper canopy of the forest.

Frothing and shrieking in insane fury, Kerchak looked about for the one he hated most, and saw him sitting on a nearby limb.

"Come down, Tarzan, great killer," cried Kerchak. "Come down and feel the fangs of a greater killer! Do mighty fighters fly to the trees at the first approach of danger?" And then Kerchak gave the apes' call of challenge.

Quietly Tarzan dropped to the ground. Breathlessly the tribe watched from their lofty perches as Kerchak charged the puny figure with a roar.

Kerchak was nearly seven feet tall. He had

short legs, but his enormous shoulders were bunched and rounded with huge muscles. His neck was so thick it made his head seem like a small ball atop a huge mountain of flesh. His snarling lips were drawn back to expose his great fighting fangs, and his little, wicked eyes gleamed with madness.

Awaiting him stood Tarzan, himself a mighty muscled animal, but his six feet of height and his powerful muscles seemed no match for Kerchak.

His bow and arrows lay some distance away where he had dropped them while showing off Sabor's hide. He confronted Kerchak now with only his hunting knife and his human intellect to offset the ferocious strength of his enemy.

As his antagonist came roaring toward him, Lord Greystoke tore his long knife from its sheath, and with an answering challenge as bloodcurdling as Kerchak's, rushed swiftly to meet the attack. He knew better than to let those long hairy arms encircle him, and just as their bodies were about to crash together, Tarzan grasped one of the huge wrists of his enemy. Springing lightly to one side, he drove his knife to the hilt into Kerchak's body, below the heart.

Before he could wrench the blade free, the ape's quick lunge to seize him had torn the weapon from Tarzan's grasp.

Kerchak aimed a terrific blow at the ape-man's head with the flat of his hand. Had it landed, it might easily have crushed in the side of Tarzan's skull—but the man was too quick. Ducking beneath it, he answered Kerchak with a mighty punch to the stomach.

The ape was staggered, and was near collapse from the mortal wound in his side, when with a mighty effort he rallied for an instant—just long enough to pull his arm free from Tarzan's grasp and get his arms around his wiry opponent. His great jaws sought Tarzan's throat, but the young lord's sinewy fingers were at Kerchak's own throat before the cruel fangs could close on the sleek brown skin.

Thus they struggled, the one to crush out his opponent's life with those awful teeth, the other to close forever the windpipe beneath his strong grasp while holding the snarling mouth away.

The greater strength of the ape was slowly prevailing, and the teeth of the straining beast were barely an inch from Tarzan's throat when, with a shuddering tremor, the great body stiffened and then sank limply to the ground.

Kerchak was dead.

Tarzan pulled out the knife that had so often made him master of those who were stronger, and planted his foot on the neck of his vanquished enemy. Once again, loud through the forest rang the fierce, wild cry of the conqueror.

The young Lord Greystoke had become King of the Apes.

CHAPTER 12

MAN'S REASON

One member of the tribe of Tarzan of the Apes questioned his authority: Terkoz, the son of Tublat. Terkoz feared the keen knife and deadly arrows enough to disobey the king in minor ways, but Tarzan knew that the dissenter was merely biding his time. Given the chance, Terkoz would attempt to win the kingship by treachery, so Tarzan remained always on guard.

For months the life of the little band went on much as before, except that Tarzan's intelligent leadership made them better fed and more content than ever before. He led them by night to the fields near the village. There they ate what they wished, but Tarzan ordered them not to destroy what they could not eat, as most apes would normally have done. So while the thieving annoyed the tribespeople, it was still worthwhile to farm there; it would not have been had the plantation been foolishly laid waste.

During this period, Tarzan paid many nighttime visits to the village to renew his supply of arrows. He soon noticed the food always left by the tree where he entered the gate, and began to eat whatever was put there.

When the villagers saw that the food disappeared overnight, they were filled with shock and dread. It was one thing to put food out to placate a god—it was unheard of for the god to actually visit the village and eat it. It seemed to confirm all of their fears and superstitions.

Moreover, the tribe was unhappy. The ongoing thefts, and the strange pranks played by unseen hands, were making them reconsider the location. Mbonga and the elders began to discuss abandoning the village for a safer site.

Presently the warriors began to hunt farther and farther south into the heart of the forest, looking for a new village site. Tarzan's tribe was now disturbed often by the hunters. New noises and new dangers signaled man's arrival. And when man comes, many of the larger animals—including the great apes—instinctively abandon the area for good.

For a short time the apes lingered near the beach because Tarzan hated the thought of leaving the treasured contents of the little cabin forever. But one day an ape discovered many tribespeople clearing space for a village near the apes' longtime watering stream. The apes would no longer stay, so Tarzan led them far inland to a spot where no human ever went.

Once every moon Tarzan would swing rapidly back through the swaying branches to have a day with his books, and to obtain more arrows. The Africans were making this harder by carefully hiding their supply at night in granaries and occupied huts. This required Tarzan to spy out the hiding place by day.

Twice he had entered huts at night while the residents slept on their mats, stealing the arrows from the very sides of the warriors. But this method was clearly too dangerous, so he began ambushing solitary hunters with his long, deadly noose, stripping them of weapons and ornaments, and dropping their bodies from a high tree into the village street at night.

Fortunately for the terrorized tribespeople, Tarzan only did such things once a month, giving them hope each time that this might be the last raid. Had it not been for these breaks, they would likely have abandoned this new village as well.

The Africans had not yet come upon Tarzan's cabin, but the ape-man dreaded that they might. After all, he took what they valued—their arrows, food, lives, and peace of mind. They might well take what he cared for—his treasured cabin. So he began to spend more and more time there and less and less with the tribe.

As a result, the community began to suffer from his neglect. Disputes and quarrels arose constantly, and the king's duty was to be present to settle them peaceably. At last some of the older apes spoke to Tarzan on the subject, and for a month thereafter he remained constantly with the tribe.

The duties of the kingship are not extensive. Perhaps Thaka comes in the morning to complain that old Mungo has stolen his new wife, Hasa. Tarzan must act as judge, and learn whom Hasa would prefer as mate, and perhaps assign compensation to the other. Then perhaps comes Tana, shrieking and bleeding, complaining that her husband Gunto has cruelly bitten her. Gunto in turn complains that Tana is inattentive to his needs and wants. Tarzan scolds them both, threatens Gunto with a death-bearing arrow if he abuses his wife in the future, and makes Tana promise to be a better wife. In any case, whatever Tarzan decides is accepted by the apes as final.

And so it goes, little family differences for the most part, which if left unsettled would lead to greater strife, and the eventual breakup of the tribe.

But Tarzan tired of the curtailment of his liberty. He longed for the sunny beach and the little cabin, with its cool interior and the endless wonders of the books. He had grown away from his people. They could not understand the strange matters that passed through the brain of their human king. Tarzan could not talk with them of the great fields of thought opened up by his reading, nor share his ambitions with them—they lacked the words.

He no longer had friends in the tribe. An adult human tends to find good companions from among intellectual equals. The tribespeople he raided were such equals, but it had never occurred to him to befriend them. Had Kala lived, Tarzan would have sacrificed all else to remain near her. But she was dead, and the playful friends of his childhood had grown into fierce, surly brutes. He much preferred the peace and solitude of his cabin to the irksome duties of leadership.

The hatred and jealousy of Terkoz, son of Tublat, was all that prevented Tarzan from resigning his kingship. He was too much the stubborn young Englishman to retreat in the face of so wicked an enemy.

Terkoz would surely be chosen leader in his place, for the ferocious brute had established his dominance over the few bull apes who had dared resent his savage bullying. Tarzan would have liked to subdue him barehanded, if possible. As an adult, Tarzan had become so strong and agile that he might win a hand-to-hand fight with the ape, except for the advantage of the latter's huge fighting fangs.

Events took the matter out of Tarzan's hands one day, leaving his future open to him. He might go or stay, with no harm to his fierce pride.

The tribe was feeding quietly, spread over a wide area, when a great screaming arose some distance east of where Tarzan lay beside a stream, fishing barehanded.

As one, the tribe swung rapidly toward the frightened cries. They found Terkoz holding an old female by the hair, beating her mercilessly with his great hands.

As Tarzan approached, he signaled Terkoz to stop. The female was the wife of a poor old ape, too elderly to protect his family.

Terkoz knew that it was against the apes' law to strike another's woman, but he was a bully. She had caught a tender young rodent. Terkoz knew that her husband could not protect her, so he had demanded the food, and she had refused. When Terkoz saw Tarzan approaching without his arrows, he continued to beat the poor female in deliberate insult to his hated chieftain.

Tarzan did not repeat his warning signal. Instead, he charged.

It was Tarzan's most terrible battle since that long-gone fight with Bolgani, the great king gorilla. Only by accident had the sharp knife saved him from death. Here the knife barely offset the gleaming fangs of Terkoz, and the ape's advantage in brute strength was offset only by Tarzan's great quickness and agility. Overall, though, Terkoz had the slight advantage.

Had no other quality influenced the battle, Tarzan of the Apes, the young Lord Greystoke, would have died as he had lived—an unknown savage beast in central Africa.

But Tarzan had that little spark which spells the difference between man and animal—reason. Only reason saved him from death that day.

They had scarcely fought a dozen seconds before they were rolling on the ground, striking and tearing in a battle to the death. Terkoz had a dozen knife wounds on his head and chest, and Tarzan was torn and bleeding. A great piece of his scalp hung down over one eye, blocking his vision.

So far, the young Englishman had been able to keep the horrible fangs from his jugular. As they both began to tire, Tarzan had an idea. He would work his way to Terkoz's back, cling there, and stab his enemy to death.

This turned out to be easier than expected, for the ape—with no idea of the tactic—made no effort to prevent it. But when Terkoz finally realized that his enemy was fastened to him in a way that made the ape's teeth and fists useless, he hurled himself about on the ground so violently that Tarzan could barely keep his desperate hold. Before he could stab, a heavy impact against the earth knocked the knife from Tarzan's hand. Now he found himself weaponless.

During the rollings and squirmings of the next few minutes, Tarzan's hold was loosened a dozen times, but then luck favored him. He gained a hold the ape could not possibly break: his right arm passed under Terkoz's arm from behind, and his right hand and forearm went behind the ape's neck. Wrestlers know this hold as the half-Nelson, and Tarzan immediately realized its value. Soon he managed a similar grip with the left arm, and Terkoz's powerful neck creaked beneath a full-Nelson.

There was no more lunging about. The two lay perfectly still on the ground, Tarzan on Terkoz's back. Slowly the bullet head of the ape was being forced lower and lower to his chest. Tarzan knew that the neck was near breaking.

Then to Terkoz's rescue came the same factor that had brought him near to death —a man's reasoning power.

"If I kill him," thought Tarzan, "what advantage will I gain? Will it not rob the tribe of a great fighter? And if Terkoz dies, he will know nothing of my supremacy. Left alive, he will always be an example to the other apes."

"KA-GODA?" hissed Tarzan in Terkoz's ear, which, in ape tongue means: "Do you surrender?"

For a moment there was no reply, and Tarzan added a little pressure, wringing a horrified shriek of pain from the great beast.

"KA-GODA?" repeated Tarzan.

"KA-GODA!" cried Terkoz.

"Listen," said Tarzan, easing up a trifle, but not releasing his hold. "I am Tarzan, King of the Apes, mighty hunter, mighty fighter. In all the jungle there is none so great.

"You have said: 'KA-GODA' to me. All the

tribe have heard. Quarrel no more with your king or your people, for next time I shall kill you. Do you understand?"

"HUH," assented Terkoz.

"And you are satisfied?"

"HUH," said the ape.

Tarzan let him up, and in a few minutes all were back at their activities, as though nothing had happened. Deep in the minds of the apes was the knowledge that Tarzan was not only a mighty fighter, but also a strange creature. With his enemy in his power, Tarzan had spared rather than killed him.

That afternoon the tribe came together as usual before darkness settled on the jungle. Tarzan, his wounds washed clean, called the old males to join him.

"You have seen again today that Tarzan of the Apes is the greatest among you," he said.

"HUH," they replied with one voice, "Tarzan is great."

"Tarzan," he continued, "is not an ape. He is not like you. His ways are not your ways, and so Tarzan is going back to the lair of his own kind by the waters of the great lake which has no far shore. You must choose another king, for Tarzan will not return."

And thus, young Lord Greystoke took the first step toward his new goal—to find other men like himself.

CHAPTER 13

HIS OWN KIND

Tarzan of the Apes, lame and sore from the wounds of his battle with Terkoz, set out for the seacoast the next morning.

He traveled very slowly, spent the night in the jungle, and reached his cabin late the following morning. Once there he rested, moving about only to gather fruits and nuts to satisfy his hunger. After ten days he was nearly recovered, except for a terrible, half-healed scar from his left eyebrow to his right ear.

While recuperating, Tarzan began a project. The skin of Sabor had lain all this time in the cabin. He tried to make it into a cape, but the hide had dried as stiff as a board. He knew nothing of tanning, so this cherished plan had to be abandoned.

Then he decided to steal garments from one of the African villagers, for it was important to Tarzan to distinguish himself from animals in every possible way. Ornaments and clothing seemed the most obvious badge of humanity, so he wore the decorations he had taken from warriors, as he had seen the men wear them.

Around his neck hung the golden chain with the diamond-inlaid locket of his mother, Lady Alice. On his back was a well-made quiver of arrows slung from a leather shoulder belt, another item taken from some vanquished warrior. His belt was made of tiny strips of rawhide, which held a homemade sheath for his father's hunting knife. Kulonga's fine longbow hung over his left shoulder.

The young, black-haired, perfectly-muscled Lord Greystoke was indeed a strange and warlike figure. His face was noble, and his clear eyes held the intelligent fire of life, but he did not know or care; he had other worries. He did not have clothing to show that he was a man, not an ape. Might he yet become an ape? Was not hair beginning to grow on his face? All apes had facial hair, but the men he had seen had almost none. True, he had seen pictures in his books of men with hair upon their lip and cheek and chin, but he was still afraid. So, almost daily, he sharpened his knife and roughly shaved the degrading mark of apehood off his face.

When he felt quite recovered from the bloody battle, Tarzan set off towards Mbonga's village. He was walking carelessly along a winding jungle trail, as he occasionally did, rather than travel at a more rapid speed through the trees.

Suddenly he came face to face with an African warrior.

The look of surprise on the man's face was

almost comical, and before Tarzan could unsling his bow, the fellow had turned and fled down the path, crying out as if to warn others.

Tarzan took to the trees in pursuit, and in a few moments came in view of three men racing madly in single file through the undergrowth. Tarzan easily passed them overhead without being heard or seen. As they sprinted, they did not note the crouching figure squatting on a low branch above their path.

Tarzan let the first two pass beneath him, but as the third came swiftly on, the quiet noose dropped about his throat. A quick jerk drew it tight. The victim screamed in agony, and his fellows turned to see his struggling body rise slowly into the dense foliage of the trees above, tongue protruding. With frightened shrieks they turned and ran as fast as their legs would carry them.

Tarzan released his prisoner quickly and silently, removing the warrior's weapons and ornaments. To his great joy, there was a handsome deerskin breechcloth. He quickly put it on. Now indeed he was dressed as a man should be. No one could doubt his high origin. How he would have liked to have returned to the apes to parade this finery before their envious gazes.

Taking the body across his shoulder, he moved more slowly through the trees toward the little fenced-in village. He needed more arrows.

As he approached the enclosure, he saw an

excited group surrounding the two fugitives. Trembling with fright and exhaustion, they could barely tell their strange tale.

Mirando, they said, had been just ahead of them when he had suddenly come screaming toward them, crying that a terrible white and naked warrior was pursuing him. The three of them had hurried toward the village as swiftly as they could.

Again Mirando's shrill cry had caused them to look back, and what they had seen was horrible— his body flying upwards into the trees, his arms and legs flailing and his tongue out. He had uttered no other sound. No other creature was in sight.

The villagers were nearly in a panic, but wise old Mbonga was skeptical. "You tell us this great story," he said, "because you do not dare to speak the truth. You do not dare admit that when the lion sprang at Mirando, you ran away and left him. You are cowards."

Scarcely had Mbonga ceased speaking when a great crashing of branches in the trees above them caused the people to look up in renewed terror. What they saw made even Mbonga shudder, for tumbling through the air came the dead body of Mirando, which sprawled with a sickening thud at their feet.

Not even the oldest of them knew of any natural flesh-and-blood creature with the ability to steal arrows, make people rise into the jungle, and launch their dead naked bodies into the midst of camp. As one, the tribespeople took to their heels. They did not stop until all were lost in the dense shadows of the surrounding jungle.

Again Tarzan came down into the village, renewed his supply of arrows, and ate the offering of food. Before he left, he took the body of Mirando and propped it up against the village gate. The dead face seemed to be peering around the edge of the gatepost toward the jungle.

Then Tarzan returned, always hunting, to the cabin by the beach.

The terrified villagers eventually dared to return to their village, past the horrible, grinning face of their dead comrade. When they found the food and arrows gone, they knew their fears had come true—Mirando had seen the evil spirit of the jungle. It all made sense: only those who saw this terrible jungle god died, and no living villager among them had seen him. The god's penalty for gazing upon his person must be death. Now they knew what to do. As long as they supplied him with arrows and food, and did not view him with their eyes, they were safe. Wise Mbonga ordered that henceforth an offering of arrows should be placed next to the food offering, and it was done.

It became a tribal tradition. To this day, if you pass that African village, you will see a tiny thatched hut at its edge. In it is a little iron pot with some food, and beside that a quiver of poisoned arrows.

When Tarzan came in sight of the beach where his cabin stood, a strange and unusual sight awaited.

A great ship floated in the harbor, and a small boat had landed on the beach.

But, most wonderful of all, a number of men like himself were moving about between the beach and his cabin. In many ways they were like the men of his picture books; their skin was light, like his own. He crept through the trees until he was quite close above them.

There were ten swarthy, tanned, angry-looking fellows. They had congregated by the boat and were arguing loudly, with much gesturing and shaking of fists.

One of them was a little mean-faced black-bearded fellow whose face reminded Tarzan of Pamba, the rat. Pamba's look-alike laid his hand on the shoulder of a huge man next to him, with whom all the others had been arguing, and pointed suddenly inland. The giant turned away from the others to look, and as he turned, the rat-faced little man drew a revolver from his belt and shot the giant in the back.

Without a sound, the big fellow threw his hands up and tumbled forward upon the beach, dead.

The sound of the firearm, the first that Tarzan

had ever heard, filled him with wonder, but not panic. The conduct of the white strangers, on the other hand, was most disturbing. It was a good thing that he had restrained his first impulse, which was to rush forward and greet these men as brothers. They were evidently no different from the Africans—no more civilized than the apes—no less cruel than Sabor.

For a moment the others stood looking at the little man and his victim. Then one of them laughed and slapped the little man on the back. There was much more talk and hand-waving, but less quarreling.

Presently they launched the boat and rowed away toward the great ship, where Tarzan could see other figures moving about on the deck.

When they had clambered aboard, Tarzan dropped to the earth behind a great tree and crept to his cabin, always keeping it between himself and the ship.

Slipping inside, he found that everything had been ransacked. His precious books and pencils were strewn about the floor. His weapons and shields and other little treasures were littered about. A great wave of anger surged through him, and the new scar on his forehead stood out crimson against his tanned hide.

Quickly he ran to the cupboard and searched in the far corner of the lower shelf. Ah! He breathed a sigh of relief as he drew out the little tin box, and, opening it, found his greatest treasures undisturbed. The photograph of the smiling young man and the puzzling little black book were safe.

Then his quick ear caught a faint, unfamiliar sound. What was that?

Tarzan ran to the window and looked toward the harbor. There he saw a second boat being lowered from the great ship into the water. Many people descended the sides of the larger vessel into the boats. They were coming back in full force.

For a moment longer, Tarzan watched while a number of boxes and bundles were lowered into the waiting boats. Then, as they shoved off from the ship's side, the ape-man took a piece of paper and pencil, and printed carefully on it until it bore several lines of clear, block letters. He affixed the notice to the door with a sharp splinter of wood. Then he gathered up his precious tin box, his arrows, and as many bows and spears as he could carry, and disappeared into the forest.

When the two boats were beached, a strange assortment of humanity came ashore. There were perhaps twenty in all. Fifteen of them were rough-looking seamen, some of whom had been ashore the first time.

The others in the party looked quite different.

One was an elderly man, with white hair and glasses. His slightly bent shoulders were draped in an ill-fitting frock coat. A shiny silk hat made his dress look even more odd in the African jungle.

The second member of the party to land was a tall young man in white. Directly behind him came another elderly man with a very high forehead and a fussy manner.

After these came a large woman clothed in many bright colors. She was the only member of the party, Tarzan noted, whose skin was dark like that of the villagers. Her eyes darted fearfully between the jungle and the cursing band of sailors unloading bales and boxes from the boats.

The last member of the party to disembark was a girl of about nineteen, and the young man stood at the boat's prow to lift her high and dry to land. She gave him a pretty smile of thanks.

In silence the party advanced toward the cabin, having evidently made a plan before leaving the ship. They came to the cabin door, the sailors in front carrying the boxes and bales, the five others behind them. The men put down their burdens, and then one caught sight of Tarzan's printed notice.

"Ho, mates!" he cried. "What's here? This sign was not posted an hour ago, or I'll eat the cook."

The other sailors gathered about, craning their necks, but few could read at all, and those only barely. One finally turned to the little old man of the top hat and frock coat.

"Hi, perfesser," he called, "come an' read the bloomin' notice."

The old man came slowly to where the sailors stood, followed by the other members of his party. Adjusting his glasses, he looked for a moment at the note and then turned away, muttering to himself: "Most remarkable—most remarkable!"

"Hey, you old fossil," cried the man who had first asked for help, "did'ja think we wanted you to read the bloomin' note to yourself? Come back here and read it out loud, you old barnacle."

The old man stopped and, turning back, said: "Oh, yes, my dear sir, a thousand pardons. It was quite thoughtless of me, very thoughtless. Most remarkable—most remarkable!"

He read it again, and probably would have turned away to think on it again, but the sailor grasped him roughly by the collar and yelled into his ear: "I said read it out loud, you old idiot!"

"Ah, yes indeed, yes indeed," replied the professor softly, and he read aloud:

> **THIS IS THE HOUSE OF TARZAN,
> THE KILLER OF MANY BEASTS AND
> MEN. DO NOT HARM THE THINGS
> WHICH ARE TARZAN'S. TARZAN
> WATCHES. TARZAN OF THE APES.**

"Who the devil is Tarzan?" cried the sailor who had ordered the reading.

"He evidently speaks English," said the young man.

"But what does 'Tarzan of the Apes' mean?" cried the girl.

"I do not know, Miss Porter," replied the young man, "unless we have discovered a runaway ape from the London Zoo who has brought a European education back to his jungle home. What do you make of it, Professor Porter?" he added, turning to the old man.

Professor Archimedes Q. Porter adjusted his glasses.

"Ah, yes, indeed. Yes, indeed—most remarkable, most remarkable!" said the professor, "but I can add nothing further to what I have already said of this truly astonishing occurrence." He turned slowly in the direction of the jungle.

"But, papa," cried the girl, "you haven't said anything about it yet."

"Tut, tut, child," responded Professor Porter indulgently, "do not trouble your pretty head with such perplexing problems," and he wandered slowly off in still another direction, eyes downward, hands clasped behind him.

"I reckon the old coot don't know no more'n we do about it," growled the rat-faced sailor.

"Watch your tongue," cried the young man, his face paling in anger. "You've murdered our officers and robbed us. We are absolutely in your power, but you'll treat Professor Porter and Miss Porter with respect or I'll break that vile neck of yours with my bare hands—guns or no guns." The young fellow stepped so close to the rat-faced sailor that the latter, though his belt held two revolvers and a huge knife, slunk back abashed.

"You damned coward," cried the young man. "You'd never dare shoot a man until his back was turned. You don't dare shoot me even then." He defiantly turned his back to the sailor and walked calmly away.

The sailor's hand crept slyly to one of his revolvers, and his wicked eyes glared vengefully at the retreating form of the young Englishman. His fellows watched him intently, but he hesitated. At heart he was an even greater coward than Mr. William Cecil Clayton had proclaimed.

Two keen eyes had watched it all from the foliage of a nearby tree. While he could not understand the spoken language, the strangers' gestures and facial expressions told him much. The rat-faced little sailor's murder of a comrade had inspired strong dislike in Tarzan, and watching him quarrel with the fine-looking young man, the ape-man liked this distant cousin of Pamba even less.

Tarzan had never seen the effects of a firearm before, but when he saw the rat-faced man fingering his revolver, he knew what to expect. The young man would be murdered, just as the huge sailor had been earlier.

Tarzan raised a poisoned arrow to his bow and aimed at the murderer, but the foliage was too thick to shoot through accurately. Instead, he launched a heavy spear from his lofty perch.

Clayton had taken but a dozen steps. Pamba's

relative had half drawn his revolver, while the other sailors watched the scene intently.

Professor Porter had already disappeared into the jungle, followed by the fussy Samuel T. Philander, his secretary and assistant.

The black woman, whose name was Esmeralda, was busy sorting Miss Porter's baggage from the pile of bales and boxes beside the cabin. The younger woman had turned away to follow Clayton, when something caused her to turn back toward the sailor.

Three things happened almost simultaneously. The little sailor jerked out his weapon and leveled it at Clayton's back; Miss Porter screamed a warning; and a long, metal-tipped African spear shot like a bolt from above and passed entirely through the right shoulder of the rat-faced man.

The revolver fired harmlessly in the air, and its owner crumpled up with a scream of pain and terror.

Clayton turned and rushed back toward the scene. The sailors stood in a frightened group, weapons drawn, peering into the jungle. The wounded man writhed and shrieked on the ground.

No one noticed when Clayton picked up the fallen revolver and slipped it inside his shirt, then joined the sailors' mystified gazing into the jungle.

"Who could it have been?" whispered Jane Porter, and the young man turned to see her standing, wide-eyed and wondering, close beside him.

"I dare say this Tarzan of the Apes is watching us all right," he answered, in a dubious tone. "I wonder, now, who that spear was intended for. If for Snipes, then our ape friend is a friend indeed.

"By jove, where are your father and Mr. Philander? There's someone or something in that jungle, and it's armed, whatever it is. Ho! Professor! Mr. Philander!" young Clayton shouted.

There was no response.

"What's to be done, Miss Porter?" continued the young man, frowning with worry and indecision. "I can't leave you here alone with these cutthroats, and you certainly can't venture into the jungle with me, yet someone must go in search of your father. He is prone to wander off aimlessly, regardless of danger or direction, and Mr. Philander is nearly as bad. Pardon my bluntness, but our lives are all in jeopardy here, and when we get your father back, we must somehow teach him that his absent-mindedness endangers us all."

"I quite agree with you," replied the girl, "and I am not offended at all. Dear old Papa would sacrifice his life for me in an instant, provided he could remember to do so. There is only one way to keep him safe, and that is to chain him to a tree. The poor dear is *so* impractical."

"I have it!" Clayton suddenly exclaimed. "You can use a revolver, can't you?"

"Yes. Why?"

"I have one. If you and Esmeralda take it and

go into this cabin, you will both be safe while I search for your father and Mr. Philander. Come, call her, and I will hurry on. They cannot have gone far."

Jane and Esmeralda did as he suggested. When he saw the door close safely behind them, Clayton turned toward the jungle.

Some of the sailors were removing the spear from their screaming leader's shoulder. As Clayton approached, he asked if he could borrow a revolver from one of them while he searched the jungle for the professor. Snipes, having found that he was not dying, had stopped screaming in agony and was berating Clayton. With a volley of curses, he ordered them not to allow the young man any firearms.

This man Snipes had assumed the role of chief after killing their former leader. None of the cutthroats had yet had time to question his authority.

Clayton's only response was to shrug his shoulders, but as he left them, he picked up the spear which had pierced Snipes. Now armed, the son of England's Lord Greystoke strode into the dense jungle.

Every few moments he called for the wanderers by name. The women in the cabin heard the sound of his voice growing ever fainter and fainter, until at last it was swallowed up by the many noises of the jungle.

Meanwhile, Professor Porter and Mr. Philander

had—at Philander's insistence—finally turned their steps toward camp. They did not realize how completely lost they were in the wild, tangled maze of the matted jungle. By pure good fortune, they were headed west, back toward the coast they had landed on.

Soon they reached the beach, only to find no boats or sailors or cabin in sight. Philander was positive that they were north of the landing beach, but in fact they were about two hundred yards south of it. It never occurred to either man to call out in hopes of attracting their friends' attention. Instead, with absolute confidence in his own faulty judgment, Mr. Philander grasped the Professor by the arm. Despite the older gentleman's weak protests, he hurried him southward—further and further from the boats.

When Jane and Esmeralda had gotten safely behind the cabin door, they immediately sought to barricade it from the inside. Esmeralda turned to search for something to use, and got her first good look at the interior of the cabin. What she saw brought a shriek of terror to her lips.

Jane turned at the cry, and saw its cause lying prone on the cabin floor—the whitened skeleton of a human. A further glance revealed a second skeleton on the bed. "What horrible place are we in?" she murmured, trying not to panic.

Jane crossed the room to look into the little cradle. She knew what she would see there even before she saw it: the tiny skeleton, in all its pitiful frailty. What an awful tragedy the silent bones proclaimed! She shuddered at what might become of her and her friends in this ill-fated cabin, haunted by mysterious and perhaps hostile creatures.

Quickly, with an impatient stamp of her little foot, she sought to shake off such gloomy thoughts. But as she did, there was a little quiver in her own voice at the thought of the three men she trusted wandering in the depths of that awful forest.

Soon the girl, acting on Esmeralda's sensible notion, found that the door was equipped inside with a heavy wooden bar for a lock. After several efforts, their combined strength enabled them to slip it into place for the first time in twenty years.

Then they sat down on a bench, with their arms around one another, and waited.

CHAPTER 14

AT THE MERCY OF THE JUNGLE

After Clayton had plunged into the jungle, the sailors of the *Arrow* decided to hasten back to the anchored vessel. There they would at least be safe from spears thrown by unseen foes. The cowardly mutineers left Jane Porter and Esmeralda ashore, barricaded in their cabin.

Tarzan had seen so much that day that his head was in a whirl. But the most wonderful sight of all was the face of the beautiful young girl.

Here at last was one of his own kind—of that he was positive. The young man and the two old men might also be, but he remained skeptical. In his experience, women were not cruel or ferocious, but both white men and black men alike were. Perhaps the only reason that these men had done no killing was that they lacked weapons. They might be very different if armed.

Tarzan had seen the young man pick up Snipes's fallen revolver and hide it away in his shirt, then slip it cautiously to the girl as she entered the cabin.

He understood none of the motives behind what he had seen, but somehow, he liked the young man and the two old men. For the girl he had a strange longing he found hard to understand. The big black woman was evidently a good friend to the girl, and so he liked her also.

The sailors, especially Snipes, he hated very much. Their gestures and expressions were evil, and told him that they were prepared to harm the rest of the party. He decided to watch closely.

Tarzan wondered why the men had gone into the jungle. It never occurred to him that anyone could get lost there. To him, the maze of undergrowth was as familiar as the main street of your hometown is to you.

When he saw the sailors row away toward the ship, and knew that the women were safe in his cabin, Tarzan decided to see what the young man was doing in the jungle. He swung off rapidly in that direction, and in a short time he heard the sounds of the Englishman calling out to his friends. When Tarzan caught up with him, Clayton was leaning exhausted against a tree, wiping sweat from his forehead. The ape-man watched him intently from his hiding place.

Clayton continued to call aloud from time to time. Tarzan finally understood that he was searching for the older men.

Tarzan was about to go and look for them himself when he caught sight of a sleek yellow hide moving cautiously through the jungle toward Clayton.

It was Sheeta, the leopard. Tarzan heard the soft bending of grasses and wondered why the young white man was not warned. How could anyone not notice the loud warning? Never before had Tarzan known Sheeta to be so clumsy. No black warrior would have been so deaf to such danger.

No, the white man did not hear. As Sheeta crouched to spring, shrill and horrible from the stillness of the jungle came the awful cry of an ape-challenge. Sheeta turned and fled crashing into the underbrush.

Clayton came to his feet with a start. Never had he heard so fearful a sound, made more frightening by the sound of some great creature plunging through the bush near him. He was no coward, but the eldest son of Lord Greystoke of England felt his heart gripped with icy fear. He could not know that only the terrifying scream had saved him, nor could he have remotely imagined that it had come from his own cousin—the rightful Lord Greystoke.

As afternoon began to fade, Clayton was disheartened and unsure what to do. Should he keep searching for Professor Porter, though it meant almost certain death in the jungle at night? Or should he return to the cabin to protect Jane and Esmeralda from their many perils? He did not want to return to Jane without her father, but he was even less keen on leaving her at the mercy of the mutineers or the hundred unknown dangers of the jungle.

Possibly, too, the professor and Philander might have returned to camp. He thought that was more than likely. Before he continued what seemed a fruitless quest, he would return and see. And so he started stumbling back through the thick underbrush in what he imagined to be the right direction.

To Tarzan's surprise, the young man was heading further into the jungle in the general direction of Mbonga's village. He must be lost. Nothing else made sense; only a fool would purposefully try to invade the African village armed only with a spear that he did not even know how to use effectively. Nor was Clayton on the old men's trail; Tarzan had already seen him cross it, fresh and plain for all to see.

Tarzan was perplexed. The fierce jungle would make easy prey of this stranger in a very short time if he were not guided quickly to the beach.

In fact, there was Numa, the lion, right now— stalking Clayton a dozen paces to the right.

Clayton heard the great body nearby, and then the beast's thunderous roar split the evening air. The man stopped with upraised spear and looked toward the awful sound. The shadows were deepening and darkness was settling in. What a fate! To die here alone, beneath the fangs of wild beasts; to be torn apart; to feel the hot breath of the brute on his face as its great paw upon his chest!

For a moment all was still. Clayton stood rigid, spear upraised. Presently he heard the rustling sound of the thing in the bush creeping stealthily toward him. At last he saw it, not twenty feet away—the long, muscular body and tawny head of a huge black-maned lion, moving slowly forward in a low crouch. As its eyes met Clayton's, it stopped, and cautiously prepared to spring.

In agony the man watched, fearful to launch his spear, powerless to flee.

He heard a noise in the tree above him. It sounded like some new danger, but he dared not take his eyes from the yellow-green eyes before him. There was a sharp twang, like a breaking banjo-string, and an arrow appeared in the yellow hide of the crouching lion.

With a roar of pain and anger the beast sprang, but somehow Clayton stumbled to one side. As he turned again to face the infuriated king of beasts, he saw an astonishing sight. Just as the lion turned to renew the attack, a half-naked giant dropped from the tree above, squarely onto the brute's back.

With lightning speed a powerful arm encircled the huge neck, actually raising the great beast from behind as it roared and pawed the air—as easily as Clayton would have lifted a pet dog.

Clayton would never forget that scene.

As the stranger's right arm lifted the lion, his left hand plunged a knife repeatedly into its body behind the left shoulder. The infuriated beast flailed and struggled uselessly.

Had the battle lasted a few seconds longer, the outcome might have been different, but it all happened too quickly. The lion scarcely had time to recover from its confusion before it sank lifeless to the ground.

Then the strange figure who had slain it stood tall upon the carcass, and throwing back his wild and handsome head, gave out the fearsome cry which had so startled Clayton moments before. It was a young man, naked except for a loincloth and a few African ornaments around his arms and legs. On his chest a priceless diamond locket gleamed against smooth brown skin.

The hunting knife had been sheathed, and the man gathered up his bow and quiver from where he had tossed them when he leaped to attack the lion.

Clayton spoke to the stranger in English, thanking him for his brave rescue and praising his impressive strength and dexterity, but the only answer was a steady stare and a faint shrug of the mighty shoulders.

When the wild man—for such Clayton now thought him—had reslung the bow and quiver, he drew his knife and deftly carved a dozen large strips of meat from the lion's carcass. Squatting down to eat, he motioned Clayton to join him.

The strong white teeth sank into the raw and dripping flesh with obvious gusto, but the uncooked meat did not appeal to Clayton. Instead he watched him, and presently it dawned on him—this must be the 'Tarzan of the Apes' whose notice had been found on the cabin door that morning.

If so, he must speak English.

Again Clayton attempted to speak with the ape-man, who replied aloud but in a strange tongue. It resembled the chattering of monkeys mingled with the growling of some wild beast.

No, this could not be Tarzan of the Apes, for

it was very evident that he spoke not a word of English.

When Tarzan finished his dinner, he rose and, pointing in a very different direction from that which Clayton had been traveling, started off that way through the jungle.

Clayton hesitated to follow him, for he thought he was being led deeper into the forest. The ape-man saw this and returned, grasping him by the coat. He pulled the Englishman along until he felt that Clayton understood, then left him to follow voluntarily.

The Englishman concluded that he was a prisoner, with no option but to accompany his captor. They traveled slowly through the jungle as the dark night fell about them. The footfalls of padded paws, the breaking of twigs and the wild calls of savage beasts all seemed to be closing in all about him.

Suddenly Clayton heard the faint sound of a firearm—a single shot, and then silence.

In the cabin by the beach, two thoroughly terrified women clung together as they crouched upon the bench in the gathering darkness.

Esmeralda sobbed, bemoaning the evil day that she had left her dear Maryland. Jane maintained outward calm but was torn by inner fears and worries. She was as afraid for the three men wandering in the depths of the jungle as she was for herself. From the dark jungle she could hear the constant shrieks, roars, barks and growls of wild creatures seeking their prey.

Now there came the sound of a heavy body brushing against the side of the cabin. She could hear the great padded paws on the ground outside. For an instant, all was silence; even the bedlam of the forest died to a faint murmur. Then she distinctly heard the beast outside sniffing at the door, not two feet away from them. Instinctively the girl shuddered.

"Hush!" she whispered. "Hush, Esmeralda," for the woman's sobs and groans seemed to have attracted whatever was just beyond the thin wall.

A gentle scratching sound was heard on the door. The brute tried to force an entrance, then stopped, and again she heard the great pads creeping stealthily around the cabin. Again they stopped—beneath the window on which the girl's terrified eyes were now glued.

The head of a huge lioness was silhouetted in the window against the moonlit sky. The gleaming eyes were fixed upon Jane in intense ferocity.

"Look, Esmeralda!" she whispered. "For God's sake, what shall we do? Look! Quick! The window!"

Esmeralda took one frightened glance toward the little square of moonlight just as the lioness emitted a low, savage snarl. It was too much for her overtaxed nerves. "Oh, God Almighty!" she shrieked, and slid to the floor in a faint.

For what seemed like forever the great brute stood with her forepaws upon the sill, glaring into the little room. Presently she tried the strength of the window-bars with her great claws, and Jane held her breath in terror. Then, to her relief, the head disappeared and she heard the lioness's great footsteps receding. But now the scratching at the door resumed, this time with increasing force until the great beast was tearing at the massive panels in an eager frenzy to get at her prey.

Had Jane known the immense strength of that door, she would have felt less fear of the lioness reaching her through it. When he built it, little did John Clayton imagine that one day, twenty years later, it would shield a fair American girl—then unborn—from the teeth and talons of a man-eater.

For a full twenty minutes the brute tore at the door with baffled cries of rage. Finally she gave up, however, and Jane heard her returning toward the window. The lioness paused there for an instant, then threw all her weight against the timeworn bars.

The girl heard the wooden rods groan beneath the impact, but they held, and the huge body dropped back to the ground below. The lioness repeated these tactics over and over, until finally the horrified woman saw a portion of the bars give way. In an instant, one great paw and the big cat's head were thrust inside the room.

Slowly the powerful neck and shoulders spread the bars apart, and more and more of the lithe body squeezed through the opening.

Jane, standing pale and rigid against the farther wall with her hand on her heart, sought frantically for some means of escape. Suddenly her hand felt the hard outline of the revolver Clayton had left with her.

Quickly she drew it, leveled it full at the lioness's face, and pulled the trigger.

There was a flash of flame, a booming roar, and an answering roar of pain and anger from the beast. Jane saw the great form disappear from the window, and then she, too, fainted, the revolver falling at her side.

But this Sabor was not killed. The bullet had merely inflicted a painful wound in one of the lioness's great shoulders. It was the surprise at the blinding flash and the deafening roar that had caused her hasty but temporary retreat. In another instant she was back at the window, clawing it with renewed fury—but with less success due to her shoulder wound.

She saw her prey lying senseless on the floor. There was no longer any resistance to be overcome. She need only worm her way inside to claim her dinner.

Slowly, she forced her great bulk, inch by inch, through the opening. Now her head was through, then one great foreleg and her good shoulder. She drew up the wounded leg in order to squeeze it through as gently as possible.

A moment more and both shoulders would be through. The long, sinuous body and the narrow hips would soon follow.

To this sight, Jane Porter again opened her eyes.

CHAPTER 15

THE FOREST GOD

The sound of the gunshot magnified Clayton's worries. While one of the sailors might have fired a weapon, he recalled that he had left a revolver with Jane. Perhaps even now she was attempting to defend herself against some savage man or beast.

Clayton could only guess what his strange captor or guide thought, but his quickened pace showed that he had definitely heard the shot. Soon Clayton fell behind as he stumbled blindly along behind him. Fearing that he would be forever lost, he called out to Tarzan, who dropped quickly out of the branches to his side.

For a moment Tarzan looked undecided. Then, stooping down before Clayton, he motioned for him to grasp him about the neck; and with his English cousin hanging onto his back, Tarzan took to the trees.

The young Englishman never forgot the next few minutes. High into bending and swaying branches he was carried. The ape-man swung with Clayton from tree to tree in dizzying arcs, threaded through mazes of interwoven limbs, and balanced high above the dark depths of the jungle like a tightrope walker. Clayton's first sensation of chilling fear soon gave way to keen admiration. This forest god was carrying him through the inky blackness of the night as easily and safely as Clayton would have strolled a London street at high noon.

And yet, for all his seeming speed, Tarzan was in reality feeling his way with relative slowness. Constantly he had to seek limbs that would hold this double weight, and the slow pace was annoying him.

Presently they came to the clearing before the beach. Tarzan's quick ears had heard the strange sounds of the lioness's efforts to force her way through the bars, and it seemed to Clayton that they dropped a straight hundred feet to earth, so quickly did Tarzan descend. Yet their landing was soft and smooth, and as Clayton released his hold on the ape-man, he saw him dart like a squirrel toward the opposite side of the cabin.

The Englishman sprang quickly after him just in time to see the hindquarters of some huge animal about to disappear through the window of the cabin. It was at this point that Jane revived from her faint.

When she opened her eyes and saw her mortal danger, Jane's brave young heart gave up its last hope. But then, to her surprise, she saw the huge animal being slowly drawn back through the window, and in the moonlight beyond she saw the heads and shoulders of two men.

When Clayton rounded the corner of the cabin to see the animal disappearing within, he also saw the ape-man seize the long tail in both hands. Tarzan braced his feet against the side of the cabin and pulled with all his might, intending to haul the beast out of the interior.

Clayton was quick to lend a hand, but the ape-man jabbered something to him in a hasty tone of command. The Englishman knew he was being given orders of some sort. Uncertain what to do, he too seized the lioness's tail and pulled with all his strength.

At last their combined efforts began to drag the great body farther and farther outside the window, and the rash bravery of the act dawned on Clayton. For a naked man to drag a shrieking, clawing man-eater from a window by the tail to save two strange women was pure heroism. For Clayton to have done so himself would have been less heroic, in his mind, because he was deeply in love with one of the women inside. In any case, he expected the lioness to make short work of them, yet he pulled with the strength of a man in love.

And then he recalled the battle between this man and the great, black-maned lion which he had witnessed a short time before, and his confidence grew. Tarzan was still issuing some sort of orders, whatever they were.

He was, of course, trying to tell this stupid man to plunge his poisoned arrows into Sabor's back and sides, and to draw the hunting knife and stab the lioness in the heart, but the man was not obeying. Tarzan dared not let go to do these things himself, for he knew that his puny companion could not hold the mighty lioness alone, even for an instant.

Slowly the lioness was emerging from the window. At last her shoulders were out, one bloodied.

And then Clayton saw an incredible thing. Tarzan, racking his brain, had suddenly recalled his battle with Terkoz. As the great shoulders came clear of the window, so that the lioness hung upon the sill only by her forepaws, Tarzan suddenly released his hold on the tail.

With the quickness of a striking rattlesnake, he launched himself full upon Sabor's back, his strong young arms seeking and gaining a full-Nelson on the beast, as he had done during his bloody wrestling victory over Terkoz.

With a roar the lioness turned completely over on her back, falling on top of her enemy; but the black-haired giant only tightened his hold.

Pawing and tearing at earth and air, the lioness rolled and thrashed in an effort to dislodge this strange attacker. But tighter and tighter drew the iron muscles that were forcing her head lower and lower onto her tawny chest.

The steel forearms of the ape-man grasped the lioness's neck tighter and tighter. Her efforts became weaker and weaker.

At last Clayton saw the immense muscles of Tarzan's shoulders and biceps stand out in cords and knots beneath the silver moonlight. There was a long, sustained and supreme effort on the ape-man's part—and Sabor's neck broke with a sharp snap.

In an instant Tarzan was on his feet, and for the second time that day, Clayton heard the bull ape's savage roar of victory. Then he heard Jane's agonized cry:

"Cecil—Mr. Clayton! Oh, what is it? What is it?"

Running quickly to the cabin door, Clayton called out that all was right, and shouted to her to open the door. As quickly as she could, she raised the great bar and fairly dragged Clayton within.

"What was that awful noise?" she whispered, shrinking close to him.

"It was the cry of the kill from the throat of the man who has just saved your life, Miss Porter. Wait, I will fetch him so you may thank him."

The frightened girl would not be left alone, so she accompanied Clayton outside the cabin to the dead body of the lioness.

Tarzan of the Apes was gone.

Clayton called several times, but there was no reply, and so the two returned to the greater safety of the cabin.

"What a frightful sound!" cried Jane. "I shudder at the mere thought of it. Do not tell me that a human throat gave that hideous shriek."

"But it did, Miss Porter," replied Clayton, "or at least if not a human throat, that of a forest god."

And then he told her of his experiences with this strange creature—of how twice the wild man had saved his life—of the wondrous strength, and agility, and bravery—of the brown skin and the handsome face.

"I cannot make it out at all," he concluded. "At first I thought he might be Tarzan of the Apes, but he neither speaks nor understands English, so that theory is incorrect."

"Well, whatever he may be," cried the girl, "we owe him our lives, and may God bless him and keep him in safety in his wild and savage jungle!"

"Amen," said Clayton, fervently.

CHAPTER 16

"MOST REMARKABLE"

On a sandy beach several miles south of the cabin, two old men stood arguing. They were hopelessly lost, trapped between the broad Atlantic and the forbidding interior of Africa. Strange noises assaulted their ears. They had wandered for miles in search of their camp, but always in the wrong direction.

At such a time, surely, one would expect all their attention to be concentrated on the vital question of retracing their steps to camp.

Instead, they were debating about the history of Spain under Islam. After several points and counter-points, Mr. Samuel T. Philander happened to turn his nearsighted gaze to the jungle. He interrupted: "Bless me! Professor, there seems to be someone approaching."

Professor Archimedes Q. Porter turned in the direction indicated.

"Now, Mr. Philander," he chided. "How often must I urge you to better concentrate your mental faculties on the sort of important problems which naturally fall to great minds? And now you display a lack of courtesy in interrupting my learned discourse for no better reason than to point out a large four-footed feline. As I was saying, Mr.—"

"Heavens, Professor! A lion?" cried Mr. Philander, straining his weak eyes toward the dim figure outlined against the dark tropical underbrush.

"Yes, yes, Mr. Philander, if you insist upon using slang, a 'lion.' But as I was saying—"

"Bless me, Professor," again interrupted Mr. Philander, looking worried, "permit me to suggest that the conquered Moors of Spain will still be available for us to discuss later, if we now postpone the discussion of their situation. When we attain a more distant view of yonder *felis carnivora*, perhaps we can resume."

In the meantime the lion had approached with quiet dignity to within ten paces of the two men, where he stood curiously watching them in the moonlight.

"Most disappointing, most disappointing," exclaimed Professor Porter in irritation. "Never before have I known one of these animals to be permitted loose outside its cage. I shall most certainly complain to the directors of the nearby zoological garden."

"Quite right, Professor," agreed Mr. Philander nervously, "and the sooner it is done, the better. Let us do so at a distance." Seizing the professor by the arm, Mr. Philander set off away from the lion.

They had gone but a short distance when Mr. Philander looked back and noted in horror that the lion was following them. He tightened his grip on the protesting professor and hurried.

"As I was saying, Mr. Philander," repeated Professor Porter.

Mr. Philander took another hasty glance rearward. The lion also had quickened his pace, and was trailing them at a fixed distance.

"He is pursuing us!" gasped Mr. Philander, breaking into a run.

"Tut, tut, Mr. Philander," the professor objected. "This sort of haste is most undignified in men of letters. Should any of our friends happen to be nearby, what will they think of us and these childish antics? Let us behave as gentlemen of learning."

Mr. Philander stole another glance to the rear. The lion was bounding along in easy leaps scarcely five paces behind.

He dropped the professor's arm, and broke into a sprint that would have done credit to any varsity track team. When the Professor caught a backward glance at the cruel yellow eyes and half-open mouth so near, he himself broke into a run, coattails streaming behind, holding onto his silk top hat.

Before them a portion of the jungle stretched out toward a narrow peninsula, and Mr. Philander headed for the sanctuary of the trees.

From the shadows of this area peered two sharp eyes, watching the race with interest.

Tarzan of the Apes found it amusing. The two men were safe enough from attack by the lion; Numa would not have let such easy prey run away if he were hungry. The lion might stalk them until his appetite returned, but if he was not provoked, more likely he would soon get bored and slink away to his jungle lair. The greatest danger was that one of the men might stumble and fall, and then Numa would pounce upon him, caught up in the joy of the kill.

So Tarzan swung quickly to a lower limb in line with the approaching fugitives. As Mr. Philander came panting beneath him, too tired to climb to safety, Tarzan reached down and got him by the collar. He easily yanked him up onto the limb by his side. In another moment he did the same for the professor.

With a baffled roar, Numa leaped unsuccessfully toward his vanishing quarry. Slow-moving, easy prey was not supposed to suddenly disappear upward into trees.

For a moment the two men clung, panting, to the great branch, while Tarzan squatted with his back to the tree-trunk. He watched them with mingled curiosity and amusement.

It was the professor who first broke the silence.

"I am deeply pained, Mr. Philander, that you

have shown such a lack of manly courage in the presence of an animal, and that your shameless fear has caused me to exert myself so abnormally in order that I might finish my statement. As I was saying, Mr. Philander, when you interrupted me, the Moors—"

"Professor Archimedes Q. Porter," broke in Mr. Philander, in icy tones, "that will be quite enough. You have accused me of cowardice. You suggest that you ran only to overtake me, not to escape the clutches of the lion. Mind your tongue, Professor! I am a desperate man, and though a patient one, my patience has about been goaded to its end."

"Tut, tut, Mr. Philander, tut, tut!" cautioned Professor Porter. "You forget yourself."

"I forget nothing as yet, Professor Porter, but, believe me, sir, I am on the verge of forgetting both your high position in the world of science and your gray hairs."

The professor sat in silence for a few minutes, and the darkness hid the grim smile that came to his wrinkled face. Presently he spoke.

"Look here, Skinny Philander," he said, in belligerent tones, "if you are lookin' for trouble, peel off your coat and come on down on the ground, and I'll punch your head just as I did sixty years ago in the alley back of Porky Evans' barn."

"Ark!" gasped the astonished Mr. Philander. "Lordy, how good that sounds! When you're human, Ark, I love you, but somehow it seems as though you had forgotten how to be human for the last twenty years."

The professor reached out a thin, trembling old hand through the darkness until it found his old friend's shoulder.

"Forgive me, Skinny," he said, softly. "It hasn't been quite twenty years, and God alone knows how hard I have tried to be 'human' for Jane's sake, and yours, too, since my other Jane passed away." Mr. Philander reached up to clasp the hand that lay upon his shoulder in the silent eloquence of friendship.

They did not speak for some minutes. The lion below them paced nervously back and forth. The third figure in the tree was hidden by the dense shadows. He, too, was silent—motionless as a statue.

"You certainly pulled me up into this tree just in time," said the professor at last. "I want to thank you. You saved my life."

"But I didn't pull you up here, Professor," said Mr. Philander. "Bless me! I quite forgot that I myself was drawn up here by some outside agency. There must be someone or something in this tree with us."

"Eh?" exclaimed Professor Porter. "Are you quite positive, Mr. Philander?"

"Most positive, Professor," replied Mr. Philander, adding, "and I think we should thank the party. He may be sitting right next to you now, Professor."

"Eh? What's that? Tut, tut, Mr. Philander, tut, tut!" said Professor Porter, edging cautiously nearer to Mr. Philander.

Tarzan of the Apes now decided that Numa had loitered beneath the tree long enough. He raised his head skyward, and there rang out the awful warning challenge of the great apes, nearly in the two old men's terrified ears. They flinched at the cry, almost losing their balance. From their perch on the limb, they saw the great lion halt his restless pacing, then slink quickly off into the jungle.

"Even the lion trembles in fear," whispered Mr. Philander.

"Most remarkable, most remarkable," murmured Professor Porter, clutching frantically at Mr. Philander to regain his balance. Unfortunately for them both, Mr. Philander's own perch was just as shaky. The additional impact of Professor Porter's body caused them both to sway together uncertainly, and then with mingled and most unscholarly shrieks, they pitched headlong from the tree, locked in frenzied embrace.

It was quite some moments before either moved, for both were positive that they must have suffered multiple fractures.

At length Professor Porter attempted to move one leg. To his surprise, it responded normally. He now drew up its mate and stretched it forth again.

"Most remarkable, most remarkable," he murmured.

"Thank God, Professor," whispered Mr. Philander, fervently, "you are not dead, then?"

"Tut, tut, Mr. Philander, tut, tut," cautioned Professor Porter. "I do not yet know with accuracy." The professor then wiggled his right arm—joy! It was intact. Breathlessly he waved his left arm above his prostrate body—it still worked!

"Most remarkable, most remarkable," he said.

"To whom are you signaling, Professor?" asked Mr. Philander excitedly.

Professor Porter made no reply to the silly question. Instead he raised his head gently from the ground and moved it around a little.

"Most remarkable," he breathed. "It remains undamaged."

Mr. Philander had not dared move, assuming that his arms, legs and back were broken. With his face partly in the mud, he watched Professor Porter's strange motions with awe. "How sad!" exclaimed Mr. Philander, half aloud. "Concussion of the head, with severe brain damage. How very sad indeed! And for one still so young!"

Professor Porter rolled over on his stomach, gingerly bowing his back until he resembled a huge tomcat near a yelping dog. Then he sat up and felt about his person.

"They are all here," he exclaimed. "Most remarkable!"

He arose, and, with a scathing glance at the motionless form of Mr. Samuel T. Philander, he said: "Tut, tut, Mr. Philander, this is no time for laziness. We must be up and about."

Mr. Philander gazed in speechless rage at Professor Porter. Then he attempted to rise, and was greatly surprised when he succeeded in doing so.

He was still bursting with anger, however, at the injustice of Professor Porter's comment, and was about to offer a heated reply when his eyes fell upon a strange figure standing a few paces away, watching them intently.

Professor Porter had recovered his shiny silk hat and replaced it on his head. Mr. Philander was pointing to something behind him. The professor turned to behold a giant, naked but for a loincloth and a few metal ornaments, standing motionless before him.

"Good evening, sir!" said the professor, lifting his hat.

For reply the giant motioned them to follow him, and set off up the beach in the direction from which they had recently come.

"I think it would be prudent to follow him," said Mr. Philander.

"Tut, tut, Mr. Philander," returned the professor. "A short while ago you were making a most logical argument to support your view that our camp lay directly south of us. I was skeptical, but you finally convinced me, so now I am positive that toward the south we must travel to reach our friends. Therefore I shall continue south."

"But, Professor Porter, this man may know better than either of us. He seems to be native to this part of the world. Let us at least follow him for a short distance."

"Tut, tut, Mr. Philander," repeated the professor. "I am a difficult man to convince, but once convinced, my decision is firm. I shall continue in the proper direction, if I must walk completely around the African continent to reach my destination."

Tarzan, seeing that these strange men were not following him, returned to them and interrupted any further argument. Again he beckoned to them, but still they stood in argument.

The ape-man lost patience with their ignorance. He grasped the frightened Mr. Philander by the shoulder, and before that worthy gentleman knew what was happening, Tarzan had tied one end of his rope securely around Mr. Philander's neck.

"Tut, tut, Mr. Philander," said Professor Porter, "it is most unseemly of you to submit to such indignities."

But soon he too had been seized and securely bound by the neck with the same rope. Then Tarzan set off toward the north, leading the now thoroughly frightened professor and his secretary.

The two tired and hopeless old men proceeded in deathly silence for what seemed like hours.

After a while, they crested a little hill and were overjoyed to see the cabin lying in front of them, not a hundred yards away.

Here Tarzan released them, and, after pointing toward the little building, vanished into the jungle.

"Most remarkable, most remarkable!" gasped the professor. "But you see, Mr. Philander, that I was quite right, as usual, and your stubbornness caused us a series of most humiliating accidents. In the future, I trust you shall allow yourself to be guided by a more mature and practical mind."

Mr. Samuel T. Philander was too much relieved at the happy outcome to their adventure to take offense at the professor's dignified gloating. Instead, he grasped his friend's arm and hastened him toward the cabin.

It was a much-relieved party of castaways that found itself reunited. They stayed awake all night sharing their various adventures and wondering about the strange protector they had found on this savage shore.

Esmeralda was positive that it was none other than an angel of the Lord, sent down especially to watch over them.

"Had you seen him devour the raw meat of the lion, Esmeralda," laughed Clayton, "you would have thought him a very curious angel."

"There was nothing heavenly about his voice," said Jane Porter, with a little shudder at the recollection of the awful roar which had followed the killing of the lioness.

"And it certainly did not agree with my previous ideas on the dignity of divine messengers," remarked Professor Porter, "when the—ah—*gentleman* tied two highly respectable scholars neck to neck and dragged them through the jungle as though they were cows."

CHAPTER 17

BURIALS

$\mathbf{B}$y morning the abandoned party was exhausted and hungry, having neither eaten nor slept in twenty-four hours. The mutineers had left them a small supply of dried meats, canned soups and vegetables, crackers, flour, tea and coffee; and these were quickly broken out.

The next task was to make the cabin livable. The first step was to remove the relics of the long-ago tragedy. Professor Porter and Mr. Philander examined the skeletons with deep interest, and identified them as those of a male and female human, likely of European heritage. The smallest skeleton received little attention; it was in the cradle, so no one doubted that it was the couple's infant.

As they were preparing to remove the skeleton of the man for burial, Clayton discovered that one of the finger bones wore a massive ring. Picking it up to examine it, Clayton cried out in astonishment, for the ring bore the emblem of the house of Greystoke.

At the same time, Jane discovered the books in the cupboard. One of them was inscribed with a name: JOHN CLAYTON, LONDON. In a second book she found the single name GREYSTOKE.

"Why, Mr. Clayton," she cried, "what does this mean? Here are the names of some of your own people in these books."

"And here," he replied gravely, "is the great ring of the house of Greystoke, which has been lost since my uncle, John Clayton, the former Lord Greystoke, disappeared. We had presumed him lost at sea."

"But how can these things be here, in this savage African jungle?" exclaimed the girl.

"It can mean but one thing, Miss Porter," said Clayton. "The late Lord Greystoke was not drowned. He died here in this cabin, and these are his mortal remains."

"Then this must have been Lady Greystoke," said Jane reverently, indicating the bones on the bed.

"The beautiful Lady Alice," replied Clayton, "of whom my parents have often spoken. She was a woman of great personal charm and virtue. Poor woman," he murmured sadly.

With deep solemnity, the bones of Lord and Lady Greystoke were buried beside their little African cabin. Between them was placed the tiny skeleton of the baby of Kala, the ape.

As Mr. Philander was placing the frail bones of the infant in a bit of sailcloth, he examined the skull closely. Then he called Professor Porter over, and the two argued in low tones for several minutes.

"Most remarkable, most remarkable," said Professor Porter.

"Bless me," said Mr. Philander, "we must tell Mr. Clayton at once."

"Tut, tut, Mr. Philander!" disagreed Professor Porter. "Let the past rest in peace."

And so the white-haired old man repeated the burial service over this strange grave, while his four companions stood respectfully about him.

From the trees Tarzan of the Apes watched the solemn ceremony, but most of all he watched the sweet face and graceful figure of Jane Porter.

He could not understand the new emotions stirring inside him. He wondered why he felt such an interest in these people—why he had gone to such effort to save the three men. But he did not wonder at all why he had saved the strange girl from the hungry lioness.

The men certainly were stupid and cowardly. Even Manu, the monkey, was more intelligent than they were. If these were his own kind, he would take less pride in his heritage.

But the girl, ah—that was a different matter. Instinct told him that he must protect her.

He wondered why they had dug a great hole in the ground merely to bury dry bones. It made no sense—no one wanted to steal dry bones. Had there been meat them he could have understood, because Dango, the hyena, and the other robbers of the jungle would get at it.

When the burial ceremony was over, the little party turned back toward the cabin. Esmeralda, still weeping, chanced to glance toward the harbor. Instantly her tears ceased, and she cried out and pointed in outrage, "Look at that low-down trash out there! They-all's abandonin' us on this island."

Sure enough, the *Arrow* was sailing slowly toward the harbor's entrance.

"They promised to leave us firearms and ammunition," said Clayton. "The merciless beasts!"

"It is the work of Snipes, I am sure," said Jane. "King was a scoundrel, but he was somewhat human. If they had not killed him, I know that he would have left us with more supplies and tools."

"I regret that they did not visit us before sailing," said Professor Porter. "I wished to request them to leave the treasure with us, as I shall be a ruined man if that is lost."

Jane looked at her father sadly.

"Never mind, Father," she said. "It wouldn't have done any good, because treasure was the reason they killed their officers and marooned us on this awful shore in the first place."

"Tut, tut, child, tut, tut!" replied Professor Porter. "You are a good child, but a naïve one, I fear," and he turned and walked slowly away toward the jungle, his hands clasped behind him, eyes on the ground.

His daughter watched him with a sad smile upon her lips, and then turning to Mr. Philander, she whispered: "Please don't let him wander off again. You know that we count on you to keep a close watch upon him."

"He becomes more difficult to handle each day," replied Mr. Philander, with a sigh and a shake of his head. "I presume he is now off to report to the Zoo's directors that one of their lions was at large last night. Oh, Miss Jane, you don't know what I have to contend with."

"Yes, I do, Mr. Philander, but while we all love him, you alone can manage him. Regardless of what he may say, the poor dear respects your great learning and good judgment. He cannot tell the difference between education and wisdom."

Mr. Philander, unsure whether he had been complimented or insulted, puzzled over this question as he turned to pursue Professor Porter.

Tarzan had seen the concern on the faces of the little group as they watched the ship depart. To him the vessel was a wonderful novelty, so he decided to hasten out to the point of land north of the harbor for a better view of it—and, if possible, to learn in which direction it went. Swinging speedily through the trees, he reached the small peninsula just in time for an excellent view.

It was a strange sort of floating house. There

were some twenty men running around on the deck, pulling and hauling on ropes. A light land breeze was blowing, and the ship had been eased through the harbor's mouth under light sail. Now that they had cleared the point, she was under full sail, headed out to sea as quickly as possible.

Tarzan watched the graceful movements of the ship in rapt admiration, and longed to be aboard her. Presently he spotted a bit of smoke on the far northern horizon, and he wondered how smoke could appear on the great water.

Apparently the lookout on the *Arrow* must also have seen the smoke, for in a few minutes Tarzan saw some of the sails being taken down. The ship turned back toward land. A man at the bow was heaving a rope with a small object at the end into the water, then hauling it back in and repeating the process. Tarzan wondered why.

At last the ship came up directly into the wind. Its sails came down, and the anchor splashed overboard. On deck, the sailors were scurrying about.

A boat was lowered, and in it a large chest was placed. Then a dozen sailors rowed it rapidly toward the beach near Tarzan's hideout. As it drew nearer, Tarzan saw the rat-faced man in the boat's stern.

A few minutes later, the boat touched the beach on the north side of the point, out of sight of the cabin. The men jumped out, lifted the great chest to the sand, and then began to argue. After some bickering and looking about, the rat-faced sailor indicated a spot beneath Tarzan's tree, and said, "Here is a good place."

"As good as any," replied one of his companions. "If they catch us with the treasure aboard, they will take it all away. We might as well bury it here and hope that some of us will escape hanging and come back and enjoy it later."

The rat-faced one now called to the men remaining at the boat, and they came slowly up the bank, carrying picks and shovels. "Hurry, you!" cried Snipes.

"Stow it!" retorted one of the men, named Tarrant, in a surly tone. "You're no admiral, you damned shrimp."

"I'm Cap'n here, you swab, an' don't forget it!" shrieked Snipes, with a volley of foul curses.

"Steady, boys," cautioned one of the men who had not spoken before. "Fightin' amongst ourselves won't get us nothin'."

"Right enough," replied Tarrant, "but it ain't a-goin' to get nobody nothin' to act important neither."

"You fellows dig here," said Snipes, indicating a spot beneath the tree. "And while you're diggin', Peter kin be a-makin' a map of the location so's we kin find it again. You, Tom, and Bill, take a couple more men and fetch the chest."

"What work are you a-goin' to do?" asked Tarrant. "Just boss us about?"

"Git busy there," growled Snipes. "You didn't think your Cap'n was a-goin' to help dig, did you?"

The men all looked up angrily. None of them liked Snipes to begin with, and since he had murdered King—the original ringleader of the mutiny—he had been ordering them about constantly. They had grown to hate him.

"Do you mean to say that you don't intend to take a shovel and lend a hand with this work? Your shoulder's not hurt so bad as that," said Tarrant.

"Not by a damned sight," replied Snipes, fingering the butt of his revolver nervously.

"Then, by God," replied the angry sailor, "if you won't take a shovel, you'll take a pickax." With that he raised his pick above his head, and with a mighty blow, he buried the point in Snipes' brain.

For a moment the men stood silently looking at the gruesome result of their fellow mutineer's grim humor. Then one of them spoke.

"Served the skunk jolly well right," he said.

The men began to dig in the soft soil, first with picks and then with shovels. There was no further comment on the killing, but the men worked more readily than they had since Snipes had assumed command.

When they had a trench large enough to bury the chest, Tarrant suggested that they enlarge it and bury Snipes on top of the chest. "It might help fool anyone who happened to be diggin' hereabouts," he explained.

This made sense, and so the trench was made wide enough for the corpse. Then a deeper hole was made in the middle for the box, which was wrapped in sailcloth and lowered in so that its top was about a foot below the bottom of the grave. Earth was shoveled in and tramped down until the bottom of the grave was level.

The men stripped the corpse of weapons and other items they wanted, then rolled Snipes's body into the hole and filled the grave. They stomped the ground flat, threw the rest of the loose dirt around the area, and spread dead brush over it for concealment.

Their work done, the sailors returned to the small boat and rowed rapidly toward the *Arrow*. The breeze had increased considerably, and as the smoke plume was now much larger, the mutineers quickly set full sails and headed away toward the southwest.

Tarzan, who had watched all this activity with interest, thought about the strange actions of these peculiar creatures. Men were indeed more foolish and cruel than the beasts of the jungle! How fortunate that he lived in the peace and security of the great forest!

And what had the chest contained? If they did not want it, why not merely throw it into the water? That would have been much easier.

Ah, he thought, but they do want it. They

have hidden it here because they intend returning for it later, as one might do with the carcass of Horta, the boar.

Tarzan dropped to the ground and began to look around. Maybe they had dropped something useful to him. Soon he discovered a shovel hidden near the grave.

He tried to use it as the sailors had done. It was awkward work and hurt his bare feet, but he continued until he found the body. This he dragged from the grave and laid aside. He kept digging until he found the chest, and this too he set aside, next to the corpse. Then he filled in the smaller hole below the grave and reburied the body, covering the site again with the underbrush.

Now he returned to the chest, which had taken four sailors to move. Tarzan picked it up as though it were empty, and with the spade slung on his back by a piece of rope, carried it off into the densest part of the jungle.

He could not easily swing through the trees with his awkward burden, but he was able to make fairly good time by keeping to the trails. For several hours he traveled north and east until he came to a thick wall of tangled vegetation; then he took to the lower branches. In another fifteen minutes he emerged into the arena where the apes had celebrated the rites of the Dum-Dum.

Tarzan started digging near the center of the clearing, not far from the drum. The ground was packed down, so it was harder work than before, but Tarzan labored until he had a hole deep enough to hide the chest from view.

Why had he gone to all this effort without knowing the value of the contents of the chest?

Tarzan had a man's figure and a man's brain, but he had an ape's upbringing. His brain told him that the chest contained something valuable, or the men would not have hidden it. Growing up, he had learned to imitate the new and unusual. Now the natural curiosity of both men and apes prompted him to open the chest and examine its contents, and he tried, but the heavy lock and massive iron band defeated even his great cunning and strength. He had to bury the chest without satisfying his curiosity.

By the time Tarzan had hunted his way back to the vicinity of the cabin, feeding as he went, it was quite dark.

A light was burning inside the little building. Clayton had found an unopened tin of oil that had originally been left with the Claytons by Black Michael, and the lamps still worked.

Tarzan was astonished to see the interior of the cabin appearing as bright as day. He had often wondered how the lamps worked. His reading and the pictures had told him what they were, but he had no idea how they could be made to produce the wondrous sunlight shown in the pictures.

As he approached the window nearest the

door, he saw that the cabin had been divided into two rooms by a rough curtain of sailcloth.

In the front room were the three men; the two older were deep in argument, while the younger, tilted back against the wall on an improvised stool, was absorbed in one of Tarzan's books. Tarzan was not particularly interested in the men, however, so he sought the other window. There was the girl. How beautiful and delicate she was!

She was writing at Tarzan's own table beneath the window. The black woman lay asleep upon a pile of grasses at the far side of the room.

For an hour, Tarzan feasted his eyes upon her while she wrote. How he longed to speak to her, but he dared not try. Like the young man, she probably would not understand him. Worse yet, he might frighten her away.

At length she arose, leaving her manuscript upon the table. She went over and sat on the bed upon which had been spread several layers of soft grasses. Then she loosened the soft mass of golden hair which crowned her head. It fell about her oval face like a shimmering waterfall in the light of a sunset, all the way below her waist.

Tarzan was spellbound.

Then she extinguished the lamp, and the cabin was wrapped in darkness. Still Tarzan watched. Creeping close beneath the window, he waited, listening, for half an hour. At last he was rewarded by the sounds of the regular breathing typical of sleep.

Cautiously he slipped his hand between the window's bars until his whole arm was inside the cabin. Carefully he felt around on the desk until at last he grasped the papers upon which Jane Porter had been writing. In silence he withdrew his hand with the precious treasure.

Tarzan folded the sheets into a small parcel, which he tucked into the quiver with his arrows. Then he melted away into the jungle as softly and as noiselessly as a shadow.

CHAPTER 18

THE JUNGLE TOLL

When Tarzan of the Apes awoke early the following morning, his first thought was of the wonderful writing hidden in his quiver. Now that it was light, he was desperately eager to read what the beautiful golden-haired girl had written.

The first glance brought bitter disappointment. He had never before wanted anything so badly, and now he was baffled by strange, sloppy handwritten characters of a sort he had never seen before. Why, they even tilted in the opposite direction from any others he had seen. Even the little bugs of the black book were familiar friends, despite their confusing arrangement, but these were altogether new bugs.

For twenty minutes he pored over them, when suddenly he began to spot familiar, though distorted shapes. Ah, they were his old friends, but badly crippled.

Then he began to make out a word here and a word there. His heart jumped for joy—he could read it! In another half hour he had made good progress, and except for an occasional unfamiliar word, he found it getting easier and easier.

Here is what he read:

West Coast of Africa, about 10x degrees south latitude (So Mr. Clayton says.)
February 3 (?), 1909.

To Hazel Strong, Baltimore, MD

Dearest Hazel:

It seems foolish to write you a letter that you may never see, but I simply must tell somebody of our awful experiences since we sailed from Europe on the ill-fated Arrow.

If we never return to civilization, as now seems likely, this will at least record the events leading up to our final fate, whatever it may be.

As you know, we were supposed to have set out upon a scientific expedition to the Congo. Papa was thought to have some wondrous theory of an ancient civilization whose remains lay buried somewhere in the Congo valley. But after we sailed, the truth came out.

It seems that an old bookseller in Baltimore discovered, between the leaves of a very old Spanish manuscript, a letter written in 1550 detailing the adventures of the mutineers of a Spanish ship. The vessel was bound from Spain to South America with a vast treasure of "doubloons" and "pieces of eight," and the letter was to his son, the captain of a Spanish merchant vessel. Many years had passed, and the old man had become a respected citizen, but his greed remained so strong that he risked all to help his son gain them both fabulous wealth.

The writer told how, a week out from Spain, the crew had mutinied and murdered every officer. In so doing, they sealed their fate, for they had slain everyone who could navigate a ship at sea.

They were blown about for two months. Dying of scurvy, starvation, and thirst, they were shipwrecked on a small island. The vessel was broken to pieces, but not before the ten remaining survivors had rescued one of the great chests of treasure. They buried it on the island, and for three years they lived in hope of rescue.

One by one they sickened and died, until only one man was left, the writer of the letter. The men had built a boat from the wreckage of the vessel, but having no idea where the island was located, had not dared go to sea.

When he was the only survivor, however, the writer became so lonely he chose to risk death upon the sea rather than madness on the isle. So after nearly a year of solitude, he set sail.

Fortunately he sailed due north, right into the path of the Spanish merchantmen plying between the West Indies and Spain. Within a week he was picked up by one of these vessels, homeward bound. He told a story of shipwreck, hardship and death on the island, but did not mention the mutiny or the buried treasure.

The merchant captain assured him that, from his description and considering the winds, he must have been stranded on one of the Cape

Verde islands, which lie off the West Coast of Africa at about 16x or 17x north latitude.

His letter described the island in detail, as well as the location of the treasure, and was accompanied by the crudest, funniest little old map you ever saw, with trees and rocks all marked by scrawled X's to show the exact spot where the treasure had been buried.

When Papa explained the real nature of the expedition, my heart sank, for I know so well how gullible the poor dear has always been. When he told me he had paid a thousand dollars for the letter and map, I feared he had been duped once again. Worse yet, I learned that he had borrowed ten thousand dollars more from Robert Canler, and had signed papers for the amount.

Mr. Canler asked for no collateral, and you know, dearie, what that will mean for me if papa cannot pay. Oh, how I detest that man!

We all tried to remain cheerful, but Mr. Philander, and Mr. Clayton—who joined us in London just for the adventure—both felt as skeptical as I.

Well, to make a long story short, we found the island and the treasure—a great iron-bound oak chest in fine shape. It was filled with gold coins, and was so heavy that four men bent underneath its weight.

The horrid thing seems to bring nothing but murder and misfortune to those who touch it, for three days after we sailed from the Cape Verde Islands, our own crew mutinied and killed every one of their officers.

Oh, it was the most terrifying experience one could imagine—I cannot even write about it. They were going to kill us too, but the leader, named King, would not let them. So they sailed south along the coast to a lonely spot with a good harbor, and here they have marooned us.

They sailed away with the treasure today, but Mr. Clayton says they will never enjoy it. Apparently King was the only mutineer who could navigate, and on the day we landed, one of the men murdered him on the beach.

I wish you could know Mr. Clayton; he is the dearest fellow imaginable, and I believe he has fallen very much in love with me. He is the only son of Lord Greystoke, and some day will inherit the title and estates. In addition, he is wealthy in his own right, but the fact that he is going to be an English Lord makes me very sad—you know how I feel about American girls who marry titled foreigners. Oh, if only he were a plain American gentleman!

But it isn't his fault, poor fellow, and in everything except birth he would do credit to my country, and that is the greatest compliment I can pay any man.

We have had the most weird experiences since we were stranded here. Papa and Mr. Philander became lost in the jungle, and were chased by a real lion. Mr. Clayton got lost, and was attacked twice by wild beasts. Esmeralda and I were cornered in an old cabin by a perfectly awful man-eating lioness. Oh, it was simply "terrifical," as Esmeralda would say.

But the strangest part of it all is the wonderful creature who rescued us. I have not seen him, but Mr. Clayton and Papa and Mr. Philander have, and they say that he is a white man with godlike physique, skin tanned to a dusky brown, strong as a wild elephant, agile as a monkey, and brave as a lion.

He speaks no English. After he performs some courageous deed, he vanishes mysteriously like a spirit.

Then we have another weird neighbor, who printed a beautiful sign in English and tacked it on the door of his cabin, which we occupy, warning us not to destroy his belongings, and signing himself "Tarzan of the Apes."

We have never seen him, though we think he is near, for when one of the sailors was going to shoot Mr. Clayton in the back, the rascal received a spear in his shoulder from some unseen hand in the jungle.

The sailors left us very little food, and our only revolver has but three cartridges left, so we do not know how we can find meat. Mr. Philander says that we can get by on the abundant wild fruit and nuts in the jungle.

I am very tired now, so I shall go to my little bed of grasses which Mr. Clayton gathered for me, but will add to this letter from day to day as things happen.

Lovingly,

JANE PORTER

Tarzan sat in deep thought for a long time after he finished reading. There were so many new and wonderful things in the letter that his brain was awhirl.

So they did not realize that he was Tarzan of the Apes. He would tell them.

In his tree he had constructed a rude shelter of leaves and branches to keep the rain off the few treasures he had brought from the cabin. Among these were some pencils. He took one, and beneath Jane Porter's signature he wrote:

I am Tarzan of the Apes

He thought that would be sufficient. Later he would return the letter to the cabin. As for food, thought Tarzan, they need not worry—he would provide.

The next morning Jane found her missing letter in the exact spot from which it had disappeared two nights before. She was mystified, but when she saw the printed words beneath her signature, she felt a cold, clammy chill run up her spine. She showed the last sheet with the signature to Clayton.

"And to think," she said, "that uncanny thing was probably watching me all the time that I was writing—ooh! It makes me shudder just to think of it."

"But he must be friendly," reassured Clayton, "for he has returned your letter and has not attempted to harm you. And, unless I am mistaken, last night he left a significant token of his goodwill outside our cabin door—I just found the carcass of a wild boar there."

From then on, nearly every day, they found some offering of food. Sometimes it was a young deer, and other times a quantity of strange, cooked food—tasty cassava cakes pilfered from the village of Mbonga—or a boar, or leopard, and once, a lion.

Tarzan's greatest pleasure was to bring food to these strangers, for that meant helping and protecting the golden-haired girl.

Someday he would venture into the camp in daylight and talk with these people by printing the little bugs on paper, but for now he was still too shy.

As they grew familiar with the area, the castaways wandered ever farther into the jungle in search of nuts and fruit.

Scarcely a day passed that did not find Professor Porter unknowingly wandering toward the jaws of death. Mr. Philander, never a vigorous man, was worn to a shadow by the ceaseless need to safeguard the professor.

A month passed. Tarzan had finally decided to visit the camp by daylight.

It was early afternoon. Clayton had wandered to the point of land at the harbor's mouth to look for passing ships. Here he kept a large pile of wood, ready to be ignited as a distress signal.

Professor Porter was wandering along the beach south of the camp. Mr. Philander was at his elbow, urging him to turn back before they became entertainment or dinner for some savage beast.

With the others gone, Jane and Esmeralda had wandered into the jungle to gather fruit, and were getting farther and farther from the cabin.

Tarzan stood in impatient silence at the door of the little house waiting for them to return. Nowadays, all he thought of was the girl he loved. He wondered if she would fear him, and the thought nearly caused him to abandon his plan. He wanted to gaze upon her and be near her, perhaps even touch her. She was his religion.

While he waited, he printed a message to her. Whether he would give it to her, he did not know, but he enjoyed seeing his thoughts expressed in print. He wrote:

> I am Tarzan of the Apes. I want you. I am yours. You are mine. We live here together always in my house. I will bring you the best of fruits, the tenderest deer, the finest meats that roam the jungle. I am the mightiest of the jungle fighters. I will fight for you. You are Jane Porter, I saw it in your letter. When you see this you will know that Tarzan of the Apes loves you.

As he stood by the door, waiting after he had finished the message, he heard a familiar sound— the passing of a great ape through the lower branches of the forest. He listened intently, and then from the jungle came the agonized scream of a woman.

Tarzan dropped his first love letter on the ground and shot like a panther into the forest.

The other men also heard the scream, and in a few minutes they all came panting to the cabin, calling out as they approached. A glance inside confirmed their worst fears.

Jane and Esmeralda were not there!

Followed by the two old men, Clayton plunged immediately into the jungle, calling to Jane. For half an hour they stumbled on, until by pure chance Clayton came upon the motionless form of Esmeralda.

He stopped beside her, feeling for her pulse and then listening for her heartbeats. She was alive. He shook her.

"Esmeralda!" he shrieked in her ear. "Esmeralda! For God's sake, where is Miss Porter? What has happened?"

Slowly Esmeralda opened her eyes. She saw Clayton. She saw the jungle all around her. "Oh, God Almighty!" she screamed.

"Where's Miss Porter? What happened?" questioned Clayton.

"Ain't Miss Jane here?" cried Esmeralda, sitting up quickly. "Oh, Lord, now I remember! It must have snatched her away," and she began to weep.

"What took her away?" cried Professor Porter.

"A great big giant all covered with hair."

"A gorilla, Esmeralda?" questioned Mr. Philander, and the three men scarcely breathed as he voiced the horrible thought.

"I thought it was the devil! Oh, but I guess it was a gorilla. Oh, my poor baby, my poor little honey," and again Esmeralda broke into uncontrollable sobbing.

Clayton immediately began to look about for tracks, but he could find nothing except a lot of trampled grasses nearby. He knew too little of woodcraft to read their meaning.

For the rest of the day they searched the jungle, but as night approached, they were forced to give up in despair. They did not even know in which direction this creature had taken Jane. By the time they reached the cabin, it was dark. The party sat silent and sad in the little cabin.

Professor Porter finally broke the silence. His tone was no longer that of the theorizing scholar. Now he spoke as a man of action, determined, but with great grief and little hope. Clayton felt the same.

"I shall lie down now," said the old man, "and try to sleep. Tomorrow at first light, I shall take what food I can carry and not return until I have found Jane."

His companions did not reply at once. Each was immersed in his own sorrowful thoughts, and all three knew what the last words meant—Professor Porter would never return from the jungle.

At length Clayton arose and laid his hand gently upon Professor Porter's bent old shoulder.

"I shall go with you, of course," he said.

"I knew that you would wish to go, Mr. Clayton, but you must not. Jane is beyond human assistance now. What was once my dear little girl shall not lie alone and friendless in the awful jungle. I shall join her, covered by the same leaves and vines, and her mother's spirit will find us joined in death as we have been in life. I alone shall go, for she was all that remained on Earth for me to love."

"I shall go with you," said Clayton simply.

The old man looked up, regarding the strong, handsome face of William Cecil Clayton intently. He read there the love that lay in the heart beneath—the love for his daughter. He had been too preoccupied with scholarly thoughts to note the signs that these young people were becoming closer and closer, but now he realized.

"As you wish," he said.

"You may count on me, also," said Mr. Philander.

"No, my dear old friend," said Professor Porter. "We should not all go. It would be cruelly wicked to leave poor Esmeralda here alone, and three of us would be no more successful than one.

"There are already enough dead things in the cruel forest. Come—let us try to sleep a little."

CHAPTER 19

THE CALL OF THE PRIMITIVE

From the time Tarzan left the great apes, the tribe was torn by continual strife. Terkoz proved a cruel king, bullying the older and weaker apes. Many of these fled with their families to the quiet safety of the far interior.

Those who remained finally became desperate to end Terkoz's brutality. One of them remembered Tarzan's parting advice:

"If you have a chief who is cruel, do not attack him alone, as the other apes do. Instead, several of you should attack him together. Then no chief will dare to be evil, for four of you can kill any chief who might rule."

The ape who recalled this wise counsel repeated it to several of his friends, and when Terkoz returned to the tribe that day, a warm reception awaited him. There were no formalities. As Terkoz arrived, five huge, hairy beasts sprang upon him.

At heart Terkoz was a coward, just as human bullies are. He did not remain to fight and die, but tore himself quickly away from them and fled into the shelter of the forest.

He tried twice to rejoin the tribe, but each time he was violently driven away. At last he gave up, and foaming with rage and hatred, turned into the jungle. For several days he wandered aimlessly, nursing his spite and looking for something weak to vent his anger upon.

It was in this state of mind that Terkoz suddenly came upon the two women in the jungle.

He was right above them when he discovered them. The first clue Jane Porter had of his presence was when the great hairy body dropped to the earth beside her, and she saw the awful face and the snarling, hideous mouth just a foot away from her.

One piercing scream escaped her lips as the brute's hand clutched her arm, and then she was dragged toward those awful fangs. But before they touched her fair throat, another mood claimed the ape.

The tribe had kept his women. He must find others to replace them, and this seemed to be a female, hairless white ape. She would be the first of his new household, and so he threw her roughly across his broad, hairy shoulders and carried her away into the trees.

Esmeralda's scream of terror mingled with that of Jane's, and then she fainted. But Jane did not. That awful face, pressing close to hers, and the stench of the foul breath in her nostrils, paralyzed her with terror, but she kept a clear head. As the brute carried her with incredible speed through the forest, she did not cry out or struggle. The attack had confused her sense of direction, and she thought they were heading toward the beach. With this in mind, she planned to conserve her energy and her voice until they were close enough to camp for to call for help.

In reality, Terkoz was carrying her ever deeper into the impenetrable jungle.

The scream that brought Clayton and the two older men stumbling through the undergrowth had led Tarzan straight to where Esmeralda lay. She was unhurt, but it was not Esmeralda he was most interested in. For a moment he scrutinized the ground below and the trees above with expert woodcraft, until the combination of his ape upbringing and his human intelligence told him the whole story just as plainly as if he had seen it all happen.

And then he disappeared into the swaying trees, following a trail no other human eye could have even detected.

At the ends of branches, when the ape swings through, the trail is easiest to see but shows less direction. Near the center of the tree, the signs are fainter, but they plainly show the direction. For example, here on this branch the fugitive has crushed a caterpillar, so Tarzan knew where that foot would next land, and there he finds a tiny spot of moisture to prove it. Over here, a branch has partly broken under the ape's weight, and the direction of the break shows the direction of travel. Or there is a shred of hair caught on the tree trunk, and he looks to see in which direction it is wedged.

He does not even need to slow down to see such signs. To him they stand out boldly against all else, but strongest of all is the scent, for Tarzan is pursuing upwind, and his nostrils are as sensitive as a hound's. Unlike most humans, Tarzan has depended on his senses all his life for his very survival, and they are as well-developed as his muscles.

So the ape-man sped quietly on after Terkoz and his prey. But Terkoz too lived by his senses, and the sound of Tarzan's approach reached his ears and spurred him to greater speed.

Tarzan pursued them for three miles before overtaking them, and then Terkoz saw that further flight was futile. He dropped to the ground in a small open glade, still grasping Jane in one great arm, prepared either to turn and defend his prize or be free to escape.

Tarzan bounded like a leopard into the arena provided by nature.

When Terkoz saw that his pursuer was Tarzan, he assumed that this was Tarzan's woman, since they were of the same kind—white and hairless— and so he rejoiced at this opportunity for double revenge upon his hated enemy.

From the description which Clayton and her

father and Mr. Philander had given Jane, she knew that it must be the same wonderful creature who had previously saved them, and she saw him as protector and friend.

When the giant ape roughly pushed Jane aside to meet Tarzan's charge, and she saw their relative sizes, her heart quailed. How could a man defeat such a mighty enemy?

Like two charging bulls they came together, and like two wolves they sought each other's throats. The long teeth of the ape battled the thin blade of the man's knife.

Jane watched. Her lithe young form was flattened against the trunk of a great tree, hands pressed tight against her rising and falling chest, eyes wide with mingled horror, fascination, fear and admiration. She watched the primeval battle of ape and man for possession of a woman: for her.

As the great muscles of the man's back and shoulders knotted with his efforts, and his huge arms held those mighty tusks at bay, the veil of centuries of civilization and culture was swept from the blurred vision of the Baltimore girl.

When the long knife drank deep a dozen times of Terkoz's heart's blood, and the great carcass rolled lifeless on the ground, it was a primeval woman who sprang forward with outstretched arms toward the primeval man who had fought for and won her.

And Tarzan?

He did not need lessons. He took his woman in his arms and smothered her upturned, panting lips with kisses.

For a moment Jane returned his kisses with half-closed eyes. For a moment—the first in her young life—she knew the meaning of love. But as suddenly as the veil had been withdrawn, it dropped again, and she was outraged. She pushed Tarzan from her and buried her face in her hands, mortified.

Tarzan had been surprised when the girl he loved had come willingly into his arms. Now he was surprised that she rejected him. He came close to her once more and took hold of her arm. She turned on him like a tigress, striking his great chest

with her tiny hands.

Tarzan could not understand it. Before the fight he had intended to hasten Jane back to her people, but that little moment was lost now in the dim past, never to return.

Since then, Tarzan of the Apes had experienced the feeling of a warm, lithe form close to him, and the taste of burning kisses from soft, perfect lips. A deep brand was seared onto his soul: it marked a new Tarzan.

Again he laid his hand upon her arm. Again she repulsed him. And then Tarzan did just what his first ancestor would have done.

He took his woman in his arms and carried her into the jungle.

Early the following morning the four other castaways were awakened by the booming of a cannon. Clayton was the first to rush out, and there, beyond the harbor's mouth, he saw two vessels lying at anchor.

One was the *Arrow* and the other a small cruiser flying French colors, its men crowding its sides, gazing shoreward. It was evident to Clayton and his companions that the gun had been fired to attract their attention if they still remained at the cabin.

Both vessels lay far from shore, and it was doubtful that their spyglasses would locate the waving hats of the little party far in between the harbor's points.

Esmeralda had thought to remove her bright red apron and wave it frantically above her head, but Clayton, fearing that even this might not be seen, hurried off toward the northern point where his signal fire lay ready for the match. After what seemed like an age, he reached the great pile of dry branches and brush.

As he broke from the dense wood and saw the vessels again, he was dismayed to see that the *Arrow* was making sail and that the cruiser was already leaving.

Quickly lighting the pyre in a dozen places, he hurried to the extreme point of the peninsula.

There he stripped off his shirt, tied it to a branch, and stood waving it back and forth above him. Still the vessels continued to leave.

He had given up all hope when, at last, the dense vertical column of smoke from his fire attracted the attention of a lookout aboard the cruiser. Instantly a dozen glasses were trained on the beach.

Presently Clayton saw the two ships come about again, and while the *Arrow* lay drifting quietly on the ocean, the cruiser steamed slowly back toward shore. At some distance away she stopped, and a boat was lowered and sent toward the beach.

As it was brought ashore, a young officer stepped out and spoke in English.

"Monsieur Clayton, I presume?" he asked.

"Thank God, you have come!" was Clayton's reply. "And perhaps it is not too late even now."

"What do you mean, Monsieur?" asked the officer.

Clayton told of the abduction of Jane Porter and the need of armed men to aid in the search for her.

"*Mon Dieu!*" exclaimed the officer, sadly. "Yesterday it would not have been too late. Now it may be better for the poor lady if she were never found. It is too horrible, Monsieur."

Other boats had now set off from the cruiser, and Clayton, having pointed out the harbor's entrance to the officer, entered his boat and directed it toward the little landlocked bay, followed by the other craft.

Soon the entire party was met by Professor Porter and Mr. Philander. Esmeralda also joined them as she wept in mingled joy and grief.

The vessel's captain was in one of the last boats to leave the cruiser. When he heard the story of Jane's abduction, he called for volunteers to accompany Professor Porter and Clayton in their search.

Every officer and man among these sympathetic Frenchmen volunteered, begging permission to join the expedition.

The commander selected twenty men and two officers: Lieutenants D'Arnot and Charpentier. A boat was sent back to the cruiser for food, packs, ammunition, and rifles.

While this was being done, Clayton asked how they had happened to anchor offshore and fire a signal gun. The commander, Captain Dufranne, explained. A month before, they had sighted the *Arrow* heading southwest under heavy sail, and when they had signaled her to come about, she had run.

They had kept her in sight until sunset, firing several shots at her, but the next morning she had vanished. They had then kept cruising up and down the coast for several weeks, and had nearly forgotten the incident. Then, early one morning a few days before, the lookout had reported a vessel in sight, tossed about by a heavy sea and apparently out of control.

As they steamed nearer to the derelict ship, they were surprised to note that it was the same vessel that had run from them a few weeks earlier. Her sails looked as if they had been set to keep her steady, but they were being torn to rags in the high wind.

On the high sea, it was a difficult and dangerous task to attempt to board her, and as no signs of life had been seen above deck, the captain decided to stand by until the wind and sea calmed. But just then a figure was seen clinging to the rail, feebly waving a signal of despair.

Immediately a boat's crew was ordered out, and with great courage, the men successfully boarded the *Arrow*. It was now a prize, but on board, the sight that met the Frenchmen's eyes was awful.

A dozen dead and dying men rolled on the pitching deck, the living intermingled with the dead. None were conscious, not even the poor devil who had signaled.

The prize crew soon had the vessel under proper sail once more, the living members of the miserable crew carried below to their hammocks. The dead were wrapped in sailcloth and secured on deck to be identified by their comrades before burial at sea.

It did not take the French officer long to learn what had caused the disaster. When water and brandy were sought to restore the men, none were found, nor any sort of food.

He immediately signaled to the cruiser to send water, medicine, and food, and another boat made the perilous trip to meet the *Arrow*. When the supplies arrived and were given to the men, several of them revived, and the whole story was told. The part leading up to the murder and burial of Snipes and the sailing of the *Arrow* was related. After that, the chase by the cruiser had frightened the mutineers so badly they had headed straight out to sea for several days after losing their pursuer. Only then did they discover that their supplies of food and water were low, so they had turned back eastward.

With no one on board skilled in navigation, their location was a matter of debate. When three days of eastward sailing did not bring sight of land, they bore off northward, believing that the high winds had blown them clear south of the southern tip of Africa. They kept on a north-northeasterly course for two days, then were overtaken by a week of calm and could not move at all. Their water was gone, and in another day they would be without food.

Conditions changed rapidly from bad to worse. One man went mad and leaped overboard.

When another died, they threw him overboard also, though some wanted to keep the corpse on board. Hunger was changing them from human beasts to wild beasts. Two days before the cruiser had rediscovered them, they had become too weak to handle the vessel, and three more men had died. Only then had the cruiser arrived.

Some recovered and told the entire story to the French commander, but the men were too ignorant to be able to tell him precisely where the professor and his party had been marooned. The cruiser had steamed slowly along the coast, occasionally firing signal guns and having lookouts scan every inch of the beach, halting at night so as to miss no part of the shoreline. The previous night had brought them off the very beach where lay the little camp they sought.

The signal guns of the afternoon before had not been heard on shore, it was now determined, because the castaways had been deep in the jungle searching for Jane Porter. Likely the crashing noises of their travel through the brush had drowned out the sound of the distant gun.

By the time the two parties had shared their adventures, the cruiser's boat had returned with supplies for the expedition.

Within a few minutes, the little body of sailors and the two French officers, together with Professor Porter and Clayton, set off on their hopeless and ill-fated quest into the untracked jungle.

CHAPTER 20

HEREDITY

When Jane realized that she was a captive, she struggled desperately at first to escape. It was no use; the strong arms only held her a little more tightly. So she gave up the futile effort, looking up through half-closed eyes at the face of the wild man above her as he strode easily through the tangled undergrowth.

The face was especially handsome—perfectly masculine, strong, uncorrupted by bad habits or brutal passions. True, Tarzan of the Apes was a killer of men and beasts, but he never killed with the brooding, poisonous hate that leaves hideous lines on the face. Mostly he killed without emotion, like the hunter, and he was more likely to smile than scowl as he did so.

One thing the girl had particularly noticed when she watched Tarzan rushing at Terkoz—the vivid scarlet mark on his forehead, from above the left eye to the scalp. But now she noticed that it was gone, with only a thin white line marking the spot.

As she ceased struggling, Tarzan slightly

relaxed his grip. Once he looked down into her eyes and smiled, and the girl had to close her own to shut out the vision of that handsome, winning face.

Presently Tarzan took to the trees. To Jane's astonishment, she felt no fear. In fact, she felt more secure now than ever before, though she was being carried—God alone knew where or to what fate—ever deeper into the untamed forest. When she worried about the future, she had but to open her eyes and look into those fine features and brave eyes for her fears to dissolve. Their owner would never harm her.

On and on they went through what seemed to Jane a solid mass of greenery, yet for this forest god, a path seemed to open constantly as if by magic, closing behind them as they passed. Scarcely a branch even scraped her.

As Tarzan moved steadily onward, his mind was occupied with many strange new thoughts. This entire situation was outside his experience, and he felt that he must meet it as a man and not as an ape. His travel through the middle heights of the jungle had helped cool the fierce passion that had overcome him before, and he now speculated on what Terkoz might have done with the girl. He knew why the ape had not killed her, and he began comparing his intentions with those of Terkoz.

True, it was the way of the jungle beasts for the male to take his mate by force, but should

Tarzan follow the laws of the beasts? Was Tarzan not a man? But what did men do? He did not know. He wished that he could ask the girl, and then he realized that her attempt to escape him was her answer.

But now they had arrived, and Tarzan of the Apes swung lightly down to the turf of the great apes' council arena. Though they had come many miles, it was still mid-afternoon, and the clearing was bathed in the dim light that leaked through the dense jungle.

The green turf looked soft, cool and inviting. The many noises of the jungle seemed like a distant echo of blurred sounds. A feeling of dreamy peacefulness stole over Jane as she sank down upon the grass where Tarzan placed her, and as she looked up at his great figure towering above her, there was a strange sense of perfect security.

As she watched him from beneath half-closed lids, Tarzan crossed the little clearing toward the trees on the far side. She admired his graceful majesty and magnificent physique. Surely there could be no cruelty or pettiness in this creature. Such a man could not have existed since God created Adam in his own image.

With a bound, Tarzan sprang into the trees and disappeared—to where, Jane wondered. Had he left her to her fate in the lonely jungle?

She glanced nervously around. Every vine and bush seemed like the lurking-place of some huge and horrible beast waiting to bury gleaming fangs in her soft flesh. Every sound seemed like the stealthy creeping of something dangerous.

How different it was now that he had left her!

For a few minutes that seemed hours, she sat with tense nerves waiting for whichever crouching thing would end her frightened misery. She almost prayed for it to hurry up and spring.

She heard a sudden, slight sound behind her. With a cry she sprang to her feet and turned to face her end.

There stood Tarzan, his arms filled with ripe, tasty fruit.

Jane reeled and would have fallen, had Tarzan not dropped his burden and caught her in his arms. She did not faint, but clung tightly to him, trembling like a frightened deer.

Tarzan stroked her soft hair and tried to comfort and quiet her. He remembered how Kala had comforted him as a child when he had been frightened by Sabor, the lioness, or Histah, the snake. Now he did as Kala had done.

Once he pressed his lips lightly to her forehead, and she did not move, but closed her eyes and sighed. She neither could nor wished to analyze her feelings. She trusted these strong arms as she would have trusted few men. She had never before known love; was this love? She wondered, and smiled.

Still smiling, she pushed Tarzan gently away.

Looking at him with a questioning smile that he found enchanting, she pointed to the fruit and took a seat on the edge of the earthen drum. She was hungry.

Tarzan quickly gathered up the fruit and laid it at her feet. Then he, too, sat beside her on the drum, and with his knife, opened and prepared the various fruits for her meal.

Together they ate in silence, occasionally stealing sly glances at one another, until finally Jane broke into a merry laugh which Tarzan joined.

"I wish you spoke English," said the girl.

Tarzan shook his head, and an expression of wistful and pathetic longing sobered his laughing eyes.

Then Jane tried speaking to him in French, and then in her halting German, laughing at her clumsy pronunciation. No response. "Anyway," she said to him in English, "you understand my German as well as they did in Berlin."

Tarzan had long since made a decision. He remembered reading of the ways of men and women in the books at the cabin. He would act as he imagined the men in the books would have acted in his place.

Again he rose and went into the trees, but first he tried to explain with hand signs that he would return shortly. Jane understood, and was not afraid this time, just lonely. She watched the spot where he had disappeared. As before, a soft sound behind her alerted her to his return, coming across the turf with a large armful of branches. Then he went back into the jungle and in a few minutes reappeared with a quantity of soft grasses and ferns.

He made two more trips, until he had quite a pile of material at hand. Then he spread the ferns and grasses on the ground in a soft flat bed, and constructed a shelter above them with branches and huge elephant's ear leaves. Finally he closed one end of the shelter with more of the same.

Then they sat down together again on the edge of the drum and tried to talk by signs.

The magnificent diamond locket that hung around Tarzan's neck had been a source of much wonder to Jane. She pointed to it now, and Tarzan removed it and handed the pretty bauble to her.

She saw that it was of superb quality, made by skilled hands and set with brilliant diamonds in a style that was now out of fashion. She also noticed that the locket opened, so she pressed the hidden clasp. The two halves opened to reveal a pair of images painted on ivory.

One was of a beautiful woman. The other might have been a likeness of the man who sat beside her, except for a difference of expression too subtle to define.

She looked up at Tarzan to find him leaning toward her, gazing on the images in astonishment. He reached out his hand for the locket and took it, examining the likenesses with obvious surprise and new interest. Clearly he had never seen them before, or even imagined that the locket opened. How in the world could this beautiful ornament have come into the hands of a wild creature of the African jungles? The resemblance of the male image to this woodland demi-god was amazing. It could be his brother or, more likely, his father.

Tarzan was still gazing intently at the two faces. Presently he removed the quiver from his shoulder, and emptied the arrows out onto the ground. He then reached into the bottom of the container and removed a flat object wrapped in many soft leaves and tied with bits of long grass.

Carefully he unwrapped it, removing layer after layer of leaves until at length he held a photograph in his hand. He pointed to the image of the man in the locket and held them up for comparison.

Now Jane was more puzzled still. The photo seemed to depict the same man as in the locket.

Tarzan was looking at her in puzzlement as she glanced up at him. He seemed to be framing a question with his lips.

The girl pointed to the photograph and then to the locket image and then to him, as if suggesting that the image was him, but he shook his head. Shrugging his great shoulders, he took the photograph from her, carefully rewrapped it, and replaced it in the bottom of his quiver.

For a few moments he sat in silence, his eyes

on the ground, while Jane studied the little locket, turning it over and over in her hand in search of clues as to its original owner.

Then she realized that the locket had belonged to Lord Greystoke, and the likenesses were of himself and Lady Alice. This wild creature had simply found it in the cabin by the beach. How stupid of her not to have thought of that solution before.

But there was no way to account for the resemblance between Lord Greystoke and this forest god. She could not imagine that this naked savage might himself be an English nobleman.

Tarzan looked up to watch the girl examine the locket. He had no idea what the faces meant, but he could read the fascination on Jane's young face. She noticed that he was watching her, and thinking that he wanted the locket back, she held it out to him.

He took it from her and placed it around her neck, smiling at her expression of surprise. Jane shook her head forcefully and tried to remove the golden links from about her throat, but Tarzan clasped her hands tightly to prevent her. At last she stopped, and with a little laugh raised the locket to her lips.

Tarzan did not know precisely what she meant, but he guessed correctly that it was her way of showing appreciation. So he rose, took the locket in his hand, bent solemnly, and pressed his lips upon it where hers had rested. It was a stately compliment—perhaps a gesture inspired by his many generations of noble blood.

It was growing dark now, and so they ate more fruit, which was both food and drink for them. Then Tarzan got up and led Jane to the little shelter, and motioned her inside.

For the first time in hours a feeling of fear swept over her, and Tarzan felt her shrink away from him.

A half-day of contact with this girl had transformed Tarzan. Now the habits and instincts bred into his forebears asserted themselves. He wanted to please the woman he loved and have her approval.

So Tarzan did the only thing he knew to reassure Jane. He removed his hunting knife from its sheath and handed it to her hilt first, again motioning her into the shelter.

The girl understood, and taking the long knife, she entered and lay down upon the soft grasses while Tarzan stretched himself on the ground across the entrance.

And this was the way the rising sun found them in the morning.

When Jane awoke, the strange surroundings confused her at first. The reality of it all slowly came back to her, and she felt a mighty wave of gratitude at her deliverance. She had been in terrible danger, and was unharmed.

She moved to the entrance of the shelter to look for Tarzan. He was gone, but this time she felt no fear. He would return.

At the entrance to her shelter she saw the imprint of his body in the grass where he had spent all night guarding her. She knew that only his protective presence had permitted her such peaceful sleep. Was there another man on earth with whom a woman could feel so safe in such a dangerous jungle? She no longer even feared lions and panthers.

She looked up to see his lithe form drop softly from a nearby tree. As he caught her eyes looking at him, his face lighted with that frank and radiant smile that had won her trust the day before.

As he approached her, Jane's heart beat faster and her eyes brightened as they had never done before at the approach of any man.

He had been gathering fruit again. Once more they sat down together to eat.

Jane wondered what his plans might be. Would he take her back to the beach, or keep her here? With a shock, she realized that she was unconcerned, even contented, sitting next to the smiling giant sharing delicious fruit. Could it be that she did not care whether or not she returned? None of it made sense. Reason told her that she should be terrified for a dozen different reasons, but instead her heart was singing and her face was smiling.

When they had finished their breakfast, Tarzan

went into the shelter and got his knife. She felt so comfortable that she had forgotten it along with her fear.

Motioning her to follow, Tarzan walked toward the trees at the edge of the arena, and taking her in one strong arm, swung to the branches above.

The girl knew that he was taking her back to her people, and she could not understand the sudden feeling of loneliness and sorrow that crept over her.

For hours they swung slowly along.

Tarzan was in no hurry. The pleasure of those dear arms about his neck was wonderful. He did not want it to end. So he purposefully took a very indirect route, halting several times for brief rests that he did not need. At noontime they stopped for an hour at a little brook to eat and drink.

It was nearly sunset when they came to the clearing. Tarzan dropped to the ground beside a great tree, parted the tall jungle grass, and pointed out the little cabin to her.

She took him by the hand to lead him there. She wanted to tell her father that this man had saved her from death and worse, and that he had watched over her as carefully as her mother might have done. But again the timidity of the wild thing in the face of human habitation swept over Tarzan. He drew back, shaking his head.

The girl came close to him, eyes pleading. She could not bear the thought of his going back into the terrible jungle alone.

Still he shook his head, and finally he drew her to him very gently and bent as if to kiss her, but first he looked into her eyes and waited for her reaction.

For just an instant the girl hesitated. Then she realized the truth, and throwing her arms about his neck, she drew his face to hers and kissed him—unashamed.

"I love you—I love you," she murmured.

From far in the distance came the faint sound of many guns. Tarzan and Jane raised their heads. Mr. Philander and Esmeralda came out of the cabin.

From where Tarzan and Jane stood they could not see the two vessels lying at anchor in the harbor.

Tarzan pointed toward the sounds, touched his chest and pointed again. She understood. He was going, and something told her that it was because he thought her people were in danger.

Again he kissed her.

"Come back to me," she whispered. "I shall wait for you—always."

He was gone. Jane turned to walk across the clearing to the cabin.

Mr. Philander was the first to see her. It was dusk, and Mr. Philander was very nearsighted. "Quickly, Esmeralda!" he cried. "It is a lioness! Let us seek safety within!"

Esmeralda was in no mood to see any more

lions, and did not wait around to verify the statement. She was inside the cabin and had the door slammed and bolted before he could finish. Unfortunately, in her haste, she had neglected to let Mr. Philander in first. "Bless me!" he cried, beating furiously upon the heavy door. "Esmeralda! Esmeralda!" he shrieked. "Let me in! I am being devoured by a lion!"

Esmeralda figured that the pounding at the door was the lioness trying to break it down to get at her, as had happened before. The memory of that event combined with the pounding racket now was too much. She felt faint, then collapsed.

Mr. Philander cast a frightened glance behind him. Horrors! The thing was quite close now. He tried to scramble up the side of the cabin, and succeeded in catching a frail hold on the thatched roof.

For a moment he hung there, clawing with his feet like a cat on a clothesline, but then a piece of the thatch came away, and with it Mr. Philander. He landed on his back. As he was falling, he remembered what he thought to be a fact: if you faked death, lions were supposed to ignore you.

So Mr. Philander lay as he had fallen, frozen in mock death. His arms and legs had been extended stiffly upward as he came to earth upon his back— his posture was undignified, even ridiculous.

Jane had been watching his antics in mild surprise. Now she laughed—a little choking gurgle of a laugh, but it was enough. Mr. Philander rolled over on his side and peered about, eventually spotting her.

"Jane!" he cried. "Jane Porter. Bless me!"

He scrambled to his feet and rushed toward her. He could not believe that she was here, alive.

"Bless me!" Where did you come from? Where in the world have you been? How—"

"Mercy, Mr. Philander," interrupted the girl, "I can never remember so many questions."

"Well, well," said Mr. Philander. "Bless me! I am so filled with surprise and delight at seeing you safe and well again that I scarcely know what to say. But come, tell me all that has happened to you."

CHAPTER 21

THE VILLAGE OF TORTURE

The search expedition toiled through the dense jungle, spread out in a line to cover the most ground. Their hope of finding Jane was dim, but the grief of the old man and the young Englishman kept the kind-hearted D'Arnot searching. It was likely some beast had devoured her, but perhaps they might find her remains.

Shortly after a noontime halt one of the men discovered a well-beaten elephant track. After consulting with Professor Porter and Clayton, D'Arnot decided to follow it. The path wound northeastward through the jungle, and the column now moved along it in single file. Lieutenant D'Arnot was leading at a quick pace, with Professor Porter lagging behind. D'Arnot was a hundred yards ahead when a half dozen African warriors suddenly appeared and surrounded him. The Frenchman shouted a warning to the group, but before he could draw his revolver, he was subdued and dragged into the jungle.

His cry of danger had alarmed the sailors, and

a dozen of them passed Professor Porter as they hurried forward to help their officer, though they did not know the nature of the danger. They had passed the spot where D'Arnot had been seized when a thrown spear pierced one man, followed by a volley of arrows. Raising their rifles, they returned fire blindly into the jungle. Soon the rest of the party caught up, halted, and fired many volleys toward the concealed foe. These were the shots that Tarzan and Jane Porter had heard.

Lieutenant Charpentier caught up from the rear of the group. Hearing the details of the ambush, he ordered the men to follow him into the tangled vegetation.

In an instant they were ambushed by some fifty warriors of Mbonga's village. Arrows and bullets flew thick and fast; then sharp African knives and French rifle butts fought brief and savage duels. Soon the natives fled into the jungle, leaving the Frenchmen to count their losses.

Four of the twenty were dead, a dozen others were wounded, and Lieutenant D'Arnot was missing. Night was falling rapidly, but worse, they could no longer find the elephant trail. There was no choice but to make camp until daylight. Lieutenant Charpentier ordered the area cleared and the gathered brush piled around them in a circle as a crude defensive barrier.

This work continued until long after dark. The men built a huge fire in the center of the clearing for light and comfort.

When all was as safe as possible from savage beasts and men, Lieutenant Charpentier posted sentries and let the men try to sleep. The groans of the wounded and the growls of beasts attracted by the noise and firelight kept many awake. Tired, hungry and miserable, they lay through the long night praying for dawn.

The two tribesmen who had seized D'Arnot had missed the fight as they hurried their prisoner away toward their village. They dragged him along, the sounds of battle growing fainter and fainter, until D'Arnot saw a good-sized clearing containing a thatched village protected by a stout fence.

Though it was now dusk, the watchers at the gate quickly saw that the returning trio included a prisoner. A cry went up within the village, and a great throng of women and children rushed out to meet the party.

Thus began a terrifying experience for the Frenchman—being dragged as a prisoner into a village of angry tribesmen. The raw memory of recent suffering was fresh in their minds. They could never forget the brutality of the soldiers of King Leopold II of Belgium, whose soldiers had driven the tribe from their home in the Congo Free State. Once they had been a mighty band; they were now a pathetic remnant. And as Leopold's men neither knew nor cared about which tribe an African belonged to, the Africans did not know or care that D'Arnot was French and not Belgian. The tribe's experience of white men was that they were the cruel servants of a far-off king, and so were their mortal enemies.

The villagers fell upon D'Arnot tooth and nail, beating and tearing at him. All clothing was torn from him, and the merciless blows fell upon his bare and quivering flesh, but he refused to cry out in pain. He breathed a silent prayer that death might free him quickly from his torture.

Death was not to come so easily, for soon the warriors forced the women away from the prisoner. The Frenchman was to be saved for more elaborate sport, and with the first wave of their anger expended, the women and children settled for taunting and spitting at him.

Presently they reached the center of the village. There, D'Arnot was bound securely to the great post, from which no man had ever been released alive. There he stayed until well after dark, when a dance of death began to circle around the doomed officer.

Half fainting from pain and exhaustion, D'Arnot watched from beneath half-closed lids. Perhaps it was delirium, or some horrid nightmare from which he must soon awake. The angry, painted faces; the sharp teeth; the shining, nearly-naked bodies; the cruel spears; for a moment he convinced himself that he must be dreaming.

The dancing, whirling bodies circled nearer. Now a spear sprang forth and touched his arm. The sharp pain and the feel of hot, trickling blood assured him that his hopeless position was all too real.

D'Arnot closed his eyes and gritted his teeth— he would not cry out. He was a soldier of France, and he would die like an officer and a gentleman.

Tarzan guessed the meaning of those distant shots. With Jane Porter's kisses still warm upon his lips, he was swinging with great speed through the forest trees, straight toward the village of Mbonga.

He was not interested in the location of the battle, which he knew would soon be over. He could not aid the dead; those who escaped would not need his help. His haste was for those who were taken prisoner, and he knew that he would find them by the great post in the center of Mbonga's village.

Many times Tarzan had seen Mbonga's raiding parties returning with prisoners, and the same thing had happened many times at that grim stake. He also knew that they seldom delayed before getting on with the ceremony, and that it was doubtful that he would be in time to do more than avenge the victims.

Night had fallen, so he traveled high through the swaying treetops, where the gorgeous tropical moon lit his dizzy pathway. Presently to the right of his path he sighted a distant blaze, which he assumed had been lit by the two castaways before they were attacked. He knew nothing of the presence of the sailors. Tarzan did not turn aside, but passed the Frenchmen's campfire half a mile away.

In a few more minutes, Tarzan swung into the trees above Mbonga's village. Ah, he was not quite too late! Or was he? He could not tell. The figure at the stake was motionless, yet the warriors were still stabbing at it. The death blow had not been struck. He could tell almost to the minute how far the dance had gone.

In another instant Mbonga's knife would sever one of the victim's ears. That would mark the beginning of the end, for soon only a writhing mass of mutilated flesh would remain. It would still be alive, but it would wish for death.

The stake stood forty feet from the nearest tree. Tarzan coiled his rope. Then suddenly above the savage cries of the dancing tribe rose the awful challenge of the ape-man.

The dancers halted as though turned to stone. The rope sped with an invisible whir high above the heads of the tribespeople.

D'Arnot opened his eyes. A huge warrior, standing directly before him, lunged backward as though felled by an invisible hand. Struggling and shrieking, his body moved quickly toward the shadows beneath the trees.

The tribe watched spellbound, eyes wide in horror.

Once beneath the trees, the body rose straight into the air and disappeared into the foliage above. It was too much. Screaming with fright, the terrified tribespeople broke into a mad race for the village gate. D'Arnot was left alone.

He was a brave man, but that terrible cry had made the hair on the back of his neck bristle. As he watched the body soar up into the trees, D'Arnot felt an icy shiver run along his spine, as though death had risen from a dark grave and laid a cold finger on his flesh. Then he heard sounds of movement at the spot where the body had vanished.

The branches swayed as though under a man's weight. There was a crash, and the African warrior plummeted down to earth and lay still. Immediately after him came a white body, but this one landed standing. D'Arnot saw a clean-limbed young giant emerge into the firelight and come quickly toward him.

What could it mean? Who could it be? It was doubtless some new creature of torture and destruction.

D'Arnot waited, his eyes locked with the frank, clear eyes of the advancing man. The French officer was not yet hopeful, but he sensed that the face did not mask a cruel heart.

Without a word Tarzan of the Apes cut the bonds which held D'Arnot. Weak from suffering and loss of blood, he would have fallen but for the strong arm that caught him.

The Frenchman felt himself lifted from the ground. There was a sensation of flying, and then he lost consciousness.

CHAPTER 22

THE SEARCH PARTY

Dawn greeted the disheartened group of Frenchmen and the two castaways.

As soon as it was light, Lieutenant Charpentier sent several teams out to locate the trail, which was soon found. He decided to return to camp for reinforcements and then resume the search for D'Arnot. The expedition promptly started back for the beach, slowed by the bodies of the four dead men as well as the walking wounded. It was late afternoon before the exhausted, burdened men reached the beach.

As the little party emerged from the jungle, the first person that Professor Porter and Cecil Clayton saw was Jane, standing by the cabin door. With a little cry of joy and relief, she ran forward to greet them, throwing her arms about her father's neck and bursting into tears for the first time since landing on this awful shore.

Professor Porter strove manfully to control his own emotions, but could not, and sobbed quietly on the girl's shoulder. Clayton, wishing not to intrude, remained to talk with the officers until their boat pulled away toward the cruiser. Then he turned back slowly toward the cabin. He was overjoyed. The woman he loved was safe. He wondered by what miracle she had been spared.

As he approached the cabin, Jane came out. She hurried forward to meet him.

"Jane!" he cried, "God has been good to us, indeed. Do tell me how you escaped!"

He had never before called her by her first name. Forty-eight hours before, she would have been overjoyed to hear it, but now it made her uneasy.

"Mr. Clayton," she said quietly, extending her hand, "first let me thank you for your brave loyalty to my dear father. He has told me of your noble self-sacrifice. We can never repay you!"

Clayton noticed the formality of her reply, but he was unconcerned. She had been through so much. This was no time to press his love upon her.

"I am already repaid," he said, "just to see you and Professor Porter both safe and together again. It was tragic to see him in such grief, though he bore it without complaint. My own sorrow was the greatest I have ever known, certainly, but his was so hopeless and pitiful. It taught me that no love can outshine that of a father for his daughter."

The girl bowed her head. There was a question in her mind, but it seemed terribly cruel to ask. These two men loved her, and had endured terrible suffering while she sat laughing and happy beside a godlike forest creature, eating delicious fruits and trading loving gazes. But love is a strange master, and human nature is still stranger, so she asked her question: "Where is the forest man who went to rescue you? Why did he not return?"

"I do not understand," said Clayton. "Whom do you mean?"

"He who has saved each of us—who saved me from the gorilla."

"Oh," cried Clayton, in surprise. "It was he who rescued you? You have not told me anything of your adventure, you know."

"But the wood man," she urged. "Have you not seen him? When we heard the shots in the jungle, very far away, he left—to aid you, I'm sure. We had just reached the cabin, and he hurried off toward the fighting."

Her pleading, tense tone told Clayton much that she did not say. He wondered vaguely why she was so anxious for news of this strange creature. He began to feel a sense of impending loss. Unknown to him, there also sprouted the first seed of jealousy toward the ape-man—to whom he owed his life.

"We did not see him," he replied quietly, then paused thoughtfully and added, "Possibly he joined his own tribe—the men who attacked us." He did not know why he had said it—he did not believe it.

The girl looked at him wide-eyed for a moment.

"No!" she exclaimed forcefully—much too forcefully, he thought. "It could not be. They were savages."

Clayton looked puzzled. "He is a strange, half-savage creature of the jungle, Miss Porter. We know nothing of him. He speaks no European tongue—and his ornaments and weapons are those of the West Coast savages. They are the only human beings within hundreds of miles, Miss Porter. He must belong to the tribes which attacked us, or to some similar group."

Jane went white. "I will not believe it," she half whispered. "It is not true. You shall see," she said, addressing Clayton, "that he will come back and prove you wrong. You do not know him as I do. He is a gentleman."

Clayton, too, was a gentleman, and gentlemen are expected not to say hurtful things to ladies. But something in the girl's hasty defense of the forest man sparked a wave of jealousy, and for the moment, he forgot how much they owed to this wild man.

"Possibly you are right, Miss Porter," he said in a patient, patronizing tone, "but I do not think that we need worry about our forest friend. Likely he is some half-insane castaway who will forget us even more quickly than we shall forget him. He is only a beast of the jungle, Miss Porter."

The girl did not answer, but she felt her heart sink. She knew that Clayton was only saying what he thought, and for the first time she began to really think about her newfound love.

Slowly she turned and walked back to the cabin. She tried to imagine her wood-god dining by her side aboard an ocean liner. She saw him tearing his food with his hands like an animal, and wiping his greasy fingers on his thighs. She shuddered. She saw herself introducing him to her friends—crude, illiterate, uncivilized—and winced.

She entered her cabin room, sat on the edge of her grassy bed and placed a hand at her throat. As she did so, she felt the hard outlines of Tarzan's locket.

She drew it out, holding it in the palm of her hand, eyes teary. Then she raised it to her lips, and crushing it there, buried her face in the soft ferns, sobbing.

"Beast?" she murmured. "Then God make me a beast, too! Man or beast, I am yours."

She did not see Clayton again that day. Esmeralda brought her supper to her, and Jane sent word to her father that she was suffering from stress and wished to rest.

The next morning Clayton left early with the relief expedition in search of Lieutenant D'Arnot. There were two hundred armed men this time, with ten officers and two surgeons, carrying supplies for a week of travel and combat. It was an angry company, determined to punish as well as rescue.

Traveling a known trail without need to

explore, they reached the site of the previous skirmish shortly after noon. From there, the elephant-track led straight to Mbonga's village. It was but two o'clock when the head of the search party halted at the south edge of the clearing.

Lieutenant Charpentier, in command, detailed the plan of attack. The force was split into three parts. One group would remain south of the village with him. Another would take up a position in front of the village gate. The third force, which had farthest to go, was to circle around and begin the assault from the north. This would be the signal for the other two forces to join in, in hopes of capturing the village without a long fight.

For half an hour, which seemed like much longer, the men with Lieutenant Charpentier crouched in the dense foliage of the jungle awaiting the signal. They watched the tribespeople working in the fields, and coming and going through the gate.

At length the signal came—a sharp rattle of rifle fire. Answering volleys tore immediately from the jungle to the west and to the south.

The natives in the field dropped their tools and broke madly for the village. The French bullets mowed them down, and the sailors charged straight past their bodies toward the gate. The assault was so sudden that the Frenchmen reached the gates before the tribe could bar them shut, and in another minute the village street was filled with armed men fighting hand to hand in a mêlée.

The African warriors held their ground for a few moments, and some of the women even fought for their homes, but the revolvers, rifles, and swords of the Frenchmen struck down the native spearmen and archers before they could do much damage. Soon the battle turned to a wild rout, and then to a grim massacre. The French sailors had seen bits of D'Arnot's uniform on several of the warriors who opposed them. They spared the children, and any women they did not kill in self-defense, but they slaughtered every male warrior of Mbonga's village.

They carefully searched every hut and corner of the village, but found no sign of D'Arnot. They questioned the prisoners by signs, and finally one of the sailors who had served in the French Congo spoke to them in the French-African dialect known to most of the coastal tribes. Even then, all they got were excited gestures and expressions of fear. At last they concluded that the tribespeople were lying to cover their guilt, and had actually killed their comrade the night before.

All hope gone, they prepared to camp for the night inside the village. The prisoners were herded into three huts and placed under heavy guard. Sentries were posted at the barred gates, and finally the village was wrapped in the silence of sleep, except for the wailing of the women for their dead.

The next morning they set out upon the return march. Their original intent had been to burn the village, but this idea was abandoned. The prisoners were left behind, weeping and moaning, but with their dwellings and village intact.

The expedition retraced its path, slowed by ten loaded hammocks. In eight of them lay seriously wounded men, while two swung beneath the weight of the dead.

Clayton and Lieutenant Charpentier brought up the rear of the column. The Englishman kept silent in respect for the other's grief, for D'Arnot and Charpentier had been close friends since boyhood. He realized that the Frenchman's grief was worsened by the knowledge that his friend's sacrifice had been in vain, for Jane had been rescued before D'Arnot's capture. D'Arnot had acted above and beyond the call of duty to help strangers and foreigners. But when he spoke of this to Charpentier, the latter shook his head.

"No, Monsieur," he said, "D'Arnot would have chosen to die in this way. I only grieve that I could not have died for him, or at least with him. I wish that you could have known him better, Monsieur. He was indeed an officer and a gentleman—a title conferred on many, but deserved by so few. He did not die futilely, for his death in the cause of a strange American girl will inspire us all to one day face our own ends more bravely—however they may come."

Clayton did not reply, but he gained a new and lifelong respect for these Frenchmen.

It was quite late when they reached the cabin

by the beach. As they approached they fired a single shot, a prearranged signal to those left behind, signifying that the expedition had been too late. Two shots would have indicated that no sign of D'Arnot or his captors had been found, while three would mean a rescue. Thus their welcoming party was a solemn one, and with few words the dead and wounded were tenderly placed in boats and rowed silently toward the cruiser.

Clayton, exhausted from several days of laborious marching and fighting, turned toward the cabin to eat and rest. By the door stood Jane.

"The poor lieutenant?" she asked. "Did you find no trace of him?"

"We were too late, Miss Porter," he replied sadly.

"Tell me. What had happened?" she asked.

"They killed him, Miss Porter," Clayton said, his face drawn with fatigue and sorrow. And then, completely out of character for him, he blurted something very unkind: "When your forest god left you, he was doubtless hurrying to help the natives."

He was sorry before he finished the sentence, though he did not know just how much it had hurt Jane. His regret was for his unjust disloyalty to someone who had not threatened any member of his party, and had saved all their lives.

The girl's head went high. "There is but one suitable reply to your statement, Mr. Clayton," she

said icily, "and if I were a man, I might make it."
She turned quickly and entered the cabin.

Clayton, being English, did not immediately
guess what the American girl meant. Only after she
was out of sight did he realize how an American
man might have responded. In the wilds of the
American West, it was said, a man insulting another could expect to have to fight with revolvers.

"Upon my word," he said ruefully, "she called
me a liar. And I fancy I jolly well deserved it," he
added thoughtfully. "Clayton, my boy, I know you
are exhausted, but that's no reason to make a fool
of yourself. You'd better go to bed."

But before he did so he called gently to Jane
through the sailcloth partition, hoping to apologize.
He might as well have addressed a sculpture. Then
he wrote a note and shoved it beneath the partition.

Jane saw the little note and ignored it, for she
was very angry and hurt, but she was also curious.
Eventually she picked it up and read it. It said:

My Dear Miss Porter:

I had no reason to suggest what I did. My
only excuse is that my nerves must be
unstrung—which is no excuse at all.

Please try to forget my harsh words. I am
very sorry. I would not have hurt YOU, above
all others in the world. Say that you forgive me.

WM. CECIL CLAYTON

"He did think it, or he never would have said
it," she reasoned, "but it cannot be true—oh, I

know it is not true!"

One sentence in the letter bothered her: "I would not have hurt *you* above all others in the world."

A week ago that sentence would have filled her with delight. Now it depressed her.

She wished she had never met Clayton. She was sorry that she had ever seen the forest god. No, she was glad. And there was that other note she had found in the grass the day after her return from the jungle, the love note signed by 'Tarzan of the Apes.' Who could he be? If he were just another wild creature of this terrible forest, to what lengths might he go to claim her?

CHAPTER 23

BROTHER MEN

When D'Arnot awoke, he found himself lying on a bed of soft vegetation beneath a little A-shaped shelter. He looked out and saw that he was in a small clearing in the jungle. He felt lame, sore and weak, and as his awareness returned, he felt every aching bruise and every sharp cut. Even to turn his head was agony, and so for a long time he simply lay still with his eyes closed.

He tried to remember what had happened before his rescue. Where was he now? Was he among friends or foes? Finally he recalled the whole hideous scene at the stake, and then passing out in the arms of the strange figure.

D'Arnot wondered what fate was in store for him. There seemed to be no one around, only the endless humming of the greatly varied life of the jungle. Soon he fell into a quiet slumber, and did not awake again until afternoon.

He again felt the strange sense of total confusion, but this time the past came back to him sooner. Looking through the opening of the shelter, he saw the muscular, tanned back of a white man squatting outside. D'Arnot thanked God that at least he had not been recaptured by the tribe of savages.

The Frenchman called out faintly. The man turned, rose, and came toward the shelter. D'Arnot thought his face the handsomest he had ever seen.

Stooping, he crawled into the shelter beside the wounded officer and placed a cool hand on his forehead. D'Arnot spoke to him in French, but the man only shook his head—sadly, it seemed. Then D'Arnot tried English, but still the man shook his head. Italian, Spanish and German brought similar responses. D'Arnot knew a few words of several other languages, including that spoken by the West African tribes, and tried them all, but it was no use.

After examining D'Arnot's wounds, the man left the shelter and disappeared. In half an hour he was back with fruit and a hollow gourd filled with water. D'Arnot drank and ate a little, surprised that he had no fever. Again he tried without success to converse with his strange nurse.

Suddenly the man hastened from the shelter, returning a few minutes later with several pieces of bark and—wonder of wonders—a lead pencil.

Squatting beside D'Arnot, he wrote for a minute on the smooth inner surface of the bark, and then he handed it to the Frenchman. D'Arnot was astonished to see, in plain block letters, a message in English:

> I am Tarzan of the Apes. Who are you? Can you
> read this language?

D'Arnot seized the pencil, then stopped. This strange man wrote English—clearly he was an Englishman, for Americans were rare in this part of Africa.

"Yes," said D'Arnot, "I read and speak English. Now we may talk. First let me thank you for all that you have done for me."

The man only shook his head and pointed to the pencil and the bark.

"*Mon Dieu!*" cried D'Arnot. "If you are English why can you not speak English?"

And then in a flash it came to him—the man was probably deaf and mute.

So D'Arnot wrote a message on the bark in English:

> I am Paul d'Arnot, Lieutenant in the navy of
> France. I thank you for saving my life, and all
> that I have is yours. May I ask how it is that one
> who writes English does not speak it?

Tarzan's reply filled D'Arnot with still greater wonder:

> I speak only the language of my tribe—the great
> apes who were Kerchak's. I understand a little
> of the languages of Tantor, the elephant, and
> Numa, the lion, and of the other folks of the
> jungle. With a human being I have never spo-
> ken, except once with Jane Porter, by signs.
> This is the first time I have spoken with anoth-
> er of my kind through written words.

This was incredible, thought D'Arnot. A full-grown man who had never spoken with a fellow man—yet could read and write. He looked again at Tarzan's message—"except once, with Jane Porter." That was the American girl who had been carried into the jungle by a gorilla.

A sudden light dawned on D'Arnot—this, then, was the "gorilla." He seized the pencil and wrote:

Where is Jane Porter?

And Tarzan replied, below:

Back with her people in the cabin of Tarzan of the Apes.

D'Arnot asked:

She is not dead then? Where was she? What happened to her?

And again, Tarzan responded:

She is not dead. She was taken by Terkoz to be his wife, but Tarzan of the Apes took her away from Terkoz and killed him before he could harm her. None in all the jungle may face Tarzan of the Apes in battle and live. I am Tarzan of the Apes—mighty fighter.

D'Arnot wrote:

I am glad she is safe. It pains me to write. I will rest a while.

And then Tarzan replied:

Yes, rest. When you are well, I shall take you back to your people.

For many days D'Arnot lay on his bed of soft ferns. The second day a fever came. D'Arnot thought that it meant infection and death. An idea came to him—he wondered why he had not thought of it before.

He called Tarzan and indicated by signs that he would write. When Tarzan had fetched the bark and pencil, D'Arnot wrote:

Can you go to my people and lead them here? I will write a message to take to them, and they will follow you.

Tarzan shook his head and taking the bark, wrote:

I thought of that on the first day, but I dared not. The great apes come often to this spot, and if they found you here, wounded and alone, they would kill you.

D'Arnot turned on his side and closed his eyes. He did not wish to die, but he felt the fever worsening. That night he lost consciousness. For three days he was delirious, and Tarzan cared for his injuries.

On the fourth day the fever broke as suddenly as it had come, but it left D'Arnot a weak shadow of his former self. He required Tarzan's assistance even to drink water.

The fever had not been the result of infection, as D'Arnot had thought. It had been a tropical disease, to which Europeans have little resistance. Such fevers generally either kill the victims, or leave them as suddenly as D'Arnot's had left him.

Two days later, D'Arnot was tottering around the amphitheater, Tarzan's strong arm preventing him from falling. They sat beneath the shade of a great tree, and Tarzan found some smooth bark that they might write on.

D'Arnot wrote the first message:

How can I repay you for all that you have done for me?

And Tarzan, in reply:

Teach me to speak the language of men.

And so D'Arnot began immediately, pointing out familiar objects and repeating their names in French, for he thought that it would be easier to teach this man his own native language.

Tarzan, of course, could not tell one language from another. So when he pointed to the word 'man' written on a piece of bark, he learned from D'Arnot that it was pronounced HOMME, and in the same way he was taught to pronounce 'ape,' SINGE and 'tree,' ARBRE.

He was an eager student, and in two more days had mastered enough French to speak little sentences such as: "That is a tree," "This is grass," "I am hungry," and the like, but D'Arnot found that French and English grammar did not mix. The Frenchman wrote little lessons for him in English and had Tarzan repeat them in French, but this greatly confused Tarzan. The languages used words very differently.

D'Arnot realized now that he had made a mistake, but it seemed too late to go back and expect Tarzan to unlearn all that he had learned, especially as they would soon be able to talk.

On the third day after the fever broke, Tarzan wrote a message asking D'Arnot if he felt strong enough to be carried back to the cabin. Tarzan was as anxious to go as D'Arnot, for he longed to see Jane again. Staying so long with the Frenchman— away from Jane— had been very hard for him, but he was of an unselfish character.

D'Arnot, quite ready to try to return, wrote: **But you cannot carry me all that way through this tangled forest.**

Tarzan laughed.

"*Mais Oui* (But I can)," he said, and D'Arnot laughed aloud to hear the phrase that he used so often glide from Tarzan's tongue.

So they set out. As had Clayton and Jane, D'Arnot marveled at the great strength and agility of the ape-man.

They arrived at the beach in mid-afternoon, and as Tarzan dropped to earth at last, his heart pounded in anticipation of seeing Jane again.

No one was in sight outside the cabin, and D'Arnot was perplexed to see that both the cruiser and the *Arrow* were nowhere in sight. Both men suddenly felt a tremendous loneliness as they strode toward the cabin. Neither spoke, yet both knew what they would find there.

Tarzan lifted the latch and pushed the great door in on its wooden hinges. It was as they had feared: deserted.

They turned and looked at one another. D'Arnot knew that his people thought him dead— but Tarzan thought only of the woman who had kissed him lovingly and now had fled from him while he helped one of her people.

A great bitterness rose in his heart. He would go away, far into the jungle, and rejoin his ape-tribe. Never would he see one of his own kind again, nor would he return to the cabin. He would abandon his great hopes of finding his own kind and becoming known as a man.

And the Frenchman, D'Arnot? What of him? He could get along just as Tarzan had. Tarzan did not want to see him any more. He wanted to escape everything that might remind him of Jane.

As Tarzan stood by the door brooding, D'Arnot entered the cabin. Many comforts had been left behind. He recognized numerous articles from the cruiser—a camp oven, some kitchen utensils, a rifle and lots of ammunition, canned foods, blankets, two chairs and a cot—and several books and magazines, mostly American.

"They must intend to return," thought D'Arnot, gaining a bit of hope. He walked over to the desk that John Clayton had built so many years before, and on it he saw two notes addressed to Tarzan of the Apes. One was in a strong masculine hand, not sealed. The other, in a woman's hand-writing, was sealed.

"Here are two messages for you, Tarzan of the

Apes," cried D'Arnot, turning toward the door—to find his companion gone.

D'Arnot looked out. Tarzan was nowhere in sight. He called aloud but got no response.

"*Mon Dieu!* (My God!)" exclaimed D'Arnot, "he has left me. I feel it. He has gone back into his jungle and left me here alone."

And then he remembered the sorrowful look on Tarzan's face when they had found the cabin empty. It had reminded him of what the hunter sees in the eyes of the dying deer he has shot. The man had been hit hard, D'Arnot realized now—but why?

The Frenchman looked about him. The loneliness and the horror of the place made him uneasy, especially in his still-weak state. To be left here alone beside this awful jungle—never to hear a human voice or see a human face—in constant dread of attack by beasts and men. It was awful.

Far to the east, Tarzan was speeding recklessly through the jungle's middle terrace back to his tribe, faster than ever before. He realized that he was trying to escape from his own thoughts, but no matter how fast he went, he could not lose them.

He passed above Sabor, the lioness, going in the opposite direction—toward the cabin, thought Tarzan. What could D'Arnot do against Sabor—or Bolgani, the gorilla—or Numa, the lion, or cruel Sheeta?

Tarzan paused in his flight.

"What are you, Tarzan?" he asked aloud. "An

ape or a man? If you are an ape, you will do as the apes would do—leave one of your kind to die in the jungle, if it suited you. But if you are a man, you will return to protect your kind. You will not run away from one of your own people, just because one of them has run away from you."

D'Arnot closed the cabin door. Though a brave man, he was alone and frightened. He loaded one of the rifles and placed it within easy reach. Then he went to the desk and took up the unsealed letter addressed to Tarzan. Perhaps it might say that his people would return. Satisfied that it would be ethical to read this letter, he opened the envelope and read:

TO TARZAN OF THE APES:

We thank you for the use of your cabin, and are sorry that you did not permit us the pleasure of thanking you in person.

We have harmed nothing, but have left many things to add to your comfort and safety here in your lonely home.

If you know the strange white man who saved our lives so many times, and brought us food, and if you can talk with him, please also thank him for his kindness.

We sail within the hour, never to return; but we wish you and that other jungle friend to know that we shall always thank you for what you did for strangers, and that we would have rewarded you both far more had you allowed it.

Very respectfully,

WM. CECIL CLAYTON

"'Never to return,'" muttered D'Arnot rue-fully, and threw himself face downward on the cot.

An hour later a noise startled him, and he listened. Something was at the door trying to enter.

D'Arnot reached for the loaded rifle and brought it to his shoulder.

Dusk was falling, and the interior of the cabin was very dark, but the Frenchman could see the latch lifting. He felt his hair rising upon his scalp.

Gently the door opened until a thin crack showed something standing just beyond.

D'Arnot sighted along the blue barrel at the crack of the door—and then he pulled the trigger.

CHAPTER 24

LOST TREASURE

When the expedition returned from the fruitless search for D'Arnot, Captain Dufranne was anxious to steam away as quickly as possible. Only Jane had resisted, and a discussion followed between them on the beach.

"No," she said determinedly, "we should not go while two of our friends are in that jungle—your officer, Captain, and the forest man who has saved every member of my father's party. I am sure that he has stayed to rescue Lieutenant D'Arnot, just as he rushed to help my father and Mr. Clayton. He is not back now only because either the lieutenant is wounded, or because he is still in search of him."

"But poor D'Arnot's uniform and belongings were found in that village, Miss Porter," argued the captain, "and the natives became very excited when questioned about this."

"Yes, Captain, but they did not admit that he was dead. As for his clothes and possessions, prisoners are often robbed even if they will not be killed later. It proves nothing. It is strong evidence, I will admit, but it is not positive proof."

"Possibly your forest man himself was captured or killed," suggested Captain Dufranne.

The girl laughed. "You do not know him," she replied, a little thrill of pride setting her nerves a-tingle.

"I admit that he would be worth waiting for, this superman of yours," laughed the captain. "I most certainly should like to see him."

"Then wait for him, my dear captain," urged the girl, "for I intend to do so."

The Frenchman would have been very surprised had he understood what she truly meant.

They had been walking toward the cabin as they talked, and now they joined the group sitting in the shade beside the cabin. The officers arose and saluted the captain, and Clayton surrendered his camp stool to Jane.

"We were just discussing poor Paul's fate," said Captain Dufranne. "Miss Porter rightly insists that we have no absolute proof of his death. On the contrary, she maintains that the continued absence of your mighty jungle friend indicates that D'Arnot is either wounded or is a prisoner somewhere else, and still needs his aid."

"It has been suggested," ventured Lieutenant Charpentier, "that the wild man may have been a member of the tribe who attacked our party—that he was hastening to aid his own people."

Jane shot a quick glance at Clayton.

"It seems vastly more reasonable," said Professor Porter.

"I do not agree with you," objected Mr. Philander. "He had ample opportunity to harm us himself—or to lead his tribe, if it were his, against us. Instead, he has consistently been our protector and provider."

"That is true," interjected Clayton, "yet we must remember that except for himself, the only human beings within hundreds of miles are hostile tribesmen. He was armed as they are, and is but one against possibly thousands. He must surely have friendly relations with them, for he could not fight so many."

"It seems likely then that he is connected with them," remarked the captain, "possibly a member of this tribe."

"And how could he have survived so long, and learned African woodcraft and the use of African weapons, without the help of Africans?" added another of the officers. "Only they truly know this country."

"You are judging him according to your own standards, gentlemen," said Jane. "An ordinary man such as any of you . . . pardon me, I did not mean it quite that way.

"Rather, I grant you that even an athletic and intelligent white man could never have survived a year alone and naked in this jungle. But this man is of greater strength and agility than even our Olympic athletes and 'strong men,' and in battle he is as courageous and fierce as a wild beast."

"He has certainly won a loyal champion, Miss Porter," said Captain Dufranne, laughing. "I am sure that all of us here would willingly face a hundred terrifying deaths to deserve the tributes of one even half so loyal—or so beautiful."

"You would understand better," said the girl, undistracted by the flattery, "had you seen him as I saw him, battling that huge hairy brute to protect me. If you had witnessed him charging the monster with no sign at all of fear or hesitation, you would have believed him more than human. Had you see those mighty muscles, forcing back those awful fangs, you too would have thought him invincible. And had you seen the kind and gentle way he treated a strange girl of a strange race, you would trust him as I do."

"You have won the debate, fair Mademoiselle," cried the captain. "This court finds the defendant not guilty. The cruiser shall wait a few days longer, that he may have an opportunity to come and thank his lovely advocate."

"For the Lord's sake, honey," cried Esmeralda. "You all don't mean to tell *me* that you're going to stay right here in this here land of animals when you all got the opportunity to escape on that boat?"

"Why, Esmeralda! You should be ashamed of yourself," cried Jane. "Is this any way to thank the man who saved your life twice?"

"Well, Miss Jane, that's all jest as you say, but that there forest man never did save us to stay here. He done save us so we all could get *away* from here. I expect he be mighty discombobulated when he find we ain't got enough sense to leave after he done give us the chance to. I hoped I'd never have to sleep in this here geological garden another night and listen to all them lonesome noises coming out of that jumble after dark."

"I don't blame you a bit, Esmeralda," said Clayton, "and you are certainly right to call them 'lonesome' noises. I never have been able to find the right word for them, but that's perfect."

"You and Esmeralda had better go and live on the cruiser," said Jane scornfully. "What would you think if you *had* to live all of your life in that jungle as our forest man has done?"

"I'm afraid I'd be a blooming failure as a wild man," laughed Clayton, ruefully. "Those noises at night make the hair on my head bristle. I should be ashamed to admit it, but it's the truth."

"It is not only the sounds, but the silences," Lieutenant Charpentier added. "I never thought much about fear before, but as we lay in the jungle there after poor D'Arnot was taken, and those jungle noises rose and fell around us, I began to think that I was a coward indeed. It was not the roaring and growling so much as it was the stealthy noises, the ones that you heard suddenly close by, but then stopped. They sounded like a great body stalking its prey, and what was worst, you did not know how close it was, or whether it was still creeping closer. And those eyes—*Mon Dieu!* I shall see them in the dark forever. Some you see, and some you only feel—and those are the worst."

All were silent for a moment, and then Jane spoke.

"And he is out there," she said, in an awed whisper. "Those eyes will be glaring at him tonight, and at your comrade Lieutenant D'Arnot. Can you leave them, gentlemen, without at least remaining here a few days longer in case they need your help?"

"Tut, tut, child," said Professor Porter. "Captain Dufranne is willing to remain, and for my part I am perfectly willing, perfectly willing—as I always have been to humor your childish whims."

"We can spend tomorrow recovering the chest, Professor," suggested Mr. Philander.

"Quite so, quite so, Mr. Philander, I had almost forgotten the treasure," exclaimed Professor Porter. "Possibly Captain Dufranne will send men to assist us, and one of the prisoners to point out the location of the chest."

"Certainly, my dear Professor, we are all yours to command," said the captain.

that they would sail early the next day.

Jane would have begged to stay longer, except that she too had begun to believe that her forest lover would not return. Against her will, she began to entertain doubts and fears. That the magnificent body could be cold and lifeless was too awful to imagine, but the views of the French officers—who were mainly unbiased—began to seem correct.

She would not believe the more awful things said about him, but perhaps he was an adopted member of some wild tribe. More unwelcome thoughts occurred to her: if he belonged to some savage tribe, maybe he had a savage wife—maybe a dozen, with many children. The girl shuddered, and when the captain announced his intention to sail tomorrow, she was almost glad.

It was she, though, who proposed that weapons, ammunition, supplies and comforts be left behind in the cabin, as gifts for the yet-unseen 'Tarzan of the Apes,' and for D'Arnot if he still lived. In reality, she hoped that her forest god might get them.

She was the last to leave the cabin, and made some trivial excuse to return one final time after the others had started for the boat. Going inside, she wrote a message for him, to be transmitted by Tarzan of the Apes; then she sealed it. Finally, she knelt down by the bed and prayed for the safety of her jungle man. Pressing his locket to her lips, she murmured:

"I love you, and because I do, I believe in you. But if I did not believe, I would still love. Had you come back for me, and had there been no other way, I would have gone into the jungle with you—forever."

CHAPTER 25

THE OUTPOST OF THE WORLD

As his gun went off, D'Arnot saw the door fly open and the figure of a man pitch headlong inside onto the floor. Panicked, the Frenchman raised his gun to fire again into the motionless form in the dim light, but then he recognized the intruder.

He had shot his friend and protector, Tarzan of the Apes.

With a cry of anguish D'Arnot sprang to the ape-man's side. He cradled Tarzan, and called his name. No response. Then D'Arnot placed his ear above the man's heart, and was overjoyed to hear its steady beating. Carefully he lifted Tarzan to the cot, then closed and bolted the door. He lit a lamp and examined the wound. The bullet had grazed the head, leaving an ugly flesh wound but no signs of a skull fracture.

D'Arnot breathed a sigh of relief as he washed and bandaged the wound. Soon the cool water revived Tarzan, and he opened his eyes to look in questioning surprise at D'Arnot. The Frenchman replied by writing a message. He explained the terrible mistake he had made, and how thankful he was that the wound was not more serious. He handed it to Tarzan.

Tarzan, after reading the message, sat on the edge of the couch and laughed. "It is nothing," he said in French. Then, his vocabulary failing him, he wrote:

> You should have seen what Bolgani did to me, and Kerchak, and Terkoz, before I killed them—then you would laugh at such a little scratch.

D'Arnot could only imagine. He then handed Tarzan the two messages the castaways had left for him.

Tarzan read the first one with a sorrowful expression. The second one he turned over and over, puzzled—he had never seen a sealed envelope before. At length he handed it back to D'Arnot. Surprised to see an adult European mystified by an envelope, he opened it and handed the letter back to Tarzan. The ape-man sat on a camp stool and read:

> **TO TARZAN OF THE APES:**
>
> Before I leave let me join Mr. Clayton in gratitude for your kindness in permitting us the use of your cabin.
>
> We are very sad that you never came to make friends with us. We so much wished to see and thank our host.
>
> There is another I should also like to thank, whose name I do not know. He did not return,

but I cannot believe that he is dead. He is the great forest giant who wore the diamond locket.

If you can, please carry my thanks to him, and tell him that I waited seven days for him to return.

Tell him also that in my home in Baltimore, in America, he will always be welcome.

I found a note you wrote me lying near the cabin. I do not know how you came to love me, for we have never spoken. If it is true, I am very sorry, for I have already given my heart to another.

But know that I am always your friend,

JANE PORTER

Tarzan sat with gaze fixed upon the floor for nearly an hour. Clearly the castaways did not realize that *he* was Tarzan of the Apes.

"I have given my heart to another," he repeated over and over to himself. Then she did not love him! But how could she have pretended to care for him in that way, raising such hopes, only to shatter them and leave him in such utter despair? Were her kisses only signs of friendship? How could he know, knowing nothing of the customs of men … and women?

Suddenly he arose, and wished D'Arnot goodnight. Then he threw himself on the couch of ferns that had been Jane Porter's. D'Arnot doused the lamp, and lay down on the cot.

For a week they mainly rested, D'Arnot coaching Tarzan in French. Soon the two men could converse quite easily. One night, as they were sitting in the cabin, Tarzan turned to D'Arnot.

"Where is Baltimore, America?" he asked.

D'Arnot pointed toward the northwest. "Many thousands of miles across the ocean," he replied. "Why?"

"I am going there."

D'Arnot shook his head. "It is impossible, my friend," he said.

Tarzan rose, went to a cupboard, and returned with a well-thumbed geography book. Opening it to a map of the world, he said: "I have never quite understood all this; explain it to me, please."

D'Arnot did so, showing him that the blue represented all the water on the earth, and the bits of other colors the continents and islands. Tarzan asked him to point out the spot where they now were. D'Arnot pointed to a place on the west African coast.

"Now point out America," said Tarzan.

And as D'Arnot placed his finger on North America, Tarzan smiled and laid his palm upon the page, spanning the great ocean that lay between the two continents.

"It is not so far," he said, "barely the width of my hand."

D'Arnot laughed. How could he explain? He took a pencil and made a tiny dot where he had pointed. "If your cabin were at the very center of this dot, you could not even see to the edges of the area covered by the dot. Do you see now how very far it is?"

Tarzan thought for a long time. "Do any white men live in Africa?" he asked.

"Yes."

"Where are the nearest?"

D'Arnot pointed out a spot on the shore just north of them.

"So close?" asked Tarzan, in surprise.

"Yes," said D'Arnot, "but it is not close."

"Have they big boats to cross the ocean?"

"Yes."

"We shall go there tomorrow," announced Tarzan.

Again D'Arnot smiled and shook his head. "It is too far. We would die long before we reached them."

"Do you wish to stay here forever?" asked Tarzan.

"No," said D'Arnot.

"Then we shall start tomorrow. I do not like it here any more, and would rather die than stay."

"Well," answered D'Arnot with a shrug, "My friend, perhaps I also would rather die than remain here. I shall go with you."

"It is settled then," said Tarzan. "I shall start for America tomorrow."

"How will you get to America without money?" asked D'Arnot.

"What is money?" inquired Tarzan.

It took a long time to make him understand even imperfectly. "How do men get money?" he asked at last.

"They work for it."

"Then I will work for it."

"No, my friend," returned D'Arnot, "you need not worry about money. I have much more money than any man needs. If ever we reach civilization, you shall have all you need."

So on the following day they started north along the shore. Each man carried a rifle and ammunition, bedding, and some food and cooking utensils. The cooking gear seemed useless and awkward to Tarzan, so he threw his away.

"But you must learn to eat cooked food, my friend," protested D'Arnot. "No civilized men eat raw meat."

"There will be time enough to learn about food when I reach this 'civilization,' " said Tarzan. "I do not like these cooking tools. They spoil the taste of good meat."

For a month they traveled north, sometimes finding food in plenty, other times going hungry for days. They saw no signs of natives, nor were they bothered by wild beasts. Their journey was easy.

Tarzan asked many questions about civilization, and learned rapidly. D'Arnot even taught him the use of the knife and fork, but sometimes Tarzan would drop them in disgust. He would then tear his food with his strong hands and teeth like a wild beast. D'Arnot would criticize him:

"You must not eat like a brute, Tarzan. I am trying to make a gentleman of you. *Mon Dieu!* Gentlemen do not eat that way—it is terrible."

Tarzan would grin sheepishly and pick up his knife and fork again, but at heart he hated them.

On the journey he told D'Arnot about the large chest he had seen the sailors bury, and how he had reburied it at the apes' gathering place.

"It must be the treasure of Professor Porter," said D'Arnot. "It is too bad, but of course you did not know."

Then Tarzan recalled the letter from Jane to her friend, which he had taken when they first came to his cabin. Now he knew what the chest contained, and its importance to Jane. "Tomorrow we shall go back after it," he announced to D'Arnot.

"Go back?" exclaimed D'Arnot. "But, my dear fellow, we have been traveling three weeks! It would require three more to return to the treasure, which you said took four sailors to carry. Months would pass before we again reached this spot."

"It must be done, my friend," insisted Tarzan. "You may go on toward civilization, and I will return for the treasure. I can go much faster alone."

"I have a safer, quicker plan, Tarzan," exclaimed D'Arnot. "We shall continue together to the nearest settlement, and there we will charter a boat and sail back down the coast to retrieve and easily transport the treasure. What do you think?"

"Very well," said Tarzan. "The treasure will still be there, and while I could fetch it now, and catch up with you in a moon or two, I will feel better not leaving you alone on the trail. When I see how helpless you are, D'Arnot, I often wonder how the human race has survived for as long as you have told me. Why, Sabor could single-handedly kill a thousand of you."

D'Arnot laughed. "You will think more highly of your species when you have seen its armies and navies, its great cities, and its mighty engineering works. Then you will realize that it is mind, and not muscle, that makes humans greater than the mighty beasts of your jungle. Alone and unarmed, no man is a match for any large beast. But if ten men are together, they combine their minds and muscles in ways the beasts cannot. Without this ability, Tarzan of the Apes, how long would you have lasted here? How do you suppose the other natives survive?"

"You are right, D'Arnot," replied Tarzan, "for if Kerchak had come to Tublat's aid that night at the Dum-Dum, I would have died. But Kerchak could never think far enough ahead to take advantage of any such opportunity. Even Kala, my mother, could never plan ahead. She simply ate what she wished, then discarded the rest. She used to think me very silly to burden myself with extra food when traveling, though when I shared it with her, she was glad to eat it."

"Then you knew your mother, Tarzan?" asked D'Arnot, in surprise.

"Yes. She was a great, fine ape, nearly twice my size."

"And your father?" asked D'Arnot.

"I did not know him. Kala told me he was a white ape, and hairless like myself. I know now that he must have been a white man."

D'Arnot looked long and earnestly at his companion.

"Tarzan," he said at length, "it is impossible that the ape, Kala, was your mother. If she were, you would look like an ape, but you do not. You are pure man—and the child of well-bred and intelligent parents, I might add. Have you not the slightest clue to your past?"

"Not the slightest," replied Tarzan.

"No writings in the cabin that might have told something of its builders?"

"I have read everything that was in the cabin except one book. It is written in a language other than English—possibly you can read it." Tarzan fished the little black diary from the bottom of his quiver, and handed it to his companion.

D'Arnot glanced at the title page. "It is the diary of John Clayton, Lord Greystoke, an English nobleman, and it is written in French," he said. He then read the twenty-year-old diary, which recorded the details that we already know—the adventures, hardships and sorrows of John and Alice Clayton, from the day they left England until an hour before he was slain by Kerchak.

D'Arnot's voice broke with sorrow as he read aloud, stopping at times to compose himself. Occasionally he glanced at Tarzan, but the ape-man sat upon his haunches, his eyes fixed stoically on the ground.

Only when the little baby was mentioned did the tone of the diary sound happy, and even that subdued joy seemed sad against the background of despair.

One entry showed an almost hopeful spirit:

> Today our little boy is six months old. He is sitting in Alice's lap beside the table where I am writing—a happy, healthy, perfect child.
>
> Though it goes against all reason, I imagine him a grown man, taking his father's place in the world—the second John Clayton—and bringing honors to the house of Greystoke.
>
> Now, as though to endorse my prophecy, he has grabbed my pen in his chubby fists, gotten ink on his little fingers, and placed the seal of his tiny fingerprints upon the page.

And there, on the margin of the page, were the partially blurred imprints of four baby fingers and a thumb.

When D'Arnot had finished the diary the two men sat in silence for some minutes.

"Well, Tarzan of the Apes, what think you?"

asked D'Arnot. "Does not this little book explain your parentage? Why, you are Lord Greystoke."

Tarzan replied, "The book speaks only of one child, which was the little skeleton in the crib. It must have starved to death. It was there when I first entered the cabin, and was never moved until they buried the family beside the cabin.

"No, that was the baby in the book—and the mystery of my origin grows deeper. Lately I have wondered whether that cabin was my birthplace, but I now believe that Kala spoke the truth," he concluded sadly.

D'Arnot shook his head. He was unconvinced by Tarzan's reasoning, and determined to somehow either prove or disprove his theory.

A week later the two men suddenly came to a clearing in the forest.

In the distance were several buildings surrounded by a strong fence. Within the enclosure, a number of Africans cultivated a field. The two travelers halted at the edge of the jungle.

Tarzan fitted his bow with a poisoned arrow, but D'Arnot placed a hand on his arm. "What are you doing, Tarzan?" he asked.

"They will try to kill us if they see us," replied Tarzan. "I prefer to be the killer."

"Maybe they are friends," suggested D'Arnot.

"They are tribespeople," was Tarzan's only reply as he re-drew his bowstring.

"You must not, Tarzan!" cried D'Arnot.

"That is no reason to kill them. *Mon Dieu!* You have much to learn. I pity the ruffian who offends you, my wild man, when I take you to Paris. Do not assume that men are your enemies until they prove it."

"Come," said Tarzan, "let us go and present ourselves to be killed," and he started straight across the field, his head high held. D'Arnot followed behind him.

Presently one of the Africans looked up, saw Tarzan in his loincloth and D'Arnot in the remnants of John Clayton's discarded clothes, and fled inside the protective fence. The rest of the gardeners followed suit. Before they reached the gate, a white man with a rifle emerged from the enclosure to investigate.

What he saw made him raise and aim his rifle, and Tarzan of the Apes would have been shot again had not D'Arnot cried loudly in French, "Do not fire! We are friends!"

"Halt, then!" was the reply.

"Stop, Tarzan!" cautioned D'Arnot. "He thinks we are enemies."

Together they advanced toward the armed man by the gate. The latter eyed them in puzzlement. "What manner of men are you?" he asked in French.

"Europeans," replied D'Arnot. "We have been lost in the jungle for a long time."

The man had lowered his rifle and now

advanced with outstretched hand. "I am Father Constantine of the French Mission here," he said. "Welcome!"

"This is Monsieur Tarzan, Father Constantine, and I am Paul D'Arnot, of the French Navy." The priest extended his hand to Tarzan, who imitated the priest's act and shook his hand. With one keen glance, the clergyman took in the superb physique and handsome face.

And thus Tarzan of the Apes came to the first outpost of civilization.

For a week they remained with the good Father before moving on, and the observant ape-man learned much of the ways of men. During their stay, African women sewed white garments for the new arrivals, so they might continue their journey properly clothed.

CHAPTER 26

THE HEIGHT OF CIVILIZATION

Another month's travel brought them to a little seaport at the mouth of a wide river. When Tarzan of the Apes first arrived, he was as timid as a wild animal, but he gradually accepted the strange noises and ways of civilization.

Soon no one could have guessed that, two short months before, the handsome 'Frenchman' laughing and chatting with them had been swinging naked through the jungle ready to pounce on and kill some unwary animal and then eat the meat raw. He was now as elegant with the knife and fork as D'Arnot, who told him: "God made you a gentleman at heart, my friend, but we want His works to show on the outside also."

As soon as they had reached the little port, D'Arnot sent word to his government that he was safe. He requested and got three months of leave from the Navy, and also asked his bankers to send funds. Even when the money arrived, there was a month's delay in going after the treasure because they could not find a vessel to charter.

During their stay at the coast town "Monsieur Tarzan" became the wonder of all because of several events, though they seemed trivial in Tarzan's eyes.

Once, a huge African had gotten drunk and was terrorizing the town. Soon his misfortune led him to the hotel porch where Tarzan sat relaxing. The drunk, brandishing a knife, made straight for a party of four men sipping cocktails. Shouting in alarm, they ran away in haste.

The drunk then spied Tarzan, and roared and charged the ape-man. Many heads peered from hiding to watch the huge African butcher the poor 'Frenchman.'

Tarzan met the rush with the joy of battle. As the African closed upon him, steel muscles gripped the wrist of the uplifted knife-hand and broke it with a swift wrenching movement, leaving the hand useless. The pain and surprise brought the drunk quickly to his senses. He cried out in agony and then dashed wildly toward the native village. Tarzan sat back down to resume his relaxation.

On another occasion, as Tarzan and D'Arnot sat dining with a group, the talk turned to lion hunting, and lions' bravery or lack thereof. Some considered lions cowardly, but all agreed that when they heard the jungle monarch's roar near camp at night, they felt much better if they were well armed. D'Arnot and Tarzan had previously agreed to keep his past secret, so no one else knew of the ape-man's familiarity with jungle animals.

"Monsieur Tarzan has not commented," said one of the party. "He is very strong, and has spent some time in Africa. Surely he must have had experiences with lions—yes?"

"Some," replied Tarzan, dryly. "Enough to know that each of you have correctly judged the lions that you have met. But you can no more judge all lions by those than you can judge all blacks by the fellow who got drunk last week, or decide that because one white is a coward, all whites are. Like yourselves, gentlemen, animals are individuals. I always assume that a lion is ferocious, and so I am never caught off my guard."

"There would be little pleasure in hunting," retorted the first speaker, "if one is afraid of the thing he hunts."

D'Arnot smiled. Tarzan afraid!

"I do not exactly understand what you mean by fear," said Tarzan. "Like lions, fear is a different thing in different men. To me, hunting is dull unless I know that the quarry can just as easily harm me. If I took a couple of rifles, a gun bearer and twenty or thirty beaters to locate the lion, I would be perfectly safe—and perfectly bored."

"Then I take it that Monsieur Tarzan would prefer to go naked into the jungle, armed only with a jackknife, to kill the king of beasts," laughed the other, good-naturedly, but with a touch of sarcasm.

"And a piece of rope," added Tarzan.

Just then the deep roar of a lion sounded from the distant jungle, as though demanding a duel. "There is your opportunity, Monsieur Tarzan," bantered the Frenchman.

"I am not hungry," said Tarzan simply. The men laughed—all but D'Arnot. He knew.

"But you are afraid, just as any of us would be, to go out there naked, armed only with a knife and a piece of rope," said the banterer. "Is it not so?"

"No," replied Tarzan. "Only a fool does something for no reason."

"Five thousand francs is a reason," said the other. "I wager you that amount you cannot bring back a lion from the jungle, naked and armed only with a knife and a some rope."

Tarzan glanced toward D'Arnot, who nodded his head. "Make it ten thousand," said D'Arnot.

"Done," replied the other.

Tarzan arose. "I shall leave my clothes at the edge of the settlement, so that if I do not return before daylight I shall have something to wear."

"You are not going now," exclaimed the gambler—"at night?"

"Why not?" asked Tarzan. "Numa walks abroad at night—it will be easier to find him."

"No," said the other, "I do not want your blood on my hands. It will be foolhardy enough if you go forth by day."

"I shall go now," replied Tarzan, and went to his room for his knife and rope.

The men accompanied him to the edge of the jungle, where he left his clothes in a small storehouse. But as he got ready to leave, they pressured him to stay—especially the man who had placed the bet. "You win," he said. "The ten thousand francs are yours if you will give up this foolish attempt, which can only end in your death."

Tarzan laughed, and in another moment the jungle had swallowed him. The men stood silent for some moments, then slowly turned and walked back to the hotel.

Tarzan immediately took to the trees, and with a feeling of exultant freedom he swung once more through the forest branches. This was life! Ah, how he loved it! Civilization offered nothing like this—it was hemmed in by rules and protocol. Clothes were shackles.

At last he was free. He had not realized what a prisoner he had been.

How easy it would be to circle back to the coast, and then head south toward his own jungle and cabin.

Now he caught the scent of Numa, for he was traveling upwind. Presently his sharp ears detected the familiar sound of padded feet and the brushing of a huge, fur-clad body through the undergrowth. Tarzan moved to a position above the unsuspecting beast and silently stalked him until they reached a spot where the moonlight illuminated the lion.

Then the quick noose dropped and tightened about the tawny throat. As he had done a hundred times before, Tarzan tied the end to a strong branch. Then, while the beast clawed for its life, the ape-man drew his knife and dropped onto the great lion's back. He plunged his long blade a dozen times into the fierce heart.

Then with his foot on the carcass of Numa, he raised his voice in the awesome victory cry of his savage tribe.

For a moment Tarzan stood, torn between love of freedom and loyalty to D'Arnot.

At last the vision of a beautiful face, and the memory of warm lips against his, dissolved the liberating imagery of his old life. The ape-man shouldered the warm carcass and took to the trees once more.

The men upon the porch had sat uneasily for an hour, too distracted to say much. "*Mon Dieu,*" said the bettor eventually, "I can endure it no longer. I am going into the jungle with my rifle and bring back that mad man."

"I will go with you," said one, and soon several others volunteered. As though the suggestion had broken the spell of some horrid nightmare, they scattered to their quarters, and then returned, heavily armed. Together they headed toward the jungle.

"God! What was that?" cried one, an Englishman, as Tarzan's savage cry came faintly to their ears.

"I heard the same thing once before," said a Belgian, "when I was in the gorilla country. My bearers said it was the cry of a great bull ape after a kill."

D'Arnot remembered Clayton's description of the awful roar with which Tarzan had announced his kills, and he half smiled in spite of the unnerving thought: this terrible cry was a friend's voice.

As the party stood near the edge of the jungle, debating how to proceed, they were startled by a low laugh nearby.

Turning, they saw a giant figure advancing toward them with a lion on its back.

Even D'Arnot was thunderstruck. It seemed impossible that the man could have so quickly slain a lion with only a knife and rope, much less carried its corpse here by himself.

The men crowded about Tarzan with many questions, but his only answer was a laugh. To him it was like praising a butcher for his heroism in killing a cow. Tarzan had killed so often for food and for safety that it seemed normal to him. But in their eyes, he was very much a hero.

He had also won ten thousand francs, for D'Arnot insisted that he keep it all.

This was very important to Tarzan, who was just realizing the power in the little pieces of metal and paper. They changed hands any time humans did almost anything. Without money, one must die. D'Arnot had told him not to worry—he had plenty. But Tarzan was also learning that people looked down on someone who accepted money without giving back something of equal value.

Shortly after the lion hunt, D'Arnot succeeded in chartering an ancient coastal freighter for the trip to Tarzan's land-locked harbor. It was a happy morning for them when the little vessel hoisted anchor and made for the open sea.

The trip was uneventful. The morning after the boat anchored in sight of the cabin, Tarzan once more donned his jungle regalia. Carrying a shovel, he set out alone for the apes' meeting-place, returning late the next day carrying the great large chest upon his shoulder. At sunrise the little vessel sailed northward out of the harbor.

Three weeks later Tarzan and D'Arnot boarded a French steamer bound for Lyons, France, and after a few days there, D'Arnot took Tarzan to Paris. The ape-man was anxious to proceed to America, but D'Arnot insisted that they must first go to Paris, though he would not tell him why this was so important.

Shortly after their arrival, D'Arnot arranged to visit an old friend who was a high official of the police department, and took Tarzan along. D'Arnot guided the conversation around to the topic of tracking down criminals. Tarzan was interested in the policeman's explanations of new methods used in criminology, especially fingerprinting.

"But skin grows, and replaces itself in a few

years, does it not?" asked Tarzan. "What value can these imprints have then?"

"The lines never change," replied the official. "From infancy to senility, the fingerprints of an individual change only in size, unless they are scarred. But if imprints have been taken of the thumb and fingers of both hands, the only way to escape identification is to lose all ten."

"It is marvelous," exclaimed D'Arnot. "I wonder what the lines of my own fingers may resemble."

"We can soon see," replied the police officer, summoning an assistant and issuing a few directions. The man left the room, but presently returned with a little hardwood box, which he placed on his superior's desk.

"Now," said the officer, "you shall have your fingerprints in a second."

He drew from the little case a square of plate glass, a little tube of thick ink, a rubber roller, and a few snowy white cards. Squeezing a drop of ink onto the glass, he spread it back and forth with the rubber roller until the entire surface of the glass was covered with a very thin and uniform layer of ink.

"Place the four fingers of your right hand on the glass," he said to D'Arnot. "Now the thumb. That is right. Now place them in just the same position on this card, here, no—a little to the right. We must leave room for the left hand. There—now the same with the left."

"Come, Tarzan," cried D'Arnot, "let's see what your fingerprints look like."

Tarzan cooperated, asking many questions of the officer. "Do fingerprints show racial characteristics?" he asked. "Could you determine, for example, solely from fingerprints whether the subject was European or African?"

"I think not," replied the officer.

"Could you tell the fingerprints of an ape from those of a man?"

"Probably, because the ape's would be far simpler."

"But someone who was part ape and part man might show evidence of either parent?" continued Tarzan.

"I should think so," responded the official, "but the science is not yet advanced enough to say exactly. I would only trust it to tell two individuals apart, for that is absolute. No two people born have ever had identical lines upon all their digits. It is very doubtful if any single fingerprint will ever exactly match any other."

"Does the comparison require much time or labor?" asked D'Arnot.

"Ordinarily but a few moments, if the prints are clear."

D'Arnot drew a little black book from his pocket and began turning the pages.

Tarzan looked at the book in surprise. Where had D'Arnot gotten his father's diary?

Presently, D'Arnot stopped at a page with five tiny smudges. He handed the open book to the policeman.

"Are these imprints similar to mine or Monsieur Tarzan's, or even identical with either?" he asked. The officer drew a magnifying glass from his desk and examined all three specimens carefully, taking notes.

Tarzan realized now why they had come. The answer to his life's riddle lay in these tiny marks. He sat leaning tensely forward in his chair, then suddenly relaxed and leaned back, smiling. D'Arnot looked at him in surprise.

"You forget that for twenty years the dead body of the child who made those fingerprints lay in the cabin of his father," said Tarzan bitterly.

The policeman looked up in astonishment. "Go ahead, captain, with your examination," said D'Arnot. "If Monsieur Tarzan agrees, we will tell you the story later."

Tarzan nodded his head. "But you are mad, my dear D'Arnot," he insisted. "Those little fingers are buried on the west coast of Africa." As he spoke, they moved over to the broad window and its view of the busy city.

"Not for certain, Tarzan," replied D'Arnot. "If you are not the son of John Clayton, then how in heaven's name did you come into that Godforsaken jungle where no white man other than John Clayton had ever set foot?"

"You forget—Kala," said Tarzan.

"I do not even consider her," replied D'Arnot.

For some time the friends stood there gazing out the window, each wrapped in his own thoughts.

"It takes some time to compare fingerprints," thought D'Arnot, turning to look at the police officer. He was astonished to see the official leaning back in his chair, hastily scanning the contents of the little black diary.

D'Arnot coughed. The policeman looked up, caught his eye, and raised his finger for silence. D'Arnot turned back to the window, and presently the police officer spoke.

"Gentlemen," he said. Both turned toward him.

"There is evidently a great deal at stake here. This comparison must be absolutely correct. I therefore ask that you leave the entire matter in my hands until Monsieur Desquerc, our expert, returns in a few days."

"I had hoped to know at once," said D'Arnot. "Monsieur Tarzan sails for America tomorrow."

"I will promise that you can send him my report within two weeks," replied the officer, "but what it will say I cannot be sure at this time. There are resemblances, yet—well, we had better leave it for Monsieur Desquerc to solve."

CHAPTER 27

THE GIANT AGAIN

A taxicab pulled up in front of an old-fashioned house on the outskirts of Baltimore. A well-built, strong-featured man of about forty stepped out. He paid and dismissed the driver. A moment later, he was entering the library of the old home.

"Ah, Mr. Canler!" exclaimed an old man, rising to greet him.

"Good evening, my dear Professor," cried the man, extending a cordial hand.

"Who admitted you?" asked the professor.

"Esmeralda."

"Then she will tell Jane that you are here," said the old man.

"No, Professor," replied Canler, "for I came primarily to see you."

"Ah, I am honored," said Professor Porter.

"Professor," continued Robert Canler in a deliberate tone, "I have come this evening to speak with you about Jane. You know—and have approved of—my intent to marry her."

Professor Archimedes Q. Porter fidgeted in

his armchair without really knowing why. Canler was a splendid match.

"But I cannot understand Jane," continued Canler. "She continues to make excuses. I always feel that she breathes a sigh of relief every time I say goodbye."

"Tut, tut, Mr. Canler," said Professor Porter. "Jane is a most obedient daughter. She will do precisely as I tell her."

"Then I can still count on your support?" asked Canler, relieved.

"Certainly, sir," exclaimed Professor Porter. "How could you doubt it?"

"There is young Clayton, you know," suggested Canler. "He has been hanging around for months. I don't know that Jane cares for him, but he has a title and wealth, and it would not surprise me if he finally won her, unless—" and Canler paused.

"Tut—tut, Mr. Canler, unless—what?"

"Unless you were to request that Jane and I be married at once," said Canler, slowly and distinctly.

"I have already suggested it to Jane," said Professor Porter sadly, "for we can no longer afford to live here as we have."

"What was her reply?" asked Canler.

"She said she was not ready to marry anyone yet," replied Professor Porter, "and that we could go and live on the tenant farm in northern Wisconsin which her mother left her. Its tenants always make a living, and it provides a trifle of profit, which they send to Jane each year. We are planning to go up there the first of the week. Philander and Mr. Clayton have already gone there to prepare the place for us."

"Clayton has gone there?" exclaimed Canler, visibly annoyed. "Why was I not told? I would gladly have gone and made all preparations."

"Jane feels that we are already too much in your debt, Mr. Canler," said Professor Porter. Canler was about to reply when the sound of footsteps was heard, and Jane was at the doorway.

"Oh, I beg your pardon!" she exclaimed, not entering. "I thought you were alone, Papa."

Canler rose and spoke. "It is only I, Jane. Won't you come in and join the family group? We were just speaking of you." He placed a chair for her.

"Thank you," said Jane formally, entering and taking the chair. "I only wanted to tell Papa that Tobey is coming down from the college tomorrow to pack his books. Papa, you must indicate which ones you can do without until fall. Please don't carry this entire library to Wisconsin, as you would have carried it to Africa, had I not put my foot down."

"Was Tobey here?" asked Professor Porter.

"Yes, I just left him. He and Esmeralda are exchanging religious experiences on the back porch now."

"Tut, tut, I must see him at once!" cried the professor. "Excuse me just a moment, children," and the old man hastened out. As soon as he was out of earshot Canler turned to Jane.

"See here, Jane," he said bluntly. "How long must this continue? You have not replied to my proposal. I want to get the license tomorrow, and for us to be married quietly before you leave for Wisconsin. I don't care for a big wedding, and I'm sure you don't either."

Jane's eyes went icy, but she did not flinch.

"Your father wishes it, you know," added Canler.

"Yes, I know," she said quietly. Then she spoke in a cold, level tone: "Do you realize that you are buying me, Mr. Canler? Buying me for a few paltry dollars? Of course you do, Robert Canler. That was the only reason you lent Papa the money for that hair-brained escapade in Africa— which nearly succeeded after all."

Canler flushed. Jane continued.

"But you, Mr. Canler, would have been the most surprised. You are a good enough businessman to have known that his venture would fail, and too shrewd to lend money for treasure-seeking, without asking for security, unless you had some other motive. You sought a greater hold on the honor of the Porter family. It would enable you to force me to marry you, without seeming to do so."

Now Canler's face paled in anger. Jane was not finished.

"You have never mentioned the loan. In any other man I would have thought that a sign of noble character. But you are devious, Mr. Robert Canler. I know you better than you think I know you. If I cannot avoid it, I shall marry you, but let the truth be known."

When he was sure she was finished, Canler arose with a cynical smile and said, "You surprise me, Jane. I thought you had more self-control and pride. Of course I am buying you. I knew that you knew it, but I thought you would rather pretend otherwise. I did not think that your self-respect would let you admit, even to yourself, that you were a bought woman. But have it your own way, dear girl," he added lightly. "I am going to have you, and that is all that interests me."

Without a word Jane turned and left the room.

Jane was not married before she left with her father and Esmeralda for her little Wisconsin farm. As her train pulled away, she coldly bade Robert Canler goodbye. He called out to her that he would join them in a week or two.

At their destination they were met by Clayton and Mr. Philander in Clayton's huge touring car. It quickly whirled them away through the dense northern woods toward the little farm, which Jane had not visited since childhood.

The farmhouse stood on a little hill a hundred yards from the tenant house. In the past three weeks, Clayton and Mr. Philander had hired a small army of building contractors. What had been a run-down shell was now a cozy little two-story house with many modern conveniences.

"Why, Mr. Clayton, what have you done?" cried Jane Porter, her heart sinking as she realized the probable cost.

"Shh," cautioned Clayton. "Don't let your father guess. If you don't tell him he will never notice, and I simply couldn't think of him living in such a terrible state. I would have liked to do much more, Jane. For his sake, please never mention it."

"But you know that we can't repay you," cried the girl. "Why do you want to put me under such terrible obligations?"

"I don't, Jane," said Clayton sadly. "If it had been just you, believe me, I wouldn't have done it, for exactly that reason. But I couldn't think of that dear old man living in such a shambles. Please believe me when I say that I did it just for him."

"I do believe you, Mr. Clayton," said the girl, "because I know you are quite generous and decent enough to have done just that—and, oh Cecil, I wish I might repay you as you deserve—as you would wish."

"Why can't you, Jane?"

"Because I love another."

"Canler?"

"No," she snapped.

"But you are going to marry him. He told me so before I left Baltimore."

Jane winced. "I do not love him," she said, almost proudly.

"Is it because of the money, Jane?"

She nodded.

"Then do I compare so poorly to Canler? I have money enough, and more," he said bitterly.

"I do not love you, Cecil," she said, "but I respect you. If I must disgrace myself by such a bargain with any man, better he be one I already despise. I would hate any man to whom I sold myself without love. You will be happier alone, with my respect and friendship, than with me and my contempt."

He did not press the matter further. But when Robert Canler's purring motorcar drew up before the farmhouse a week later, William Cecil Clayton wished only to commit murder.

An uneventful but uncomfortable week passed at the little Wisconsin farmhouse. Canler pressured Jane to marry him at once, and eventually she grew so infuriated with the hateful pressure that she agreed. The next day, Canler would drive to town and bring back the license and a minister.

Clayton had wanted to leave as soon as the plan was announced, but the girl's tired, hopeless look made him remain. He could not desert her, and he consoled himself with the hope that something might yet happen. In his heart, he knew that he could kill Canler for the slightest reason.

Early the next morning Canler set out southward for town. There was smoke lying low over the forest in the east. A forest fire had raged there for a week, but they were in no danger as yet.

About noon Jane started off for a walk. Clayton wanted to join her, but respected her spoken wish to be alone.

In the house, Professor Porter and Mr. Philander were discussing some weighty scientific question. Esmeralda dozed in the kitchen, and Clayton, heavy-eyed after a sleepless night, fell into a fitful nap on the living-room couch.

To the east the black smoke clouds rose higher, then suddenly shifted rapidly westward—toward the farm. The tenants were at the market in town, leaving no one to notice how quickly the fire was approaching.

Soon the flames had spanned the road to the south and cut off Canler's return. Another shift of the wind pushed the forest fire to the north, then blew back. For a moment the fire stood still, as if held on a leash.

Suddenly, out of the northeast, a large black car came careening down the road.

With a jolt it stopped in front of the cottage, and a black-haired giant leaped out, ran up onto the porch and directly into the house. On the couch lay Clayton. The interloper started in surprise, but bounded to the sleeping Englishman's side, shaking him roughly by the shoulder.

"My God, Clayton, are you all mad here? Don't you know you are nearly surrounded by a forest fire? Where is Miss Porter?"

Clayton sprang to his feet. He did not recognize the man, but he understood the words and ran to the porch. "Heavens!" he cried, and then, dashing back into the house, "Jane! Jane! Where are you?"

In an instant Esmeralda, Professor Porter and Mr. Philander joined the two men. "Where is Miss Jane?" cried Clayton, seizing Esmeralda by the shoulders and shaking her roughly.

"Oh, Mister Clayton, she went for a walk!"

"Hasn't she come back yet?" he demanded. Without waiting for a reply, Clayton dashed out into the yard, followed by the others. "Which way did she go?" the black-haired giant demanded of Esmeralda.

"Down that road," cried the frightened woman, pointing south toward a mighty wall of roaring flames.

"Put these people in the other car," shouted the stranger to Clayton, "and get them out of here by the north road. Leave my car here. If I find Miss Porter, we will need it. If I don't, no one will need it."

Clayton hesitated. The strange man was insistent: "Do as I say!" And with that, the lithe figure bounded across the clearing toward the northwest, where there were no flames.

"Who was that?" asked Professor Porter.

"I do not know," replied Clayton. "He called both me and Esmeralda by name, and he apparently knew Jane, because he asked for her."

"There was something most startlingly familiar about him," exclaimed Mr. Philander, "And yet, bless me, I never saw him before."

"Tut, tut!" cried Professor Porter. "Most remarkable! Who could it have been, and why do I feel that Jane is safe, now that he has set out in search of her?"

"I can't tell you, Professor," said Clayton soberly, "but I know I have the same odd feeling. But come," he cried, "we must get out of here ourselves, or we shall be shut off," and the party hastened toward Clayton's car.

When Jane turned homeward, the smoke seemed alarmingly close, and as she hastened northward, she nearly began to panic. It seemed to her that the rushing flames were rapidly moving to block her return to the cottage. Soon she had to turn into the dense thicket and attempt to circle around to reach the house. Before long she realized that this was no use. She must return to the road and run for her life southward, toward the town.

She did so, but had gone only a short distance when she saw her retreat was also cut off. An arm of the main blaze had shot out a half mile south of its parent to cross this tiny strip of road. She halted in horror before the new wall of flame. It would be no use trying again to force her way through the woods. In a matter of minutes, the entire space between the north and the south would be a seething mass of billowing flames.

Calmly the girl kneeled down in the dust of the roadway and began to pray. "Dear Lord," she began, "I ask that You give me strength to meet my fate bravely. Please deliver my father and friends from this awful dea—"

Suddenly she heard her name being called aloud through the forest:

"Jane! Jane Porter!" It rang strong and clear, but in a strange voice.

"Here!" she called in reply. "Here! In the roadway!"

Through the upper branches of the trees, she saw a figure swinging toward her with great speed.

A veering of the wind blew a cloud of smoke around them, obscuring everything and stinging her eyes. Suddenly she felt a strong arm around her, then a feeling of being lifted up. She felt the rush of the wind and the occasional brush of a branch as she was carried along.

She opened her eyes. Far below her she saw the undergrowth and the hard earth. All around her was the waving foliage of the forest.

From tree to tree the giant figure carried her, and it seemed to Jane that she was reliving her African jungle experience in a dream. Oh, if it were the same man who had done likewise on that other day . . . but that was impossible! Yet who else in the whole world was capable of this?

She stole a sudden glance at the face close to hers, and then she gave a little frightened gasp. It was he!

"My forest man!" she murmured, "No, I must be delirious!"

"Yes, your man, Jane Porter. Your savage man has come out of the jungle to claim his mate—the woman who ran away from him," he added almost fiercely.

"I did not run away," she whispered. "I made them wait a week for you to return. You did not."

They were beyond the fire now, and he descended and set her down. Side by side they walked back in the direction of the cottage. The wind had now pushed the fire back on itself— another hour like that, and it would burn out.

"Why did you not return?" she asked.

"I was nursing D'Arnot. He was badly wounded."

"Ah, I knew it!" she exclaimed.

"They said you had gone to join the tribes-people—that they were your people."

He laughed. "But you did not believe them, Jane?"

"No . . . what shall I call you?" she asked. "What is your name?"

"You first knew me as Tarzan of the Apes," he said.

"Tarzan of the Apes!" she cried—"and that was your note I answered when I left?"

"Yes, whose did you think it was?"

"I did not know. But it could not be yours, for Tarzan of the Apes had written in English, and you could not understand a word of any language."

Again he laughed. "It is a long story, but it was me. I could not speak, but I could write —and now D'Arnot has made matters worse by teaching me to speak French instead of English. Come," he added, "jump into my car; we must overtake your father. They are only a little way ahead."

As they drove along, he continued, "Then when you said in your note to Tarzan of the Apes that you loved another—you might have meant me?"

"I might have," she answered, simply.

"But in Baltimore—oh, how I have searched for you!—they told me you might be married by now. That a man named Canler had come up here to wed you. Is that true?"

"Yes."

"Do you love him?"

"No."

"Do you love me?"

She buried her face in her hands. "I am promised to another. I cannot answer you, Tarzan of the Apes," she cried.

"You have answered. Now, tell me why you would marry one you do not love."

"My father owes him money."

Suddenly Tarzan recalled the letter he had read—and the name of Robert Canler, and the hint of trouble which, at the time, he had not understood. He smiled.

"If your father had not lost the treasure, you would not feel bound by your promise to this man Canler?"

"I could ask him to release me."

"And if he refused?"

"I have given my promise."

He was silent for a moment. The car was plunging recklessly along the uneven road, for the fire showed threateningly at their right, and another change of the wind might sweep it across this one avenue of escape. Finally they passed the danger point, and Tarzan slowed down.

"What if I were to ask him?" ventured Tarzan.

"He would pay no attention to a stranger," said the girl. "Especially one who wanted me himself."

"Terkoz paid attention," said Tarzan, grimly.

Jane shuddered and looked fearfully up at the giant figure beside her, for she remembered the great ape he had killed in her defense.

"This is not the African jungle," she said. "You are no longer a savage beast. You are a gentleman, and gentlemen do not kill in cold blood."

"I am still a wild beast at heart," he said, in a low voice, as though to himself.

Again they were silent for a time.

"Jane," said the man, at length, "if you were free, would you marry me?"

She did not reply at once. He waited patiently.

She tried to collect her thoughts. What did she know of this strange creature at her side? What did he know of himself? Who was he? Who were his parents? His very name suggested a mysterious origin and a savage life.

Could she be happy with this jungle dweller? Could she find anything in common with a husband whose life had been spent in the treetops of an African jungle? One who had spent his time fighting with fierce apes? Who had torn his food from still-quivering, fresh-killed prey and sunk his strong teeth into raw flesh, while his comrades growled and fought over their share?

Could he ever rise to her social level? Could she bear to think of sinking to his? Would either be happy in such a horrible mismatch?

"You do not answer," he said. "Are you afraid of hurting me?"

"I do not know how to answer," said Jane sadly. "I do not know my own mind."

"You do not love me, then?" he asked, in a level tone.

"Do not ask me that. You will be happier without me. You were never meant for the formal restrictions of society—civilization would annoy you, and you would soon long for the freedom of your old life. I am as totally unsuited to that life as you are to mine."

"I think I understand you," he replied quietly. "I shall not urge you, for your happiness is more important than my own. I see now that you could not be happy with . . . an ape," he added bitterly.

"Don't," she protested. "Don't say that. You do not understand."

But before she could go on, a sudden turn in the road brought them into the midst of a little town.

Before them stood Clayton's car, surrounded by the party he had brought from the cottage.

CHAPTER 28

CONCLUSION

At the sight of Jane in Tarzan's car, everyone cried out in relief and delight. Tarzan of the Apes stopped to let her out, and Professor Porter caught his daughter in his arms.

For a moment no one noticed Tarzan, sitting silently in his seat. Clayton was the first to remember, and turned to extend his hand.

"How can we ever thank you?" he exclaimed. "You have saved us all. You called me by name at the cottage, but I do not seem to recall yours. You seem very familiar, like someone I knew long ago under different conditions."

Tarzan smiled as he shook Clayton's hand.

"You are quite right, Monsieur Clayton," he said, in French. "Please pardon me if I speak to you in French. I am just learning English, and I understand it better than I speak it."

"But who are you?" insisted Clayton in French.

"Tarzan of the Apes."

Clayton started back in surprise. "By Jove!" he

exclaimed. "It is true." Professor Porter and Mr. Philander pressed forward to add their thanks to Clayton's.

The party now entered the modest little hotel, where Clayton soon arranged lodging and meals. They were sitting in the little, stuffy parlor when Mr. Philander happened to look out the window and caught sight of an approaching automobile chugging toward the hotel. It parked next to their cars.

"Bless me!" said Mr. Philander with a shade of annoyance. "It is Mr. Canler. I had hoped, er—I had thought—er—how very happy we should be that he was not caught in the fire," he ended lamely.

"Tut, tut! Mr. Philander," said Professor Porter. "Tut, tut! I have often instructed my pupils to count to ten before speaking. Were I you, Mr. Philander, I should count at least a thousand, and then maintain silence."

"Bless me, yes!" conceded Mr. Philander. "But who is the religious-looking gentleman with him?"

Jane blanched.

Clayton moved uneasily in his chair.

Professor Porter shifted his glasses nervously.

Esmeralda muttered.

Only Tarzan did not understand.

Presently Robert Canler burst into the room. "Thank God!" he cried. "I had feared the worst, Clayton. I was cut off on the south road and had to circle far around. I thought we'd never reach the cottage."

No one seemed excited. Tarzan eyed Robert Canler as Sabor eyes her prey.

Jane glanced at him and coughed nervously. "Mr. Canler," she said, "this is Monsieur Tarzan, an old friend."

Canler turned and extended his hand. Tarzan rose and gave a gentlemanly bow worthy of D'Arnot's teaching but did not seem to see Canler's hand, nor did Canler appear to notice.

"This is the Reverend Mr. Tousley, Jane," said Canler, turning to the priestly gentleman behind him. "Mr. Tousley, Miss Porter."

Mr. Tousley bowed and beamed. Canler introduced him to the others.

"We can have the ceremony at once, Jane," said Canler. "Then you and I can catch the midnight train in town."

Tarzan now understood. He glanced over at Jane, but did not move. The girl hesitated. The room was tensely silent. All eyes turned toward Jane, awaiting her reply.

"Can't we wait a few days?" she asked. "I am a nervous wreck. I have been through so much today."

Canler could feel the hostility of the entire party. The façade came away, and his tone became rough. "I am tired of being played with, and I will wait no more. Jane, you have promised to marry me. Now, I have the license, and here is the preacher. Come, Reverend Tousley and Jane. There are plenty of witnesses—more than enough," he added disagreeably.

He then took Jane Porter by the arm and started to lead her toward the waiting minister.

Scarcely had he taken a single step when a heavy hand closed on his arm with a grip of steel. Another hand shot to his throat, and in a moment he was being shaken high above the floor, as a cat might shake a mouse.

Jane turned in horrified surprise toward Tarzan.

As she looked into his face, she saw the same crimson band upon his forehead that she had seen once before in faraway Africa, when Tarzan of the Apes had battled the great ape Terkoz to the death. She knew what was on his mind. With a little cry of horror, she sprang forward to plead for restraint—not for Canler's sake, but to save Tarzan from the penalty for murder.

Before she could reach them, however, Clayton had jumped to Tarzan's side and was trying to drag Canler from his grasp. With a single sweep of one mighty arm, the Englishman was hurled across the room, and then Jane laid a small firm hand upon Tarzan's wrist, and looked up into his eyes.

"For my sake," she said.

The grasp upon Canler's throat relaxed. Tarzan looked down into the beautiful face before him.

"Do you wish this to live?" he asked in surprise.

"I do not wish him to die at your hands, my friend," she replied. "I do not wish you to become a murderer."

Tarzan removed his hand from Canler's throat and glared at him. "If you value your life, you will release her from her promise."

Canler, gasping for breath, nodded.

"Will you go away and never bother her again?"

Again the man nodded his head, his face distorted by mortal fear.

Tarzan released him in the direction of the door. In another moment Canler was gone, along with the terrified preacher.

Tarzan turned toward Jane. "May I speak with you for a moment, alone?" he asked.

The girl nodded and started toward the door leading to the hotel's porch. She went out to await Tarzan, thus missing the conversation which followed.

"Wait," cried Professor Porter, as Tarzan was about to follow. The giant halted.

Professor Porter said, "Before we go further, sir, I would like you to explain your actions. What right, sir, did you have to interfere between my daughter and Mr. Canler? I had promised him her hand, sir, and regardless of our personal likes or dislikes, sir, that promise must be kept."

"I interfered, Professor Porter," replied Tarzan, "because your daughter does not love Mr. Canler. She does not wish to marry him. That is enough for me to know."

"You do not know what you have done," said Professor Porter. "Now he will doubtless refuse to marry her."

"He most certainly will," said Tarzan, pleased. "And further," he added, "your pride will take no harm, Professor Porter, because you will be able to pay the Canler person in full the moment you reach home."

"Tut, tut, sir!" exclaimed Professor Porter. "What do you mean, sir?"

"Your treasure has been found," said Tarzan.

"What—what are you saying?" cried the professor. "You are mad, man. It cannot be."

"It is, though. It was I who stole it, not knowing either its value or its owner. I saw the sailors bury it, and ape-like, I had to dig it up and bury it again elsewhere. When D'Arnot told me what it meant to you, I returned to the jungle and recovered it. The treasure had caused so much crime and grief that D'Arnot suggested I not bring it over here with me, so I have brought a letter of credit instead. Here it is, Professor."

Tarzan pulled out and handed an envelope to the astonished professor. "Two hundred and forty-one thousand dollars. The treasure was most carefully appraised by experts, but should there be any question in your mind, D'Arnot himself bought it and is holding it for you, should you prefer the treasure to the credit."

"To the already great burden of our obligations to you, sir," said Professor Porter, with trembling voice, "is now added this greatest of all services. You have given me the means to save my honor."

Clayton, who had left the room a moment after Canler, now returned.

"Pardon me," he said. "I think we had better try to reach town before dark and take the first train out of this forest. A local fellow just rode by and said that the fire is moving slowly in this direction."

This announcement broke up further conversation. The party went out, collected Jane, and headed for the cars. Clayton took Jane, the professor and Esmeralda in his car, while Tarzan took Mr. Philander with him.

"Bless me!" exclaimed Mr. Philander, as the car moved off after Clayton. "The last time I saw you, you were a truly wild man, skipping among the branches of a tropical African forest. Now you are driving me along a Wisconsin road in a French automobile. Bless me, but it is most remarkable!"

"Yes," assented Tarzan. Then, after a pause: "Mr. Philander, do you recall the details of the finding and burying of three skeletons found in my cabin?"

"Very distinctly, sir, very distinctly," replied Mr. Philander.

"Was there anything strange about any of those skeletons?"

Mr. Philander eyed Tarzan narrowly. "Why do you ask?"

"I must know," replied Tarzan solemnly. "Your answer may solve a mystery, and cannot do any harm. I have been wondering about those skeletons for the past two months. To the best of your knowledge, sir, were the three skeletons you buried all human skeletons?"

"No," said Mr. Philander, "the smallest one, the one found in the crib, was the skeleton of an anthropoid ape, a species related to the chimpanzee and gorilla."

"Thank you," said Tarzan.

In the car ahead, Jane was thinking frantically.

She had guessed why Tarzan had asked to speak privately with her, and she knew that she must soon answer him. He was not the sort of person one could put off, and somehow that made her wonder if she feared him. Could she love someone she feared?

In the far-off jungle, she realized, she had been under a spell. Here in rural Wisconsin, she was not. Nor did the neatly-dressed young Frenchman—for so he seemed—appeal to the primal woman in her in the way the godlike forest man had.

Did she love him? She did not know—now.

She glanced at Clayton out of the corner of her eye. Was he not everything she could want—a man of class and refinement, a man who met her social expectations, a proper mate? Would any civilized woman not crave his love?

Could she love Clayton? She could see no reason why not. Jane was not coldly calculating by nature, but her heritage and upbringing had combined to teach her to reason even in matters of the heart.

She had been swept off her feet by the strong arms of the young giant in the distant African forest, and again today in the Wisconsin woods. It now seemed to her that she herself had reverted to basic human nature in this: the deep appeal of primitive man to primitive woman.

If he were never to touch her again, she reasoned, she would never feel attracted to him. She had not loved him, then. It had been nothing more than a passing delusion, brought on by excitement and personal contact. If she should marry him, their future relations would not always be so exciting; the power of contact would dull with familiarity.

Again she glanced at Clayton. He was very handsome, every inch a gentleman—a husband to be proud of.

And then Clayton spoke. A minute sooner or later, and it might have changed three lives, but fate caused him to speak at just the proper moment.

"You are free now, Jane," he said. "Won't you marry me? I will devote my life to making you happy."

"Yes," she whispered.

That evening in the little waiting room at the station, Tarzan caught Jane alone for a moment.

"You are free now, Jane." he said. "For your sake, I have become a civilized man, and have crossed oceans and continents to come to you. For your sake, I will be whatever you want me to be. I can make you happy, in the life you know and love best. Will you marry me?"

For the first time she realized the depths of the man's love—all that he had accomplished in so short a time solely for love of her. Turning her head, she buried her face in her arms.

What had she done? In fear that she might give in to the pleas of this giant, she had burned her bridges behind her. Afraid of making one terrible mistake, she had made a worse one.

There was no answer but complete honesty. She told him all from the beginning, word by word, without attempting to hide or condone her error.

"What can we do?" he asked. "You have admitted that you love me. You know that I love you, but I do not know your social rules. I shall leave the decision to you, for you know what will be best for your eventual welfare."

"I cannot tell him, Tarzan," she said. "He, too, loves me, and he is a good man. I could never face you nor any other honest person if I broke my promise to Mr. Clayton. I shall have to keep it— and you must help me bear the burden, though we may not see each other again after tonight."

The others were entering the room now. Tarzan turned toward the little window, but he did not see the outdoors.

Instead, he looked inside himself, and saw a patch of greenery surrounded by masses of gorgeous tropical plants and flowers, backed by mighty trees and capped with the blue of the African sky. In the center of the lovely scene sat a young woman on a little mound of earth, and beside her sat a young giant. They were eating delicious fruit, looking into one another's eyes and smiling. They were very happy, and all alone.

His daydream was interrupted by a station messenger, who entered and asked: "Pardon me, but is there a gentleman by the name of Tarzan present?"

"I am Monsieur Tarzan," said the ape-man.

"Here is a cablegram from Paris for you, forwarded from Baltimore."

Tarzan took the envelope and tore it open. The message was from D'Arnot. It read:

Fingerprints prove you Greystoke.

Congratulations.

D'ARNOT

As Tarzan finished reading, Clayton entered and came toward him with extended hand.

Here was the man who had Tarzan's title, and Tarzan's estates, and was going to marry the woman whom Tarzan loved—the woman who loved Tarzan. A single word from Tarzan would vastly change this man's life. It would take away his title and his lands and his castles.

It would also take them away from Jane Porter.

"I say, old man," cried Clayton, "I haven't had a chance to thank you for all you've done for us. It seems as though you've had your hands full, saving our lives in Africa and here in America, too.

"I'm awfully glad you came here. We must get better acquainted. I've often thought about you, you know, and your remarkable situation. If it's any of my business, how the devil did you ever get into that wild jungle?"

"I was born there," said Tarzan, quietly. "My mother was an Ape, and of course she couldn't tell me much about it. I never knew who my father was."

AFTERWORD

About the Author

Everyone has heard of Tarzan, but few know much about his creator, one of the great pioneers of modern fiction: Edgar Rice Burroughs.

This adventure author's amazingly productive life can be divided neatly into halves: To use some images from *Tarzan*, Edgar Rice Burrough's first thirty-seven years were spent banging into one tree after another. But he spent his remaining thirty-eight years swinging through them with all the grace of his most famous literary creation.

Ed, as his family called him, was born into the comfortable middle-class family of George and Mary Evaline Burroughs in Chicago, Illinois on February 23, 1875, the youngest of four boys. George and Mary Evaline had married while George was a Union officer during the Civil War, and they were now highly respectable pillars of Chicago society. Ed's later actions would show his parents to be very patient and loving people.

Ed was a likable boy with a happy enough childhood. He was a bit of a troublemaker, but the constant flow of diseases through the school system in those days did far more harm to Ed's education than his inability to behave. In the late 1800s the flu was much deadlier than it is today, and Ed got sick often. Mr. and Mrs. Burroughs feared for their son's life in the crowded, polluted city, so when he was sixteen, they sent him packing to the brand-new state of Idaho to live a healthier life in the clean air of his uncle's cattle ranch.

It was a loving move, but a naïve one that they would soon regret. The adventuresome teen loved the rough-and-ready life of Idaho. The cowboys of 1891 were often gamblers, outlaws in hiding, or worse; and Ed had a fine time listening to their tall tales. Basically, Ed was a sixteen-year-old boy learning from men to get into man-sized trouble. His uncle did not protest, but his parents were another matter. Hanging around with shady characters and learning bad habits was not what they had in mind for their son, and they hurried him back to the Midwest.

Mr. and Mrs. Burroughs then tried sending their son to two different boarding schools, and the reports on his wild behavior only increased their worries. In those days, wealthy people with bad-boy sons often sent their sons away to private military schools for straightening out. Accordingly, in early 1892 Ed was packed off to the Michigan Military Academy for his high school education. That wasn't any help either. While Ed liked the idea of military life, it had too many rules and regulations, many of which he broke. As a cadet, he rose in rank only to find himself in trouble again. He was good at football and popular with his peers, but that did not help his grades and his behavior, which ranged from mediocre to bad. Only his father's influence enabled Ed to graduate.

After graduation, Ed taught briefly at the academy. It hardly suited his taste for adventure, and he soon joined the United States Cavalry. He was sent to the then-Arizona Territory in 1896 and discovered that peacetime Army life was mostly about manual labor. He hoped to become an officer, but his tendency toward poor health dictated otherwise, and he was discharged in 1897.

For the next three years, Ed went from art school in Chicago to his uncle's ranch to running a small business in Idaho. Then, after ten years of turning down his proposals, in 1900 his childhood sweetheart Emma Hurlbert agreed to marry him; they eventually had two sons and a daughter together. For the next twelve years, the future giant of fiction and his family barely managed to scrape by. At one point, they had to pawn Emma's jewelry to buy food. Ed bounced from job to job during that time, from office manager to railroad policeman to salesman, and he even applied without success to become an officer in the Chinese Army. While borrowing money to pay rent and feed his family, Ed could not have imagined what a different future awaited him.

In 1910, Ed made a cynical but practical decision. Having read a lot of 'pulp fiction'—typically romances, westerns, and other action-packed writing not generally considered literature—he decided he could write similar stories. In 1911 Edgar Rice Burroughs sold his first written work, introducing John Carter as the hero of *Under the Moons of Mars*. This led to a series of adventures now considered science fiction classics. Burroughs had finally found his calling.

Shortly thereafter, in 1912, Burroughs sold *Tarzan of the Apes* to a magazine for $700. It was published in book form in 1914 and soon sold over a million copies—a remarkable number for the times. Burroughs went on to write a total of twenty-six books about the ape-man. They succeeded beyond his wildest expectations, and they capture readers' imagination to this day.

We can probably thank Hollywood for some of Tarzan's popularity. Not everyone knew how to read a book, but almost anyone could go to a movie, even if they could not read the subtitles. In 1918, when movies were still silent, the first *Tarzan* film was produced. When the Olympic swimming hero Johnny Weissmuller began to play the ape-man in 1932, and sound was added to movies, Tarzan became what Luke Skywalker or Indiana Jones would later become: not merely a hero, but a household name.

No one seemed more surprised by his success

than Burroughs himself. He was a refreshingly candid man who disliked bragging. In his own words: "I have been successful probably because I have always realized that I knew nothing about writing and have merely tried to tell an interesting story entertainingly."

Burroughs's later life included a divorce and remarriage, a stint as a town mayor, and the purchase of a California ranch called "Tarzana," which in 1928 became the name of a town that thrives to this day. Burroughs was playing tennis with his son in Hawaii on December 7, 1941, when the smoke began to rise from the bombing of Pearl Harbor by Japan. At 66, he was too old to enlist in the Army, but not too old for adventure; he went to work as a war correspondent, and even flew along on bombing missions with the Army Air Corps.

Edgar Rice Burroughs passed away in 1950 of a heart ailment; fittingly, he was reading a comic book in bed at the time.

His greatest adventure hero, Tarzan of the Apes, lives on, probably for generations yet to come.

About *Tarzan of the Apes*

'Pulp fiction.' 'Dime novels.' 'Trash.'

Wait just a minute. Something doesn't add up. How does a story like *Tarzan of the Apes* go from 'pulp fiction'—in its day, the bottom of the literary scale—to a classic that any librarian today expects to see on the shelves?

First and foremost has to be that great magnet for the mind: high adventure. The *Tarzan* stories have always been long on action and drama. As the hero, Tarzan experiences non-stop adventure; there are battles to fight, enemies to stalk, and quests to fulfill—sometimes at the same time. There's also plenty of adventure for the other characters, too, from the Frenchmen crashing through the African brush to the tribesman Kulonga to the scholarly Professor Porter and his sidekick Mr. Philander. For Jane and her companion, Esmeralda, the entire trip is an exciting adventure, although not always in the way they might have liked. Adventure can be emotional, too, as we see with Tarzan's first shaky steps toward his dream of love. It's hard to find a page of the story that isn't concerned either with planning, experiencing, or recovering from an adventure.

But there's more to the saga of Tarzan than great suspense and action. The character of Tarzan also develops in ways many readers can relate to. His learning to read brings growth, and we experience the joy with which he deciphers the "little bugs" that ultimately turn out to be the alphabet. We also see how reading leads him to a new understanding of himself and others. His emotional growth begins with his mother Kala's unselfish maternal love, which teaches him to love in return. We see how caring for others lives on in his behavior long after Kala is dead and he has avenged her death. When Tarzan becomes king of the tribe, he decides that he will not tolerate abuse of the older and weaker apes. He has developed a code of ethics that leads him to protect the weak and to keep predators at bay. He clings so tightly to this ethic that even when he grieves over his abandonment by Jane, he returns to protect D'Arnot from possible harm. With the freedom to do as he wishes, he chooses to be a man of principle.

Another aspect of freedom for Tarzan is the dangerous yet beautiful jungle, where he can depend upon his instincts and strength to survive and rule. But then Tarzan experiences a force even greater than his precious freedom in the wild: romantic love. The love that Tarzan learned from Kala lives on in his heart, like a spark waiting for fuel to transform it into a blaze. His first sight of Jane, in a moment of crisis and triumph, is like gasoline on that spark. It flares up into a beautiful passion of romance, and from that day forward, all he desires is to earn and deserve Jane's love. When he suspects that he never really had that love, he is crushed and runs away to grieve.

Then through his French companion D'Arnot, Tarzan finds a new way to express his love for Jane. The light of that love leads the ape-man to discover and master a whole new world of languages, habits, and places. And when Jane's heart seems to be given to another, Tarzan must decide how to best express his love for her. So while *Tarzan of the Apes* is a great adventure story, it is equally a love story, complete with rivalry, tragedy, and suspense. It is no surprise that the Tarzan story endures on so many reading lists to this very day.